W9-AVH-579

"A...wedding?" she croaked.

Marissa's mouth dropped open. She wanted to bolt from the room. Perhaps Jed had read her mind, because he kept a hand firmly on her shoulder.

"Yes," General Sanchez replied. "It's short notice, but my people will love the excuse for a fiesta. First thing in the morning I'll contact the village priest and the woman who sees to the bride's instruction."

This wasn't happening. This man wasn't planning her wedding and intending to carry out the plans tomorrow. Yet he was. Married to Jed? Impossible.

And to think that she'd been forced into this situation.

REBECCA YORK

USA TODAY bestselling author Ruth Glick published her one hundredth book, *Crimson Moon,* a Berkley Sensation, in January 2005. Her latest 43 Light Street book is *The Secret Night,* published in April 2006. In October she launches the Harlequin Intrigue continuity series SECURITY BREACH with *Chain Reaction.*

Ruth's many honors include two RITA® Award finalist books. She has two Career Achievement Awards from *Romantic Times BOOKclub* for Series Romantic Suspense and Series Romantic Mystery. *Nowhere Man* was the *Romantic Times BOOKclub* Best Intrigue of 1998 and is one of their "all-time favorite 400 romances." Ruth's *Killing Moon* and *Witching Moon* both won the New Jersey Romance Writers Golden Leaf Award for Paranormal.

Michael Dirda of *Washington Post Book World* says, "Her books...deliver what they promise—excitement, mystery, romance."

Since 1997 she has been writing on her own as Rebecca York. Between 1990 and 1997 she wrote the Light Street series with Eileen Buckholtz. You can contact Ruth at rglick@capaccess.org or visit her Web site at www.rebeccayork.com.

REBECCA YORK
Till Death Us Do Part

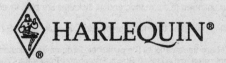

HARLEQUIN®

TORONTO • NEW YORK • LONDON
AMSTERDAM • PARIS • SYDNEY • HAMBURG
STOCKHOLM • ATHENS • TOKYO • MILAN • MADRID
PRAGUE • WARSAW • BUDAPEST • AUCKLAND

If you purchased this book without a cover you should be aware that this book is stolen property. It was reported as "unsold and destroyed" to the publisher, and neither the author nor the publisher has received any payment for this "stripped book."

ISBN-13: 978-0-373-36064-2
ISBN-10:   0-373-36064-9

TILL DEATH US DO PART

Copyright © 1995 by Ruth Glick and Eileen Buckholtz

All rights reserved. Except for use in any review, the reproduction or utilization of this work in whole or in part in any form by any electronic, mechanical or other means, now known or hereafter invented, including xerography, photocopying and recording, or in any information storage or retrieval system, is forbidden without the written permission of the publisher, Harlequin Enterprises Limited, 225 Duncan Mill Road, Don Mills, Ontario, Canada M3B 3K9.

All characters in this book have no existence outside the imagination of the author and have no relation whatsoever to anyone bearing the same name or names. They are not even distantly inspired by any individual known or unknown to the author, and all incidents are pure invention.

This edition published by arrangement with Harlequin Books S.A.

® and TM are trademarks of the publisher. Trademarks indicated with ® are registered in the United States Patent and Trademark Office, the Canadian Trade Marks Office and in other countries.

www.eHarlequin.com

Printed in U.S.A.

Directory

43 LIGHT STREET

	Room
ADVENTURES IN TRAVEL	204
ABIGAIL FRANKLIN, Ph.D. Clinical Psychology	509
INNER HARBOR PRODUCTIONS	404
THE LIGHT STREET FOUNDATION	322
KATHRYN MARTIN-McQUADE, M.D. Branch Office, Medizone Labs	515
O'MALLEY & O'MALLEY Detective Agency	518
LAURA ROSWELL, LL.B. Attorney at Law	311
SABRINA'S FANCY	Lobby
STRUCTURAL DESIGN GROUP	407
NOEL ZACHARIAS Paralegal Service	311
L. ROSSINI Superintendent	Lower Level

CAST OF CHARACTERS

Marissa Devereaux—She'd walked into a deadly trap. Now only one man could save her, if she dared accept the bargain he offered.

Jed Prentiss—The former Peregrine agent had taken an assignment that might get him killed.

Miguel Sanchez—The general had an iron grip on San Marcos. How far could Marissa and Jed trust him?

William Johnson—What was the Texan really doing in San Marcos?

Louis Rinaldo—The tough-looking Minister of Development had worked his way up from street-gang member to cabinet officer.

Thomas Leandro—The balding professor spouted Marxist doctrine, but where were his loyalties?

Pedro Harara—The banker was waiting for Marissa to make a false step.

Madre Flora—How much influence did the wise old woman wield on General Sanchez's fiefdom?

Clarita Sanchez—Was the general's daughter jealous enough to kill Marissa?

Chapter One

It required effort to keep the smile on his face.

With his thoughts in sudden turmoil and his fingers tightening dangerously around a tumbler of planter's punch, Jed Prentiss stared across the crowded room at the woman with the upswept golden curls. Was that Marissa? Here to screw things up for him—*again.*

The minister of economic development asked him a question, and he replied automatically in Spanish. At the same time he shifted slightly to the right to catch another look at the blonde through the crowd.

She turned with a graceful motion to put a champagne flute down on a passing waiter's tray, and he got a glimpse of her face. He was right. It was Marissa Devereaux. He'd recognize that silky hair anywhere. It crowned a heart-shaped face with innocent-looking blue eyes, a petite nose and a mouth that could twist facts and half truths together so adroitly you didn't know you'd been had until the middle of the next week.

In fact, she was almost as good at undercover work as he was. Except that she took foolish chances. As if she had nothing to lose.

Damn! She was the last person he wanted to see. What the hell was she doing in San Marcos—much less at a party being held at Miguel Sanchez's town house? What possible reason would San Marcos's army commander in chief have for inviting her? Jed couldn't think of one.

After promising that he'd talk with the minister about mining loans later in the week, he excused himself and made his way across the room. The nearer he got to Marissa, the more burningly aware of her he became. He couldn't possibly be close enough to smell her perfume, yet he imagined the scent of gardenia drifting toward him. She was wearing a little black dress that she probably didn't think of as sexy. But it emphasized her narrow waist and sassy little hips. He hadn't seen the front, but he knew it would be clinging to her high, firm breasts.

He scowled. He'd better keep his mind on business.

He could see she was finishing a conversation with Thomas Leandro, the outspoken university professor who'd made his reputation with pie-in-the-sky blueprints for turning the Central American republic into a socialist paradise. The professor was on Jed's list, too. But he could wait.

When Leandro went off toward the buffet table, Jed stepped into Marissa's path. Her cheeks took on a hint of heightened color, and her blue eyes widened and darkened: but the momentary lapse was her only betrayal of surprise—or anything else.

No matter how many times they met, he was never prepared for her reaction to him. As if she were suppressing strong emotions she didn't want him to read—or couldn't acknowledge. Whenever he'd tried to find out what was going on below the surface of those beautiful blue eyes, they had iced over. The rebuffs had hurt his ego. He'd vowed never to let it happen again.

"Jed. How nice to see you. Are you here on behalf of the Global Bank?"

Smooth, he thought. As if they were nothing more than friendly colleagues who traveled in the same business circles.

"Yes," he replied, matching her coolness.

They studied each other carefully.

What was she planning for the evening, he wondered. Did she already know he'd be prowling the same turf? Or was she as unpleasantly surprised as he had been? Only one of them was going to leave the capital city with the evidence he'd come to steal. He was going to make damn sure of that.

"You're a long way from Baltimore," he remarked.

She hesitated before replying. "Yes."

"So what brings you to San Marcos?"

"Oh, you know. My usual. I'm scouting out off-the-beaten-track vacation locations for Adventures in Travel."

"Latch onto anything exciting?"

"I should be able to set up a jungle trip to some partially excavated Mayan ruins. And there are excellent snorkeling and diving opportunities along the coral reef. I think I can guide visitors to a stingray feeding location."

"Sounds dangerous."

"Not when you know what you're doing."

"Be careful."

"Oh, I will."

"I didn't realize you knew Miguel Sanchez."

"I don't. Ted Bailey at the embassy was kind enough to get me on the guest list."

"Then you're on assignment for the State Department?"

"No."

It was a good bet she was lying. He knew she often mixed undercover work for Victor Kirkland at State with travel agency research. He was about to probe a little further when one of the uniformed staff approached them.

"Señorita Devereaux?"

"*Sí.*"

"*Teléfono para usted.*"

She gave Jed an apologetic look. "I'll see you later."

"Expecting an important call?"

For a split second she looked as if she weren't sure how to reply. Then she shrugged and followed the man who had delivered the message.

As Jed watched the servant lead her toward a back hall, he wondered if there was some way he could listen in on the phone conversation.

He'd memorized the floor plan of the house. There was another access to the hall, from a door off the enclosed patio.

As if he had nothing more important to do than get a breath of fresh air, he wandered casually toward the French doors.

When he stepped onto the stone terrace, the tropical night, rich with the scent of flowers, enveloped him. It took several moments for his eyes to adjust to the darkness. As they did, he went very still. Marissa had come out the side door he'd been heading for and was walking rapidly toward the far wing of the house where the office complex was located. The office complex that was strictly off-limits to everyone except Sanchez and his handpicked staff. Jed had heard stories of summary executions of suspected spies caught there.

Didn't Marissa know the risk she was taking? For that matter, didn't she know there was a guard? Jed's gaze probed the darkness.

There was *supposed* to be a guard. He didn't seem to be in sight. Had Marissa taken care of him? Jed cursed under his breath. This was just the kind of audacious maneuver she was so good at pulling off.

He was about to follow her; then, before he could, he saw a figure ooze out of the shadows like a night creature crawling out from under a rock. Without making a sound, the man padded after her.

The hair on the back of Jed's neck stood on end as if a cold breeze had blown across the patio. Marissa was in deep banana oil. Unless he could stop her before she reached the office wing.

ABOVE THE SOUND of the mariachi band playing at the party, Marissa thought she heard a voice nearby. Her whole body went rigid while she waited for a large hand to clamp down on her shoulder. When the blow didn't fall, she sprinted the rest of the way to the office wing. The heavy door was unlocked. That had been part of the deal. Jerking it open, she threw herself inside and stood with her shoulders pressed against the carved mahogany.

The door at her back gave her only a partial feeling of security. Now that she was here, she wished she'd come up with some other plan to get the information Victor wanted. Even for her, this was taking a hefty chance.

But it should work out all right.

She'd paid enough bribes to supplement the San Marcos military budget for six months.

Still, as she struggled to bring her breathing into normal range she peered down the hallway searching for signs of life. The place was as silent as a tomb. The only illumination came from a pair of ornate sconces that looked as if they held fifteen-watt bulbs. Since the electricity in San Marcos was likely to be off for half of any twenty-four-hour period, the low wattage made sense. Probably Sanchez was using his own generating plant and needed the bulk of his power supply tonight for the party.

Her high heels sounded like a flamenco dancer as she

started down the polished tile passageway. Slipping off her pumps, she looked nervously over her shoulder, half expecting to see Jed Prentiss behind her striding down the hall to catch up. If anyone bollixed up things tonight, it would be him!

All she'd needed a half hour ago, as she was psyching herself for this raid, was to glance up and discover him stalking his way toward her like a jaguar about to pounce on a tethered goat.

Her hands clamped down so tightly on her evening bag that her fingernails dug into the expensive fabric. When she realized what she was doing, she loosened her grip. She'd come here to do a job. And she would finish it and reappear at the party before anyone noticed she was missing.

As she began to tiptoe down the hall again, shoes in hand, she cursed herself for not knowing more about Jed's recent activities. Then again, she hadn't had time to brush up on every agent who'd worked in Latin America before she'd come to San Marcos. She'd better stop obsessing about him before she made some kind of fatal mistake.

With a quick glance at her watch, she saw that three minutes had elapsed since she'd ducked out of the party. That left only a little more than fifteen to get in and out of here with the goods Victor was paying her to bring home.

At least Sanchez's office was on the ground floor, she thought as she turned the corner and started for the end of the hall. She felt less exposed as soon as she'd stepped into the anteroom and quietly shut the door behind her.

The room was spartan, with a secretary's desk, a few wooden chairs and some filing cabinets. Marissa gave them only a quick glance. The good stuff was in Sanchez's private office under lock and key.

Victor had briefed her on the likely places to look, so she went straight to his desk and knelt behind it. His most confidential files were in the two bottom drawers. Willing steadiness into her hands, she extracted a small case from her evening bag. What appeared to be a manicure set was really a set of lock-picking tools. A quick look through the contents of the first drawer told her that she'd struck out. And she only had ten minutes left.

Teeth clenched, she worked the other lock. Then she came across a stack of coded papers neatly filed in manila folders. She couldn't read the text. But this was what Victor had told her to look for.

Adrenaline pumped through her veins as she placed the first one in the center of the desk blotter and got out the small camera disguised as a lipstick. Methodically she began snapping pictures of the incriminating letters and other documents.

She was almost finished when a noise in the hall made the hair on her scalp bristle.

Someone was coming!

Sweeping the papers into the folder, she had them back in place and the drawer locked again in fifteen seconds.

Now all she had to do was get out of here. And quickly. A desperate glance at the barred window told her she wasn't going to escape in that direction. With camera and evening bag clutched in her hand, she bolted for the only other possibility—the general's private bathroom.

"*¿ERES TU?*"

Jed stopped dead on the path, just managing to avoid crashing into a young Hispanic woman who had stepped out of the darkness to block his progress.

"Let me by," he answered in Spanish, only half hearing her words as he tried to push past her to get to Marissa.

Her fingers clamped onto the sleeve of his dinner jacket. "Jed. It's really you. I thought at first I'd made you up."

She stopped abruptly, looking furtively from side to side as if she were terrified of being overheard. The urgency of her touch arrested him, and he peered at her more closely. There was something familiar about her face. But on the darkened patio he couldn't place her.

"I must—"

"It's Clarita," she interrupted. "Don't you know me? I'm so glad you came back to see us."

The features resolved themselves into familiar lines. Clarita. Miguel Sanchez's daughter. She was more mature now. A girl on the verge of womanhood. She'd been eleven when Jed had been here six years ago helping the general train his troops. He'd recognized her as the neglected child of a rich man who had more important things to do than worry about his offspring's happiness. When he'd come home from the training camp with Miguel on the weekends, he'd tried to make a small difference in the little girl's life.

"I heard them talking about you, so I took a peek at the guest list for the party," she told him. "I knew you would be here. Like old times. When everything was simple." Her tone was high and wistful, as if she longed for the past.

"Clarita, I can't stay here and talk to you now."

She continued as if she hadn't heard. "It's all right. Do you remember how you taught my parrot to say 'no sweat'?" she asked eagerly. "He still remembers. Come see."

While she prattled on about the fun they'd had together, time was ticking by for Marissa. She had disappeared minutes ago—along with the man who was following her.

He forced a false heartiness into his response. "It's great

to see you again, but I have important business to take
care of. We'll talk later. Okay?" Gently but firmly he dis-
engaged Clarita's fingers from his sleeve and started toward the offices at a rapid clip, praying he wasn't too late.

She stayed right behind him. "No!"

The strangled rasp was like fingernails scraping across
a blackboard.

"I'll come right back, *niña,*" he promised, using the old
endearment.

"I'm not a little girl anymore! And you must not go
into the office wing. I know the rules. It's not allowed.
They'll shoot you if they catch you."

"It's okay. The general knows," he lied. Anything to
set her mind at ease.

"I don't think so." She looked almost frenzied as she
reached to grab hold of him again. "Jed, I can't let you
do it."

He peered into her eyes and knew instinctively that if
he tried to wrench himself away she'd start to scream.
Then every guard in the place would come charging onto
the patio to find out what he was doing to her. And when
Marissa came back out, they'd be here waiting for her.

He began talking in a low, soothing voice, telling Clarita
it was all right. Telling her that nothing was going to happen to him. That he'd come back to her in a few minutes.

But all the time he was talking, he had the sick feeling
that he was already too late.

MARISSA'S GAZE DARTED around the little room as she
locked the door behind her.

There was a small window. But it was also barred.

Someone rattled the knob and began to pound on the
door.

"Come out of there!" a voice commanded in Spanish.

"Just a minute," she answered in the same language, expecting a large fist to splinter the wood.

Sink. Toilet. Medicine cabinet. Tile floor.

Marissa looked down at the camera still clutched in her hand. If she didn't want to get caught with the incriminating evidence, she'd have to flush it down the toilet. If it would go down the toilet. Or maybe she could just flush the film.

"Come out or I'll shoot through the door," the angry voice demanded.

Desperate now, she thrust her hand into her purse to check for the empty film wrapper. Her fingers closed around the small zip-lock container in which she'd stowed the pills that were supposed to keep you from getting Montezuma's revenge.

It was big enough to hold the camera. Did she dare?

Ignoring the pounding on the door, she emptied the pills into the toilet bowl. Then she slipped her camera and film wrapper into the bag, squeezed out the air and sealed the strip across the top. Working as quietly as she could, she lifted the lid on tank and thrust the plastic bag inside, hardly able to breathe as she watched it sink to the bottom.

The whole operation seemed to take hours. She knew only seconds had passed as she flushed the pills away and rustled her clothing as if she were putting herself back together after using the facilities.

"You have ten seconds, or I'll shoot."

"No. Please." Marissa didn't have to fake the panic rising in her voice as she tried to unlock the door. The mechanism stuck, and her fingers stung as she twisted the lever.

As soon as she'd snapped the lock open, the doorknob flew out of her hand. Wide-eyed, she backed away, staring at the man who stood with a gun trained on her chest. He wasn't wearing a uniform, but he had the look of a policeman.

"I said come out of there." With his free hand he grabbed her wrist and yanked her roughly out of the bathroom. "What were you doing in El Jefe's office?" he snapped.

"What a question. You can see what I was doing. The ladies' room was occupied." Even as she did her best to look embarrassed, she was evaluating the odds of getting away from an armed man. Not good. "I had to find another quickly. It was an emergency."

"No one is allowed in this wing of the house."

"I'm truly sorry. I didn't know."

"How did you get in?"

She gestured vaguely. "I—I just walked through the door."

"It was locked!"

"No." She shook her head as if she were a bewildered tourist caught trying to snap a forbidden picture of the treasures in the cathedral. But her heart was pounding so hard that she could hardly catch her breath.

He kept the gun pointed at her while he picked up the phone, dialed a number and spoke into the receiver.

His voice was low, his Spanish rapid. But she caught enough to know that her goose was cooked. He was calling for reinforcements.

When he returned his full attention to her, his eyes were hard.

Marissa tried to swallow, but her mouth was too dry.

Pointedly he looked down at her stocking feet and then at the shoes she'd set down on the desk. "You're going to give me some straight answers, *señorita,* or you *are* going to be truly sorry."

Chapter Two

Jed heard several pairs of feet hammer against the paving stones. He whirled and cursed as four khaki-clad soldiers moving in tight formation came dashing along the path from the direction of the guard station. They all carried machine guns, and they looked as if they were on their way to the offices to foil an assassination attempt.

"Holy mother!" Clarita whispered a more ladylike version of Jed's muttered exclamation. Her eyes grew large, and the blood drained from her face. "I told you," she whispered. "It's dangerous to go there."

"They're not after you." Jed reached out to put a reassuring hand on her shoulder. She ducked away from his grasp and ran toward the bedroom wing of the house.

She had the right idea, Jed thought as he watched her disappear into the safety of the interior. He should probably blast out of here, too, while the blasting was good. He knew how Miguel Sanchez treated spies and how his twisted logic could quickly turn a friend into an enemy.

He glanced toward the lighted windows of the reception hall, wondering if anyone else had heard the guards. The guests were all drinking and eating and talking as before. Apparently the mariachi music had drowned out the sounds from the patio. Or perhaps no one chose to acknowledge the disturbance.

He was on his own. And so was Marissa.

His chest tightened as he strode rapidly after the soldiers.

One of them was standing at attention in front of the door of the office wing. Too bad it wasn't a man he'd helped train.

"*¿Qué pasa?*" he asked.

"This area is off-limits, *señor.*"

"I'm Jed Prentiss, a good friend of General Sanchez."

The guard shifted the machine gun in his grasp, as if he were unsure about aiming the gun at a good friend of *El Jefe*. Yet he obviously had his orders. "You'd better go back to the party."

Jed stood his ground.

The sentry, who'd probably never had his authority questioned before, looked uncomfortable.

The stalemate lasted less than a minute—until the rest of the armed contingent returned. The soldiers were escorting a man in civilian clothes who had a firm hold on a woman's arm.

It was Marissa.

Until Jed actually saw her being frog-marched down the hall, he realized he'd been hoping against hope that some other crisis had prompted the summoning of the guards.

Her face was paper white. It went a shade paler when she spotted him with the sentry, and he knew in that instant that she was thinking he was the one who'd turned her in.

"What's he doing here?" the civilian snapped.

"He says he's a good friend of *El Jefe*, sir."

"Go back where you belong," the man in charge said in clipped tones.

All at once the perfumed air of the tropical night was

suffocating. This wasn't the good old U.S. of A. where you were presumed innocent until proven guilty. This was the sovereign republic of San Marcos where a two-bit official could slap you in jail and throw away the key on the word of an underworld informant.

Hands resting easily at his sides, Jed summoned up his most guiltless look. "My name's Jed Prentiss. I helped the general set up his training program at *Conquista Fuerte*."

"So you say."

"You can check it out easily enough." Jed risked shifting his gaze from the man to Marissa. Her body was rigid, her breath shallow. He suspected that if she unstiffened her knees, she'd topple to the ground. His green eyes locked with her blue ones, and he saw how hard she was struggling not to fall apart. He could feel her terror. It cut through his vital organs like a machete blade. And he knew that until a few moments ago she hadn't dreamed how much trouble she could get into in the nominally democratic republic of San Marcos.

He wanted to tell her she'd been a damn fool to raid the office of a general who wielded power with the zeal of a medieval king. At the same time he wanted to wrest her from her captor, fold her into his arms and spirit her out of danger like the hero of an action-adventure film. It was an exceedingly fleeting fantasy. Even with the element of surprise, all he'd get for the grand gesture was a bullet in the back.

"If she's a spy, I'm a Saudi Arabian sheikh," he said. "I was talking to her a few minutes ago at the party. She's a scared-stiff travel agent who wandered into the wrong part of the house."

"Perhaps." The undercover man didn't sound as if he gave the explanation much credence.

"Please. I didn't do anything. Please let me go," Marissa implored.

Jed's mind scrambled for any sort of leverage he could use. If he claimed Marissa was a friend of his, he'd probably get himself detained for questioning. But maybe he still had enough influence with Sanchez to save her. "Let me speak to the general."

"He's in a meeting."

"I'll wait."

"No. You will stop poking your nose in where it doesn't belong."

"The general will want—"

"*I* will arrest you along with this female spy if you're not out of here in five seconds."

Marissa's eyes were bleak. "You'd better leave," she murmured to Jed.

"*¡Silencio!* You will not speak to each other."

Jed hated to abandon her like this. But he'd run out of options. The only thing he could do was offer her a word of comfort. "Everything will be all right. I'll tell the American embassy what's happened."

She acknowledged the help with the barest of nods, but her expression was starting to glaze over.

The man holding her arm jerked her sharply. She winced as he led her toward a door on the far side of the patio. The last view of her he had was of her rigid back and the blond curls he'd first spotted across the crowded reception.

As the guards trotted Marissa away, one of the guests from the party pressed back into the foliage of the bird of paradise tree where he was standing. Eyes narrowed, he'd been watching the scene on the patio with acute interest.

He'd seen Prentiss slip out of the reception room minutes after Devereaux had also disappeared. And he'd made a silent bet with himself that the two events were no coincidence. It was gratifying to confirm that he was right. Also a bit unsettling.

Devereaux had told everybody who would listen that she was a travel agent. Prentiss was supposed to be on a fact-finding mission for the Global Bank. But it appeared the two of them had more compelling reasons to be in San Marcos. Also, it seemed they knew each other, although neither one had admitted as much. Probably they were working together. And it looked as if Devereaux had gotten caught with her hand in the cookie jar, so to speak.

His lips thinned. Had she discovered anything incriminating before they'd bagged her? He'd have to find out quickly. And make sure she didn't get a chance to talk.

For several seconds he enjoyed watching Prentiss stand with his hands clenched at his sides. At least he had the satisfaction of knowing the bastard was sweating. But the man in the bushes didn't let the pleasure show on his face.

Deep in thought, he left his hiding place and strode toward the mansion. He'd never met Prentiss, although he'd heard of him. He was a once-top agent who was now washed up in the intelligence business. The rumor was he'd lost his nerve. But he'd toughed it out just fine with Sanchez's man.

Too bad. Prentiss and Devereaux were another problem he'd have to solve before he made any final decisions about Sanchez. But right now he'd better get in touch with his man in Junipero Province to make sure nothing out of the ordinary was happening out there.

JED STUDIED CASSANDRA Devereaux, noting the strain etched into her profile. She looked so much like Marissa— so much that it was painful.

"Would you tell the others what you told me?" she asked in a strangled voice.

It had been three days since Marissa was taken away by Sanchez's guards. Jed had arrived at Cassie's renovated East Baltimore row house at five in the afternoon, given her a summary of her sister's predicament and collapsed into bed for a few hours of badly needed sleep. While he'd been conked out, she'd made half a dozen phone calls, and he was damn impressed with the group of people she'd so quickly assembled.

He looked around the living room at the circle of faces.

He knew Jason Zacharias, of course. They'd worked together on a number of undercover assignments, including the time he'd come to rescue Jason and his wife Noel from a Scottish megalomaniac—and Jason had ended up saving him. The other women of 43 Light Street and their husbands were strangers. But he knew they were Marissa's friends. He'd always thought of her as so cold. But he could see from the faces around him that they were all deeply concerned about the turn of events in San Marcos. And they'd do anything they could to get her out of this mess.

He was especially struck by the couple sitting close together on the couch. She was Jo O'Malley, who'd been introduced as a private detective. He was Cameron Randolph, an electronics genius. Jo was expecting their first child, and it was obvious how happy they were about the pregnancy. Still, Jo had cancelled a prenatal appointment to attend this meeting.

"Start at the party," Cassie requested.

Jed did, skipping over his personal reactions to Marissa and sticking with the facts, "I went straight from Sanchez's to the American embassy, but they couldn't do anything until nine the next morning. By then it was already too late to complain that an American citizen named Marissa Devereaux was being held incommunicado by General Miguel Sanchez.'' He shifted in his chair.

"Too bad the embassy didn't get right on it. I checked with the San Marcos Department of Immigration the next day and found out that no one named Marissa Devereaux had entered the country in the past three weeks—the legal limit for a renewable tourist visa.''

Jo's eyes narrowed. "Somebody must have been working overtime searching for her entry visa. But it paid off. If she's not legally in the country, there's no way to lodge any kind of official complaint.''

"You've got it,'' Jed agreed.

"I've been burning up the phone lines to the State Department,'' Cassie added. "Marci was on an undercover assignment for our old boss—Victor Kirkland. He was willing to speak off the record because I've still got my security clearance. He says he's sorry, but he can't do anything to help her because State can't acknowledge her mission.

"Can the U.S. State Department really operate that way?'' The question came from a woman sitting in the corner. Small and delicate, she had curly brown hair and big brown eyes that seemed to stare right through Cassie. Her name was Jenny Larkin, and she was blind. Jed had wondered at first what she was doing at the meeting, since it was obvious that she had less experience than the others with the unofficial workings of government—or with detective work. But he'd quickly discovered that her analytic mind and phenomenal memory were an asset to the group.

"I'm afaid they can do whatever they want to, as long as they don't get caught,'' Cassie explained. "But I'm not going to let Victor get away with stonewalling me.''

Jed admired her defiant posture, but he didn't hold out

much hope from that quarter. He knew the rules. And so did Marissa. She'd taken a job where it was understood she was on her own if there was trouble.

Until now, Abby Franklin had been silent. "What else have you got for us?" she asked him.

"After the scam at Immigration, I didn't expect to find a record of a Marissa Devereaux checking in to a hotel. But I put it around that I'd be at the Café Primo and that I was willing to pay for information about a blond *gringa* travel agent who might have been in Santa Isabella within the past few days.

"I got lucky with a *portero* from El Grande who remembered commenting on Marissa's snorkeling equipment. He took her to room 345."

"So you let yourself in and had a look around the premises," Jo guessed. Jed was pretty sure she'd have done exactly the same thing. Before her pregnancy, anyway.

"Right. The room had been ragged out. But the maid had forgotten to replace the notepad by the phone. The top sheet looked clean. But I could make out the impression of the previous message, which was the name of a taxi company and Miguel Sanchez's address."

"I couldn't go into court with that," Dan Cassidy muttered. As an assistant state's attorney, he knew the rules of evidence.

Cassie slammed her fist against the arm of her chair. "I've been begging Marci for years not to keep taking these assignments. I told her this one was too dangerous. Damn her. What's wrong with her? Does she *want* to get herself killed?" She shot Abby a pleading look.

The woman shifted uncomfortably in her chair. "There are reasons why she takes risks other people would consider unacceptable."

Startled, Jed stared at the attractive brunette. She'd been

introduced as a psychologist. And, like most headshrinkers, she'd shut up and let everyone else do the talking. It sounded as if she'd been seeing Marissa professionally. Remembering the way Marissa had always struggled to hide her emotions from him, he was seized with sudden regret that he'd never tried to understand her; he'd only reacted to what he perceived as her cold arrogance.

"Is that all you're going to say?" Cassie persisted, her voice fierce. "Won't anybody stick their neck out for Marci?"

"It's not a matter of sticking my neck out," Abby said gently. "You know it would be a breach of professional ethics to talk about the things Marissa and I have discussed at her therapy sessions."

Cassie looked down at her hands.

"You think someone betrayed Marissa?" Jenny asked Jed.

"I know she wouldn't have crossed the patio unless she'd been assured it would be empty. There could have been a backup security system only Sanchez knows about. Even a silent alarm," Jed observed. "Or someone at the party could have spotted her heading for forbidden territory and alerted security."

"Who?" Cassie snapped.

"Any of over a hundred guests. She was talking to Thomas Leandro just before she left. But there were a lot of other people there. One of them might have jumped at the chance to do the general a favor. Or it could be someone with his own ax to grind. Pedro Harara, the president of the Banco Nacional, doesn't much like American women."

"Why not?" Cassie asked.

"He married one who caught him in bed with his secretary and took him for several million dollars when she moved back North again.''

The laughter around the room cut some of the tension.

Jed answered more questions, gave more opinions and assessments, all the while trying to keep certain pictures out of his mind—pictures of what could be happening to Marissa. He couldn't allow emotion to cloud his judgment. And he dared not let his private fears show on his face because that might panic the group.

Jason had been silent through most of the discussions, letting the others ask questions. Then he began to formulate a plan.

''Too harebrained,'' Jed snapped when the security expert had finished.

''Do you have a better idea?''

''Give me a little time to think.''

MARISSA SHIFTED uncomfortably on the narrow bunk. It was made of wooden planks and topped with a straw tick that prickled where it touched her skin. Not very comfortable, but at least the mattress wasn't resting directly on the unwashed stone floor.

She shuddered. She'd been in this tiny cell for three days, and she knew she was in danger of coming unglued. After the scene on the patio, two women had strip-searched her before she'd been locked up.

It had been humiliating, but thank God they hadn't found anything incriminating. Now she was praying that her hasty addition to Sanchez's toilet tank didn't gum up the works.

At first she'd huddled on the bunk, expecting the general to interrogate her as soon as possible. But minutes of waiting had turned into hours. Was he researching her background before he called her upstairs—to give himself an advantage?

That theory had gone out the window as hours dragged into days. She still hadn't seen the general. Or anyone else, since the guards were shoving her meager meals of rice and beans through a slot in the door.

Some of her clothes and her bag of toiletries preceded the food on her second afternoon. Wondering if anyone was watching on a hidden camera, she changed out of her rumpled black dress into cotton slacks and a T-shirt. The knowledge that someone had been in her hotel room wasn't comforting. Nor was the lack of response to any of the pleas and questions she'd shouted through the door.

What kind of mind game was Sanchez playing, anyway?

It was hard not to feel completely abandoned, but she didn't allow herself to lose hope. Still aware that someone might be spying on her, she furtively took some of the items from her cosmetic kit and slipped them into her pocket. If she was very lucky, she'd get a chance to use them.

Then, for as long as she could keep moving, she did what exercises she could manage without getting down on the squalid floor in her tiny cell. After fatigue claimed her, there was nothing to do but lie on the bunk and think.

First she tried to figure out how she'd gotten caught. Most likely the dirty rat who'd taken her money to unlock the door to the office complex and disappear for twenty minutes had turned her in. Or he could have gotten nailed himself. Or someone else at the party besides Jed might have figured out what she was doing.

Thomas Leandro? The balding professor who spouted Marxist doctrine and combed what hair he had in a swirl around his glossy dome. In a strong wind, he looked like a bird's nest that had blown out of a tree.

Pedro Harara? The five-foot-three banker who dressed like a character in a thirties gangster movie and wore a girdle to hide his paunch. He'd almost put her to sleep standing up with his scintillating discussion of international fund transfers.

Louis Rinaldo? The tough-looking minister of development who'd worked his way up from street gang member to cabinet officer. He wore three gold rings on his fingers to prove he'd made it.

Or what about the man who called himself William Johnson, the one with the horse face and the drawl that stretched all the way to Texas? She had no idea who he was or what he was doing at the party, but she'd had him on her list to check out. Too bad she'd never gotten a chance.

The only guest she was sure hadn't given her up to *El Jefe* was President Juan Palmeriz. San Marcos's elected leader hated Sanchez and was praying for an excuse to get him out of power. But his fear of a coup was so great that he didn't go to sleep at night without first looking under the bed.

After hours of fruitless speculation, Marissa felt as if she'd go insane if she didn't have someone to talk to. Maybe that was what Sanchez wanted. And she wasn't going to give him the satisfaction of breaking her. So she began to make up long silent conversations with various friends and enemies.

She mentally discussed with Abby the character defects that had gotten her into this mess. Abby kept saying it wasn't her fault; she wished she could be as sure.

She railed at Victor Kirkland for sending her on a mission that, in retrospect, had been foolhardy.

She tried to rehearse plausible answers to the questions

Sanchez was eventually going to ask her. If he wasn't simply planning to let her rot here.

But when she felt most alone and terrified, she talked to Jed Prentiss. Particularly at night when it was dark and he couldn't see her face.

She knew that was a silly contrivance. He wasn't even in the cell with her. She wasn't sure she could trust him. She didn't even know whether he was still in San Marcos. Yet it was somehow very comforting to lie in bed and mentally whisper to him in the dark, as if they were lovers instead of uneasy rivals.

Somebody turned me in. Was it you? She posed the question to him in her mind for the dozenth time, holding her breath as if she really were waiting for his answer.

I wouldn't do that, honey bee.

She wanted to believe him with all her heart. For the time being, she gave him the benefit of the doubt.

You're the only one who knows what's happened to me.

Yeah.

Are you doing anything to get me out of here?

She waited in the blackness, her mind forming the answer she wanted to hear: he was moving heaven and earth to spring her from this cell. But it was hard to have much faith in wishful thinking. Or anything else.

She closed her eyes and allowed herself to imagine that he had shifted to his side, that he had put his muscular arms around her so that they lay on the bunk spoon fashion. She sighed and scooted a little closer, almost swearing she could smell the spicy after-shave he wore, feel the hard wall of his chest against the back of her head. She pictured his broad shoulders and the sun-streaked hair that always made him look as if he'd climbed out of a lifeguard's chair. It was so good to delegate some of the fear and uncertainty to him. To let him give her his protection.

She longed to ask more of him. Gently she touched her finger to her lips, stroking back and forth with a feather-light touch, imagining what it might be like to kiss him. A little shiver went through her. She'd wanted to taste his mouth. A couple of years ago she'd finally admitted that to herself. Almost every time they met, she looked at his lips. But there was no such thing as sharing a chaste kiss with a man like Jed. He would want more.

Vivid images invaded her mind, and she could feel her body trembling. In the darkness she struggled for control— for the calm center of her soul where she was in charge of her life. It took longer than usual. Her emotions were in too much turmoil, her nerves too raw. But finally her will prevailed the way it always did.

Years ago she'd figured out what was necessary for her survival. Like the way she'd acted to keep Jed at arm's length. She knew he'd been puzzled at first. The perplexity had changed to a mixture of anger and hurt. That had made her ache inside. She'd wanted so badly to erase the wounded look from his eyes.

But he frightened her too much. He was too male. Too assertive. Too much a creature of the tough, aggressive habits he'd developed during long years as an undercover agent.

He was too dangerous for her. The wrong kind of man entirely. If she was going to dare a relationship with any-one, it should be with a mild, unthreatening guy who wouldn't make demands. Who'd let her set the pace. Yet fate kept throwing her into Jed's path in various Latin American countries where they were both doing under-cover work. And every time they met, she felt like a moth being drawn to a flame.

But it was different now. Here, in this cell, where she was so defenseless and alone, she was too weak to give up the small amount of comfort she gained by pretending he was lying in back of her, his body shielding hers, ready to overpower the guards when they finally opened the door. With a soft sigh she closed her eyes and hugged her arms around her shoulders.

JED LEANED BACK in the comfortable wing chair in Abby Franklin's office at 43 Light Street. The setting was tastefully soothing, and he tried to fit in by crossing his legs easily at the ankles and sipping at the mug of coffee she'd offered him. Probably he wasn't fooling Dr. Franklin. This crack-of-dawn meeting was his last stop in Baltimore before he decided whether or not to risk his life on a mission that had about a fifty-percent chance of succeeding.

"I appreciate your getting together with me so early," he said, setting down the mug.

"*I* appreciate your volunteering to get Marissa out of San Marcos."

"I'm not exactly working for free."

Abby ignored the clarification. "Now that we know for sure that the State Department won't do a damn thing, you may be her only chance."

"You might have to come up with another alternative. I haven't decided whether I'm going to take the job."

"Jason thinks you're the one who can do it."

He ignored the vote of confidence and sprang a question on her. "Is Marissa just a danger to herself? Or to others, as well?"

"She's not a danger to herself," Abby retorted.

"You told Cassandra her sister takes crazy chances."

"That's a loose interpretation of what I said."

"You have to tell me what's going on in Marissa's head before I make a commitment."

Abby looked regretful. "Jed, she trusts me not to talk about our sessions. I can't betray her confidences to you."

"Not even to save her life?"

Abby paused before replying. "Let me put it this way. If you go back to San Marcos knowing certain things about her that she hasn't chosen to reveal to you, she'll sense it—and react negatively. And she'll never trust either one of us again."

"Let *me* put it *this* way," he countered. "Your group of conspirators has hatched a very flaky plan. And when I get to San Marcos, I'm not going to be able to clue in Marissa. She'll have to take my opening moves on blind faith. Then the two of us are going to have to pull off a performance worthy of the stars in a Gilbert and Sullivan operetta. Is she up to that? Or will she get both of us killed?"

Abby knit her fingers together in her lap. "Jed, I can't tell you very much. But perhaps you've sensed that she has strong feelings for you."

"Yeah. She hates me."

"Hardly."

"Then what?"

"You have to work that out for yourself."

"I may not get the chance. From the way she looked at me when the guards took her into custody, I'd be willing to bet she thinks I'm the one who turned her in to Sanchez."

"You're describing a situation in which she was under a great deal of stress. She's had some time to think things through." Abby leaned forward. "Jed, some very rough things have happened to Marci in her life. Things she hasn't even been able to discuss with her sister. She's done what she had to do to survive, and she's come a long way.

I've thought for several months that you might be able to help her."

"She's discussed *me* with *you? What the hell did she say?"

"I'm sorry. I shouldn't have let that slip out." Abby flushed. "I'm not going to answer any more questions about my patient. What else did you come here to talk about?"

Jed shifted in his chair, looking from the tasteful prints on the wall to his hands and then toward the window. Everywhere but at Abby's face. He could get up and leave on cue. Or he could make a grab for the brass ring. "You're too perceptive."

"That's what they pay me for. But this session is free of charge."

He forced a laugh. It sounded strained and nervous. "You mentioned that everything that's said here is strictly confidential."

"Yes."

"So if I wanted to discuss something about myself and I wanted to keep it quiet, it wouldn't go any further."

"That's right."

He almost cut and ran. Then he figured he didn't have anything to lose. If he didn't want to, he never had to see Abby Franklin again. "There's a reason why I might be putting Marissa in danger by taking this assignment. I mean, something in *my* background that might make me a risky choice."

When Abby's expression remained neutral, he continued. "Did Marissa tell you I used to be hooked up with a supersecret spy organization?"

"Yes. She didn't tell me the name," she added.

"She probably doesn't know I was asked to resign." He

heard his voice turn gritty as he struggled to keep his face from betraying the depths of his humiliation.

"That was rough on you," Abby murmured.

"Yeah," he whispered.

"So did you really come here to tell me you're no good at your job?"

"I am good at it!"

"But you're the wrong man for the rescue mission?" Abby persisted.

"Maybe."

"I'm willing to give you my professional judgment."

"I found out seven years ago."

"Found out what?"

He clenched his hands on the arms of the chair so he wouldn't bolt from the room. With his emotions under equally rigid restraint, he told Abby Franklin the secret that had been eating him alive.

ROUGH HANDS shook Marissa awake, and she couldn't hold back a startled scream.

"Let's go," a gruff voice ordered in Spanish.

"Wh—what's going on?" she answered in the same language.

"*El Jefe* has sent for you."

Marissa's heart began to pound. With no warning, she was going to be interrogated by the man whose office she'd been caught burglarizing. Had he found the camera in the toilet tank? Was that why he was finally sending for her? She ran a nervous hand through her hair. "Would you let me have a minute alone?"

He shrugged and stepped outside the door, giving her some privacy.

Quickly she used the toilet in the corner of the cell and washed her hands and face, wondering how unkempt she looked after three days in a cell. She expected to be escorted upstairs to the general's office, and braced herself accordingly. Her eyes widened as she was led outside to a gray Chevy van parked by the delivery entrance. Two guards hustled her inside. Yanking her foot to the right, they cuffed her ankle to a ring that had been welded to the floor. Hardly standard equipment from Chevrolet.

"You said *El Jefe*—"

"*¡Silencio!*"

She pressed her lips together as the man slid onto the bench seat beside her. He kept a machine gun cocked under his arm. His companion climbed into the driver's seat and started the engine. After ten minutes it was clear they were heading out of the city. Going west, according to a road sign.

Marissa knew that Sanchez had a *finca* in Colorado Province. Calling it a farm was an understatement, since it occupied more than twenty thousand acres. Despite the heat and humidity, she shivered. In the capital *El Jefe* was a powerful man but not entirely above the law. At his outlying estate he was the lord of the manor. He could do anything with her that he wanted, and no one would ever dig up the facts.

A cold sweat broke out on her skin. Involuntarily, her foot jerked against the cuff.

"Sit still," the man with the gun muttered.

She went rigid.

The scenery changed from overcrowded urban to jungle in almost the blink of an eye. However, she knew from her extensive research on Sanchez and the local area that the two-lane road they took was one of the best paved in San Marcos, undoubtedly for the general's benefit. Marissa had come this way a few days ago on the trip she'd told Jed about—to visit some newly discovered Mayan ruins being excavated by a team from the University of New Mexico.

What would Jed do if he were in a spot like this, she wondered. Somehow, on all the dangerous missions she'd undertaken for the State Department, she'd never pictured herself getting captured. Shot, maybe; put out of her misery with one clean bullet. But not abducted. She shuddered, admitting for the first time that she should have known better.

Every ten or fifteen miles the jungle gave way to a village of thatch-roofed, bamboo huts strung out along the road. More than once a stray cow or goat wandered onto the pavement, and the driver honked furiously. Each time Marissa tensed as she entertained the guilty hope that the speeding van might collide with one of the animals. If the vehicle was forced to stop, she might have a chance to escape.

There were no such fortunate incidents with the livestock. But Marissa's lucky break came about a mile and a half past one of the villages when the van blew a tire. Cursing, the driver had to wrestle the vehicle to the far right side of the blacktop, since there was no real shoulder. When he opened the back door, he discovered there was no jack. He cursed again.

The two men—who turned out to be named Jose and Jorge—argued in rapid Spanish, each accusing the other of being responsible for getting them into this fix. Jorge, the one who'd sat with her in the back seat, lost the shouting match and ended up trotting back to the village. Jose climbed out and ambled into the shade of a kapok tree. Nearby several goats grazed.

It was only about eight in the morning, but the temperature in the disabled van was already rising to steam-bath proportions.

"You're not going to leave me in here, are you?" Marissa called through the open window.

"He's got the key." Jose pointed in the direction of his retreating companion before pulling his cap over his face and settling down for a nap.

Thank God they'd been too confident to search her, Marissa thought as she slipped her hand into her pocket and extracted one of the items she'd hidden—her spare manicure set. And thank God she knew a lot about the terrain, both from several previous jungle expeditions and extensive reading.

Working quietly and stealthily, she began to probe at the lock on the cuff that secured her ankle to the floor of the van. Every so often she glanced up at Jose. He looked as if he were asleep.

Her hands were shaking so badly that it took several tries to open the lock. Finally it yielded.

Her breath slowed as she looked through the window of the van. Was this whole thing a setup? An excuse to shoot the prisoner attempting to escape?

She didn't know. But she'd made her decision. Considering what could be waiting for her at Sanchez's estate, she had to try to get away while the getting was good.

After one last furtive glance at the guard, she ducked low and slipped out the open door.

The moment her feet hit the pavement she was crouching and running toward the safety of the trees.

Chapter Three

Marissa muffled her sob of relief as she reached the concealing foliage on the other side of the road. Quickly she slipped farther into the shadows.

She'd gotten free. But that was only the first step. Not a living soul in this part of San Marcos was going to risk Sanchez's wrath by helping her. Her only hope was to reach the American archaeologists at the Mayan ruins, explain what had happened and hope they had the resources to get her out of the country.

That meant she'd have to get far enough away from the van to risk crossing the road, then head north. Going back seemed like a bad idea, since she might run into Jorge. So she continued toward Sanchez's estate and tried to stay more or less parallel to the blacktop.

However, she soon found it was impossible to travel in a straight line without a machete to slash her way through the dense foliage. In addition, she had to move carefully, since she was trying hard not to leave a trail the guards could follow.

The jungle was alive with other dangers, too. The archaeologists had told her about killing a coral snake near the ruins. Since there was no antidote for their venom, a bite meant death within minutes. All she could do was break a dead branch from a small tree to use as a defensive weapon.

Her clothing was soaked with perspiration, but she kept moving at a steady pace, detouring around tarantula holes and the huge hills of the leaf-cutter ants, who could make mincemeat of human flesh as easily as they denuded trees.

When she judged she was half a mile from the van, she sprinted across the road. Then she headed north, using the position of the sun as a guide. Every time she heard a noise in the underbrush, she expected Jorge or Jose to lunge from behind a palm tree. But so far so good.

Marissa pushed herself as hard as she could through the bugs and heat and plants that seemed to grab at her clothing as if they had an agreement with the soldiers to slow her progress. Eventually she had to stop and rest. Wishing that she had a hat and some insect repellent, she reached out a hand to steady herself against a slender tree trunk.

It was an unfortunate move. The bark was covered with thorns. She yelped in pain, and high above her in the trees a colony of howler monkeys reacted. Mortally offended by what they considered the invasion of their territory, they began to protest loudly. She might as well have been standing next to an air raid siren.

She started off again at the fastest pace she could manage. But she was a whole lot less optimistic than she'd been a few minutes ago. She'd been counting on her pursuers not knowing where to look for her. The monkeys had given them a road map.

JED TRIED TO RELAX in the airline seat. At least he was flying to San Marcos first class this time, so there was enough room to stretch his legs.

Of course, there would be plenty of space to stretch out if he and Marissa came home in wooden boxes.

He grimaced. Abby Franklin could pay the funeral expenses, since she'd listened to his story and then made him believe he'd be okay if he took certain precautions. He'd left her office feeling better about himself than he had in years. After a little reflection, he realized how good she was at her job. What she'd really done was the equivalent of patching up a combat soldier and sending him back into battle. But he'd understood her motives. She was convinced that he was the only person with the right set of qualifications to extract Marissa from Sanchez's clutches.

The flight attendant came by and asked him if he wanted a drink. He ordered a bourbon and water. Maybe the liquor would help him sleep—like the rest of the passengers on the red-eye flight to Santa Isabella. Most of them looked as if they were going to San Marcos to visit relatives or relax in an unspoiled tropical paradise. *He* was flying into one of the trickiest assignments of his undercover career.

And he might have to change the rules as he went along if things didn't work out the way Marci's friends thought they would.

Marci. Ever since he'd heard her sister use the nickname, he'd started to think of her like that. It was part of his changing image of her, as if he were dealing with two different women. Marissa was cold and aloof, tough and sophisticated. She'd taken plenty of undercover jobs, and she knew the risks.

Marci was another matter entirely. His face softened as he considered her. She was fragile and vulnerable, shy and a bit naive. She pretended she knew all the rules. In fact, she'd conned *him* pretty well over the past few years, and he was a damn good judge of people. But all along she'd been hiding behind Marissa's tough exterior, hoping no one would notice her.

He pressed his knuckles against his teeth. Now that

Abby and Cassie had given him the right clues, he couldn't understand why he hadn't recognized the symptoms. She was like him, hiding some shameful secret she didn't want anyone to know. Something so bad that it made her reckless—even a little foolhardy—*as if she didn't believe her life was worth much.*

Too bad for her Abby had slipped and revealed more than she should. Or had she? His eyes narrowed as he went back over the scene in the psychologist's office, examining the nuances. Abby had told him she thought he'd be good for Marci. Had that been a calculated maneuver? Part of her plan to get him on her side?

He sighed. Whatever it was, it had worked. It had even starting him wondering if he and Marci could help each other, since neither of them felt there was much to lose.

Of course, Marci was one thing. Marissa was quite another. Getting close to *her* could be a disaster. He'd always known that Marissa Devereaux and Jed Prentiss would be an explosive combination. Either it would be damn good or they'd end up tearing each other apart.

Still, he felt a sense of tingling anticipation that made it difficult to sit still in the airplane seat. One of the reasons he was going back to San Marcos was to find out once and for all what would happen if he let her know he was attracted to her. This time Marissa wasn't going to be able to duck away from him or give him that cold look he now realized was a protective mechanism. Not if she was going to follow the script that the Light Street group had written for her. No, if she wanted to save her hide she was going to have to work with him—up close and very personal.

MARISSA KEPT PUTTING one foot in front of the other even though she'd long since reached the point of exhaustion. Yet she knew she had to put as much distance as she could between herself and the spot where she'd stirred up the howler monkeys.

So far Sanchez's goons hadn't shown. But she wasn't going to breathe easy until she reached the relative safety of the archaeological dig.

She hoped she could get there before nightfall. The jungle during the day was dangerous enough. When the sun went down, it would be pitch-dark and twice as perilous. She'd have to find a tree she could climb and wait for morning before she could risk moving around again. And that wouldn't save her from poisonous tree frogs or snakes. Or the predators that would smell her fear or hear her shivering. Aside from the dangers, when the temperature dropped, her perspiration-soaked clothing was going to feel like a cold compress.

But that was hours away. Her immediate problems were heat and thirst. She'd had nothing to drink but a few gulps of water in her cell that morning. And even with the high humidity, she was getting dehydrated from the jungle heat.

She hadn't crossed any streams, and she knew they would be a risky proposition out here, where she could pick up some nasty parasite while slaking her thirst. But there were hollow vines that were full of water. When she found one, she slashed it off with her penknife and gratefully tipped the cup end to her lips.

She'd taken several swallows when the sound of a branch snapping behind her made her whole body go rigid. Dropping the vine, she made a dash for a nearby thicket. But she didn't get more than a few feet before a muscular arm hooked itself around her neck.

Before her scream had died away she felt the point of a machete pressed against the small of her back.

"Be still, and you won't get hurt," a harsh voice she

didn't recognize instructed in Spanish. She'd been caught, but not by Jorge or Jose.

He was in back of her, so she couldn't see his face or gauge his resolve. As she breathed in the acrid scent of his sweat, she struggled to keep a lid on her fear. It helped a little to remind herself of her martial arts training. He wouldn't be expecting any fancy maneuvers on her part. And the first thing to do was make him think she was completely at his mercy. "What are you going to do to me?" she croaked.

Instead of answering, he called out loudly, "I've found the woman they're looking for."

Moments later he was joined by a friend dressed in the faded cotton trousers and shirts that San Marcos's peasants wore. He, too, was carrying a machete.

"I'm nothing to you. Please, let me go," she begged.

The one who held her began to march her toward the road.

"I just want to get back—home." The last part came out as a choked cry.

"The soldiers want you," he said, as if that settled the matter. *"Vámonos."*

"I'll pay you," she tried in desperation.

"We don't want your money," the second one answered. "They will be angry with the village if I don't bring you in. They might burn us out or kill our animals."

She understood then that there was no use pleading with these men or trying to bribe them. If they didn't obey the wishes of the soldiers, they would be inviting the wrath of *El Jefe.*

Her captors gave her no opportunity for escape.

In minutes they emerged from the shade of the jungle onto the hot surface of the road. The van from which she'd escaped was parked a hundred yards or so farther on, and she saw immediately that the soldiers had repaired the flat tire. Jose and Jorge were lounging against the vehicle, one on either side. It did nothing to lift her spirits to find out she'd been slogging through rough terrain half the morning, and they'd been riding along in comfort.

When the villagers delivered her up to Jorge, he gave her a look that was equal parts relief and anger.

"*Puta,*" he growled, his hands balled into fists. "What the hell do you think you're doing causing so much trouble? You're going to be sorry."

She braced herself for a blow, but none came. Maybe he didn't want to have to explain how the prisoner had gotten injured. Pivoting away, he honked the horn several times in rapid succession.

When he turned back to her, his anger was under better control. Methodically he began to search her, his hands lingering on her body in a way that made her want to throw up. When he found her knife and the other tools, he gave her a thunderous look.

"This will make the general very angry."

She raised her chin. "You wouldn't be stupid enough to tell him your prisoner got away, would you?"

"Why not?" The question was from Jose, who had come around the van to stand behind her.

"Because he won't be angry only at me. He's going to wonder why you were careless enough to let a woman in a leg iron slip out of your hands."

The two men exchanged a quick, whispered conversation. At least Marissa had the satisfaction of knowing she'd rattled them badly. And maybe her ploy would keep them from talking about the morning's misadventure.

Jorge cuffed her wrists behind her back before he shoved her into the van. The vehicle lurched away in a cloud of exhaust that enveloped the villagers who were standing several yards away watching the spectacle.

As JED pressed his foot down on the old Land Rover's accelerator he was thinking about the two best features of the road to *El Jefe's finca*. There were no potholes. And there weren't any cops on motorcycles who were going to stop him for speeding. Which was a damn good thing, because he was driving as if the devil was in pursuit.

He slowed marginally as he approached a village, alert for cows with a death wish. But at this time of day they were all lazing in the shade while the egrets picked the bugs from their hides.

As soon as he'd cleared the populated area, Jed accelerated again. He'd shown up at Sanchez's offices in Santa Isabella that morning pretending that he wanted to get together with his old buddy, since they hadn't connected at the party the other night. He'd been told that the general was at his country estate.

Determining the whereabouts of the female prisoner being held incommunicado had been a little trickier. But he'd been lucky enough to run into one of the men he'd trained six years ago. The fellow had made lieutenant, and he attributed much of his military success to Jed's guidance.

As they talked about old times and present duties, Jed asked if the general was loading them up with special assignments. He found out that two guards had taken a good-looking blond woman out to the hacienda the previous morning.

With his heart pounding, he'd gotten out of the conversation as quickly as possible. Five minutes later he had hit the road to Sanchez's estate, trying like hell not to think about what he might find. But he couldn't stop some pretty vivid pictures from jumping into his mind. He'd once walked into a session when *El Jefe* had been demonstrating interrogation techniques on prisoners captured from the revolutionary army.

As he sped west the sky turned to navy blue, and the wind began to blow. A tropical storm was rolling in. He hoped it held off until after he arrived at the *finca,* or the driving rain might slow him to a crawl.

Two miles from the main gate he was stopped at a checkpoint. Again he was damn lucky. It still wasn't raining, and another of his old comrades was on duty. He was passed through on the assumption that Sanchez knew about the visit. He hoped he didn't get the guard in too much trouble.

If things were the same as they'd been six years ago, an electrified fence and another guard station were ahead. Jed's hands tightened on the wheel. Even if they were best buddies, it was doubtful that the sentry up ahead would allow him to pass without authorization from *El Jefe*.

But what if the general was interrogating his prisoner? If he was busy with Marissa, he'd probably left strict orders not to be disturbed because he wouldn't want to break the rhythm of the session.

A sick feeling rose in Jed's throat. Too bad this Land Rover wasn't armor plated so he could steamroll the guardhouse and hope that Sanchez would come out to investigate the disturbance.

As it turned out, the sentry's attention wasn't focused on the road but on the nearby field that *El Jefe* used for disciplinary action. The trees at the edge of the parade ground bent and swayed. The wind tore at the shirts and trousers of soldiers in the field marching in formation as if preparing for a formal drill. Not likely in a gale condi-

tion. No, this was no practice session. He recognized the
configuration. It was a firing squad.

His blood turned to ice when he spotted the prisoner
being marched to a stake facing the troops. It was Marissa.

Chapter Four

Jed gunned the engine of the Land Rover and barreled through the checkpoint. The wooden arm on the barrier snapped like a fence rail in a hurricane. Behind him he heard the sentry bellowing in surprise, then anger.

"¡Basta! Or I'll shoot."

Jed didn't stop. Half expecting a volley of machine gun bullets to plow into the vehicle, he kept his foot pressed on the gas. A few seconds later he decided the guard was no fool. *El Jefe* himself was in an open car on the field. Any shots would endanger the general's life.

However, Jed was taking no chances. As quickly as he could, he put the troops between himself and the sentry. When the vehicle zoomed onto the grass, their precise formation dissolved into disarray. Some men stopped in their tracks, a few kept marching. Most broke into a run as if they'd been scattered by the rising wind. It would have been comical if Jed had been watching it on a movie screen. But this wasn't make-believe. It was Marissa's life.

The only soldiers who weren't aware of the disturbance were the ones escorting her toward the wooden stake about fifty yards away. Marissa walked between the uniformed men with her head held high and the breeze blowing the hair back from her face. She made it look as if she was the one in charge, not they. What was it costing her to march to her death with such composure?

As he watched, he felt a hard knot of anxiety inside his chest burst into sharp pieces, sending pain stabbing through his lungs. Lord, what if he'd been a few minutes later?

Behind him he could hear Sanchez snapping out angry orders. Then a troop of running feet hammered toward the Land Rover. Jed didn't wait for the squad to reach him. Screeching to a stop, he jumped out of the vehicle. Marissa wasn't out of danger yet. Neither was he. But he proceeded with what he hoped looked like unswerving confidence.

"Change of plans," he barked in Spanish.

At the sound of his voice, the men holding Marissa dropped her arms and whirled.

She was thrown off balance. Swaying in the gale, she turned on shaky legs and stared around uncomprehendingly as if she'd suddenly awakened from a nightmare and wasn't sure she was really conscious or where she was.

He saw her eyes snap into focus and zero in on him. He wasn't surprised as they widened the way they always did when the two of them first met. Yet this time he knew there was more behind the look than usual. He saw panic, relief and disbelief all warring with each other.

"Jed?" His name was a mere wisp of sound on her trembling lips.

"Come to get you out of this mess, honey bee." He was surprised to be struggling with the rough quality of his own voice. Momentarily, he was as shaken as she.

Tottering on shaky legs, she took a step toward him. At the same time she made a tiny, muted sound that was half sob, half exclamation.

Chaos swirled around the two of them. But it seemed to fade into the background. Marissa was the sole focus of his attention. And she was looking at him with the same intensity.

Closing the distance between them in a few sure strides, he caught her in his embrace and held her tightly, achingly aware of how small and fragile she felt. Like a fluttering bird he'd freed from a trap.

She slumped against him. He wasn't sure when she took hold of his shoulders, but he felt her fingers digging into his flesh so hard that he knew he would see the marks when he got undressed that night. Then her whole body began to tremble.

He bent his head and spoke low and urgently in her ear, glad that the wind gave them a measure of privacy. "It's all right. I'm here. I'm not going to let anything happen to you," he told her, his hands stroking through her hair and up the icy flesh of her arms as he tried to warm her with his touch, tried to project a sense of absolute confidence that he wished he could feel. He'd pictured a dozen harrowing scenarios. But not *this*. "I've got a way to protect you, honey."

His name sighed out of her once more, drawing his attention to her mouth. It looked so soft, so vulnerable, so exposed that he had to kiss her. Seeing his intent, she stiffened and made a startled exclamation. Afraid she was going to push him away, he tried to hold on to her with his gaze. This was the moment of greatest danger, the moment she could give away the whole shooting match.

"Marci, no."

She stared up into his eyes, hers so large and questioning that he could have gotten lost in their blue depths. Perhaps he was as dazed as she, because something strange happened. He knew where he was—on the parade ground, surrounded by uniformed soldiers. But the men and their surroundings had faded into the background so that he was conscious only of Marci. He sought something vital from her as his lips moved against her. At the same time he felt his own vulnerability rise to the surface as if he were the one in need of aid and comfort.

In that instant everything changed. The stiffness left her spine, and she went soft and pliant in his arms. In reaction, his emotions changed from protective to hungry. He drank in her sweetness even as she swayed against him, clinging to him like a lost kitten trying to grasp something solid. But he was as lost as she.

Later he realized that it all must have happened in mere seconds. On the field it felt as if they had stepped out of time into a private space of their own. As they clung together, nothing existed for him besides Marissa and the contact of his mouth against hers. His body against hers. The urgent movement of her hands up and down his back.

Her lips opened under his, and he took advantage of the surrender. He tasted passion, heard a low murmur in her throat that made the blood in his veins run hot.

Then in the space of a heartbeat he sensed her change, as he felt her remember who she was and who he was and that there was a reason—whatever it was—that she had never allowed him this close before.

He longed to bring her back to him. Longed to use every lover's trick he'd ever learned to recapture her heady response, but he realized with a start that they weren't alone and that a harsh voice had intruded into their reality.

The voice rose above the wind. "Arrest this man."

Jed's attention snapped instantly back to the here and now. Marissa went taut in his arms.

Soldiers with guns moved into position around them, cutting off any avenue of escape. But then, Jed had never thought this rescue was going to be easy. Ignoring the troops, he turned and focused on the man who had given the order.

Miguel Sanchez had the grace to look astonished. "Jed?"

"Sé, mi amigo."

Some of the squad had recognized him, and he heard his name whispered in the circle of startled faces as he shifted Marissa to his side.

"What is the meaning of this?" *El Jefe* demanded. "What are you doing here interfering in my private business?"

"I apologize for arriving unannounced. But I can't allow you to execute an innocent woman. Particularly when she's my fiancée."

"Your *what?*" Sanchez bellowed, any pretense of calm vanishing.

Marissa's reaction was no less violent. Her body jerked in Jed's arms. Raising her head, she searched his face, her eyes wide and startled. And so tantalizingly beautiful that he was almost undone. But he managed to remember why he was here and why it was so important to hang on to his wits.

"My fiancée. The woman I'm going to marry." He repeated the words very slowly and very evenly, and not only for Sanchez's benefit. Marissa needed time to take in the information.

"That's impossible. She's a spy!" the general growled. "She escaped into the jungle, and my men had to recapture her."

"Oh, yeah?"

"Do you know who sent her?"

"Nobody sent her. There's obviously been some kind of mistake," Jed countered. He'd been acting on pure instinct when he'd driven headlong in front of the troops.

Now he looked at the stake that had been waiting for Marissa and was unable to keep from shuddering. "This is no place for a civilized discussion. Why don't we go back to the hacienda and talk about it before we all get drenched."

Sanchez nodded—a single, curt movement of his head—and began striding toward his jeep. Jed started to lead Marissa to the Land Rover, but the general's voice stopped him. "No." *El Jefe* spoke over the wind, his voice raised so the assembled troops could hear. "I insist you ride with me, *amigo*. One of my men will bring your vehicle and put it in the garage."

Jed didn't bother to argue. His life and Marissa's depended on their getting a chance to communicate. But defying Sanchez at this moment was an even surer ticket to destruction.

Marissa still looked dazed as he helped her into the jeep's back seat. At first she nestled against him like an injured animal. But he felt her coming back to life as *El Jefe* barked orders to the squad. He sensed her struggling to pull herself together, but there was only so much he could do to help without giving away the story line to their attentive audience. When the jeep lurched forward she sat up straighter and squirmed in the seat, trying to put some distance between them. Jed suspected that his leg pressed to hers was making it difficult for her to think. But he held her firmly, aware that Sanchez kept shifting his gaze from the road to glance with interest in the rearview mirror at the engaged couple in the back seat.

"I was worried about you, honey," Jed murmured, keeping Marissa close to him and stroking his lips against her temple.

The caress made her shiver, and he wondered if the melting moment in his arms had been a figment of his imagination. No, for a few incredible seconds she'd kissed him like a lover. But he could put that down to disorientation—and a spontaneous reaction to the man who'd snatched her from the jaws of death.

He ached to find out if her surge of emotions had come from more than fear and gratitude. But that discovery would have to wait for another time and place. "I hope you're feeling more like yourself," he murmured, knowing the statement was only partly true. Lord, what he wouldn't give for a few hours with the woman who had come alive in his arms.

She swallowed. "Yes."

"Good girl." He patted her knee, anticipating her response to the intimate gesture. She jumped, and he knew he had gotten her full attention. As much for Miguel's benefit as hers, he began to speak in a half amused, half worried voice. "So I leave you alone for a couple of hours and you get yourself in a real mess again. Cassie and Abby and Sabrina and everybody else are going to be worried sick when they hear about this. Or maybe we shouldn't even tell them."

Her head whipped toward him. "How do you know—?"

His hand tightened on hers, and he clamped down on her sentence before she could give anything away. "How did I know you were here, honey bee? A combination of detective work and luck." He raised his voice and addressed Sanchez. "You weren't really going to shoot my lady love, were you, you old devil?"

"I was still weighing the pros and cons."

"Oh, yeah?"

"There was always the chance that a last-minute reprieve might loosen her tongue."

Marissa made a strangled sound.

They were approaching the stretch of jungle that separated the hacienda from the military complex. Miguel turned onto a hard-packed dirt road that wound past banana trees, tall ferns and countless jungle plants Jed couldn't name. They were all swaying wildly, raining leaves down on the jeep. And the sky was black as midnight. Jed expected the rain to begin pelting them any second.

When Sanchez leaned forward and picked up a portable phone, Jed pressed his fingers tightly over Marissa's.

She looked at him and nodded. And he knew she was functioning on a higher level. She understood that while the other man's attention was focused on giving orders for their reception, they had partial privacy. Still, Jed took the precaution of keeping his tone light and garrulous. "Don't let him fool you into thinking he's harmless."

She glanced toward the front seat. "I won't."

In the dim light he turned her face toward him. "Did he hurt you?" he whispered.

"Not physically."

He let out the breath he'd been holding. "You were in the prison complex in Santa Isabella?"

"Yes. In solitary confinement. I didn't see a living soul until two men brought me here yesterday."

Jed glanced up to see that Miguel was staring at them intently in the mirror again. Probably he'd only used the phone call to see what they would do when they thought his attention was elsewhere.

Just then they emerged from the forest. The wind suddenly died and the sun came out again. A good omen, Jed told himself, wishing he believed in omens.

They headed for a high adobe wall softened with festoons of blooming purple and orange bougainvillea. But the metal gate was all business. Jed watched as Sanchez pressed a remote control that slid the barrier open, interested to find that security had become more automated since his time. The modernization could be helpful if they had to make an unexpected getaway. Electronic devices could be disabled.

However, when they passed the dog kennel, his hopeful thoughts turned gloomy. Electronics were one thing. The pack of Dobermans that patrolled the grounds at night was another thing altogether.

The barking of the Dobermans stabbed through the last of the fog shrouding Marissa's brain. She gave Jed a quick sideways glance, marveling that he could appear so calm. Trying to follow his example, she sat up straighter and looked around, aware of her surroundings with a sudden aching clarity. The sun had come out from behind the clouds, and the whitewashed walls of the hacienda were bathed in the warm afternoon light. The wind had died to a gentle whisper. And she wasn't dead.

When she shuddered, Jed's arm tightened around her, and she had the uncanny sensation that he understood what she was feeling.

She looked down, hoping he wasn't reading *everything* in her mind. For her own equanimity she struggled to rationalize what had happened between them out there on the field—or more specifically what had happened to her. *His* part was easy enough to grasp. He was a normal man. She'd tumbled into his embrace, and he'd taken advantage of the situation.

But she'd behaved in a manner that was so totally alien that she could only explain it one way: she'd been living in a nightmare that would end with her own death, and just when she'd lost all hope, Jed had come charging to her rescue. She'd been so off balance that she'd let herself feel things she'd been afraid of for years. Particularly with him. Convulsively, she knit her hands together. Perhaps holding tight to her own flesh could bring back the perfect control she'd relied on for so long.

"It's okay," he whispered, and she wondered if he was still following her thoughts.

"Umm." With Jed's thigh pressed against hers and his grip firmly on her shoulder, it was impossible to think clearly, but she clamped down hard on her instinctive urge to pull away. She knew Sanchez was watching, and they had to keep playing by the script Jed had tossed her.

He'd told the general that they were engaged! How were they ever going to pull it off? How could they possibly act as if they were madly in love? As if they were lovers? Contemplating that led to memories of his kiss, which made her heart lurch inside her chest. Perhaps the most disturbing thing of all was that she still felt a tingle of awareness between them like a humming electric current. It had started when he'd kissed her, and she wanted to pretend it wasn't there. But she was coming to realize she couldn't wish it away.

Jed's arm was around her shoulder, but he was leaning forward responding to a question from the general. As she switched her focus to the conversation flowing so easily in Spanish, she realized for the first time how close the two men must have been.

"So why didn't you come to me when Marissa was first apprehended?" Sanchez asked.

"I tried. Ask that undercover man who took her into custody on the patio. He wasn't letting anyone through to you."

"He had his orders. But you should have let me know she was your woman."

Jed laughed. "I remember how you close ranks when you think you've been crossed. For all I know, you were going to assume *I* was part of a plot against you. Then you would have arrested me as well as her. And we'd both be up the creek without a paddle."

"You've got a point," *El Jefe* conceded.

The give-and-take between the men continued. Marissa missed a number of allusions that must have referred to events they both remembered well. She didn't much like being excluded, but she had enough sense to keep her mouth shut and let Jed remind the general of their old bond. She'd rather have the State Department on the job. But Victor Kirkland wasn't the one who had shown up to win her freedom. It seemed that Victor had tossed her to the wolves, and Jed had stepped in. Perhaps his friendship with the general might be the only thing that would get her out of here.

Or was that what was really going on, she wondered with a sudden little jolt. Jed had appeared out of nowhere like a knight in shining armor. But the rescue could have been staged, too. And he could be counting heavily on her vulnerability.

She swallowed painfully. Were Jed and Sanchez putting on a performance for *her?* Was this all part of some diabolical plan to get her to talk about what she'd found in the general's office? Did they think that if she wouldn't tell Sanchez anything, she'd spill the beans to Jed?

But if he was here to trick her, what about the familiar way he'd mentioned Cassie and Abby and Sabrina? He'd met her sister when they'd all been on an assignment together in Colombia. But he'd never met any of the other women from 43 Light Street. He'd made it sound as if they were all working together to get her out of here. Yet that could be faked, as well—when there was no way to get in touch with anyone whose name he'd mentioned so casually.

She had sense enough to know she was too off balance to make any coherent judgments. Her head swam with plots and counterplots as the jeep pulled up in front of the hacienda, where two guards in dress uniforms snapped to attention. She saw the curtains move at one of the windows and wondered who was watching. Jed helped her out of the jeep and kept his arm around her, guiding her toward the house.

Before they reached the front door, it opened. A teenage girl with long dark hair and liquid brown eyes came hurrying out. She had Miguel's features, and Marissa remembered that his dossier had mentioned a daughter and a long-dead wife. But there had been hardly any information about either one.

The girl stopped a few feet from the group.

"Clarita, you're not supposed to be out here," Sanchez said in a voice that raised the hairs on the back of Marissa's neck. If he could speak that way to his daughter, what might he do to a female prisoner?

The girl merely shrugged, clearly accustomed to his intimidating manner. "I'm not one of your soldiers. I don't have to follow orders."

"Everyone in this house follows my orders."

"Yes. And unfortunately everyone in San Marcos, too."

It was a dangerous response, Marissa thought as she waited to see what *El Jefe* would do. She couldn't imagine he was enjoying this little scene. His face contorted. "We'll discuss it later."

The girl looked as if she were about to say something more. At the last moment she turned toward Jed, her expression softening. "You came back to us. I knew you would after I saw you the other night."

"I have business with your father."

As the girl's gaze swung from Jed to Marissa and back

again, she went through another rapid change of mood. This time her eyes held a mixture of bewilderment and hurt. "I'm sorry I ran away from you on the patio. I thought you came to see me, and we'd have fun together again. Like in the old days."

Jed seemed perplexed, no more equipped for this scene than Sanchez. "I do want to see you."

"Then why do you have your arm around the woman prisoner? Why are you protecting her from my father?"

"Marissa is my fiancée."

The girl's expression went from questioning to fury in the space of a heartbeat. "She can't be."

"I fell in love with her. And I came here to bring her home."

"Oh." Several seconds of silence ticked by before Clarita tipped her head toward Marissa. "Are you good in bed? Is that what he likes about you?"

"That's enough," Sanchez roared. "Go to your room this instant before you embarrass yourself further."

Marissa stood with her cheeks burning while the girl turned and flounced away. Before she reached the house she pulled a hibiscus blossom off a nearby bush, crushed it in her hand and tossed it onto the pavement.

"I'm sorry," the general muttered as he watched his daughter disappear. "I'm having some trouble with her. But you can be sure she will be punished for that outburst."

Despite her own embarrassment, Marissa murmured, "I think she needs your love, not your anger."

"What do you know about it?" Sanchez snapped.

"I know what it's like to be raised by an army officer who doesn't have much time for his family."

"Well, you know nothing about *this* family, *señorita!*"

Marissa was instantly sorry she hadn't thought before she'd spoken.

"Come inside," *El Jefe* commanded. "We have more important business to discuss than my daughter."

When the general turned his back, Jed gave Marissa a warning look. She nodded tightly, acknowledging her mistake. But despite Clarita's angry words, Marissa's heart had gone out to her. She knew what it was like to feel trapped in a home where love was the last consideration. Bowing her head, she climbed the stairs. Inside, the wide front hall of the hacienda was cool and spacious and furnished like the grand entrance to a museum of colonial art.

The general was limping slightly as he escorted his visitors to the back of the house.

Marissa wondered what was wrong with his foot. He was obviously making an effort not to let his pain slow him down as he escorted them into an office. Glancing around her, she noticed the effort made to blend splendor and practicality. The desk and cabinets looked like valuable antiques, the chairs and sofas were of soft leather. French doors led to a large courtyard, alive with flowering plants.

El Jefe sighed as he took a seat behind a wide desk under the window. The desk rested on a slightly raised platform, giving the effect of a judge's bench towering over a courtroom.

With the option of putting some blessed space between herself and the general, Marissa remained standing near the door. Jed sprawled on one of the sofas as if he'd spent many relaxed evenings in the room. "Your gout acting up?" he asked.

Sanchez nodded tightly.

"Sorry."

"You're one of the few people who knows about it. If

the press got hold of the story, they'd say it came from rich food and decadent living.''

"Well, *I* know it's inherited from your grandfather. The secret's safe with me.''

Marissa expected Sanchez to look relieved. Instead, *El Jefe*'s eyes narrowed dangerously as he studied Jed. "Is it? I trusted you once. But this business with the woman has given me some strong doubts. You claim she's your fiancée. But I've had news of you from time to time, and this is the first I've heard you were engaged. So what are you up to? Is this all some trick to get me to let her go? Or should I have you both arrested and thrown into the cells downstairs while I find out what's really going on?'

Chapter Five

Marissa's knees buckled. Before she toppled over, she clamped a steadying hand against the back of a chair.

Jed didn't move except to look directly at Sanchez. For an endless moment there was only silence in the room. Then Jed laughed deep in his throat. "You know better than to try shock tactics on me."

"Do I? Well, how about this scenario? What if you're both spies—hired by our esteemed president Palmeriz to bring me down," Sanchez answered, his voice icy.

"Palmeriz! He doesn't have the guts to go against the commander in chief of the army. You could flood the capital with your troops and capture him before he gets out of the presidential palace."

Sanchez shrugged. "Perhaps, but I have other enemies. Men who would love to benefit from the power I've worked hard to consolidate."

"And they all know I'm not loco enough to try and put something over on you," Jed answered.

"For enough money, you might take the gamble."

"Money's no good to me in the grave. You know I never risk my hide taking foolish chances."

Sanchez relaxed a degree. "I also know you don't stay

in one place for long. You expect me to believe you intend to settle down with Señorita Devereaux?"

"Hardly."

The general raised a questioning eyebrow.

"Settling down wasn't what I had in mind," Jed continued easily. "I'm sure you've researched Marci's background. She's a travel agent who specializes in setting up trips to adventure locales. She's a very exciting woman." He chuckled. "In fact, she's very talented in a variety of delightful ways."

Marissa's hands tightened on the back of the chair. She knew the remark was intended to get the general's mind off spying and onto more intimate aspects of her relationship with Jed. Unable to meet *El Jefe*'s speculative gaze, she turned toward her temporary fiancé, who was also looking at her. She felt her face grow hot and her pulse accelerate.

She couldn't penetrate Jed's deadpan expression. But when he held out his hand, she recognized her cue. What's more, she'd just been given a very pointed lesson that her life might depend on acting the part Sanchez was expecting. Crossing the rug, she curled herself onto the sofa beside Jed as if snuggling up to him was the most natural thing in the world, as if it didn't make her heart beat so fast that she was in danger of passing out.

She drew in a deep breath and plunged into her assigned part, mustering what she hoped was an intimate look. "I wish we had some time alone. I'd like to tell you how glad I was to see you come driving up in that Land Rover." Her voice was pitched low, but not low enough for the general to miss.

Jed reached up to stroke a wayward strand of her hair back into place. "Honey bee, I was real glad I got there when I did."

The rough quality of his voice made the sentiment sound real. So real that she longed to drag him from the room and start asking questions. Personal questions.

Then, over his shoulder, she saw Sanchez watching them, and it suddenly came home to her how well matched the two men were. Superficially they weren't much alike. The general had dark hair, dark eyes and a dark complexion set off by a thin mustache. Jed's hair was sun streaked, his eyes green, his complexion golden from the sun. Yet the two of them had a lot in common. They were both dangerous and ruthless and accustomed to doing what needed to be done. She had to hope that Jed played by civilized rules. The general was different. Here at his *finca* he held absolute power. And as Lord Acton had so aptly put it, absolute power corrupts absolutely.

One of Jed's hands stroked her shoulder possessively, sending little shivers along her nerve endings. With the other he gestured toward Sanchez. "You haven't exactly been treating my fiancée like an honored guest."

"Until a little while ago, I didn't know she belonged to you."

Marissa pressed her lips together to keep from snapping back a retort that the concept of women as property had gone out with the Middle Ages. Except maybe in San Marcos. Then Jed plucked a twig out of her hair, and she was suddenly aware of how she must look. She was still wearing the rumpled slacks and shirt from her jungle adventure. And she hadn't even washed or brushed her hair in days. Automatically she tried to move away from Jed. He kept her firmly in his grasp, his hand continuing to move over her shoulder.

When he forced her closer, she willed her body not to stiffen in his embrace. She hoped she was making it seem natural as she closed her eyes and leaned her head against his chest. She hoped she looked like a woman who was letting her man take charge. So much of this charade rested on his shoulders, and over the past few minutes it had begun to sink in that he had put himself in a great deal of danger for her. "I'm sorry I got myself into this mess. I'm sorry I got *you* into it, dear heart." She swallowed, wondering where the endearment had come from. It had simply seemed like the right thing to say.

Jed gave her a crooked little smile, no doubt congratulating her on the improvisation. "I think it's going to work out."

When he grazed his thumb across her palm, she winced.

He was instantly alert, turning her hand over. They both stared down at the raised red circle in the center.

"I don't like the looks of that. What did you do?" Jed demanded.

She flushed. "Forgot the first rule of jungle survival. Never sit on anything, touch anything or lean on anything before you have a good look at it. I closed my hand around some thorns."

Jed lifted her palm, inspecting the welt and probing at it with his thumbnail.

Marissa struggled not to grimace again. "I tried to get it out, but it broke off."

"Well, I'm not going to take a chance on an infection, honey." He looked toward Sanchez. "Let me have your first aid kit."

The general didn't move for several seconds. Then, to Marissa's surprise, he opened one of his lower desk drawers and pulled out a small metal box.

Jed got up to retrieve it. "Thanks."

The smell of antiseptic filled Marissa's nostrils as he sterilized a needle and then her palm before cradling her hand in his left one. "It may hurt."

"It's okay."

She clamped her teeth together, but as Jed began to probe, she drew in several sharp breaths.

He raised the needle from her flesh. "Sorry."

"It's the only way to get it out. Just do it as fast as you can." She held on to the edge of the sofa with her free hand, focusing on Jed as she tried to shut out the pain.

"You're doing great," he murmured, working carefully. But the thorn was deep, and he couldn't get under it without stabbing into her.

She kept her eyes fixed on his face, watching the way his features contorted in concentration—and concern.

"I don't like hurting you," he muttered.

"I know."

She breathed out a long sigh when he finally freed the thorn and swabbed the wound with more antiseptic. This time the liquid stung.

When it was all over, he stroked his hand across her damp forehead. "Good girl."

She nodded wordlessly. She'd never imagined that Jed Prentiss could be this caring, this gentle. But then, a lot of things had changed in the past few days. And not just her perceptions of Jed. Too much had happened too quickly for her to ever be the same again.

For several heartbeats the room was completely silent. Then Jed cleared his throat, and she reminded herself that she was in no state to be making any sweeping pronouncements.

He addressed himself to Sanchez. "Marci's already paid heavily for her innocent mistake. And I don't mean only this wound. She's had three days in one of your filthy cells. Now I'd like to take her home and do my damnedest to wipe this nightmare out of her head." He sounded sincere, but she'd better keep remembering that this was as much a performance on her part as anything else.

The general's features tightened. "If she made an *innocent* mistake, why did she run away the first chance she got?"

"I was scared," Marissa replied instantly. "I know prisoners brought here have 'disappeared'—as they refer to it in Santa Isabella."

El Jefe didn't deny the accusation. "So you've researched me. You're quite thorough for a *travel agent.*"

"I always collect a great deal of information on a country before I decide it's safe for American tourists."

Sanchez let the answer hang in the air.

"Marci is a resourceful woman. I wouldn't expect her to pass up a chance to get herself out of a sticky situation. She'd been held for days, after all, and it looked like no one was doing anything. However, I can see your point of view, too, Miguel. I understand why you have some doubts about her. But I hope you'll make an exception in her case. Out of friendship for me."

"I have to consider San Marcos before myself."

"I know that. So I've come prepared to offer you something in exchange for Marci. Louis Rinaldo has told me how anxious the government is to develop the copper mining potential in Junipero Province. I'm sure the Global Bank will accept my recommendation of a six million dollar loan for the project."

"Rinaldo wasn't supposed to talk about the copper deposits!" the general snapped.

"No?" Jed sounded genuinely puzzled. "I thought your government was looking for a way to beef up exports."

"We are. But I prefer to keep reports on our natural resources confidential until we're ready to go ahead with a project."

Marissa glanced from Jed to Sanchez. The general's objection didn't make sense. How could you get a loan if you weren't willing to let your banker know how you planned to spend the money?

A buzzer sounded, and Marissa jumped.

Sanchez picked up the phone. After listening for several seconds he spoke in low, rapid Spanish into the mouthpiece. Then, replacing the receiver, he stood. "You'll have to excuse me. I'm needed elsewhere."

Jed also rose, bringing Marissa with him. With his free hand casually in his pocket, he stood facing the general.

"We'll talk about this later," Sanchez said, halfway out the door before he had finished the sentence.

"Convenient," Jed muttered under his breath.

When two armed guards entered, she felt Jed's fingers close around her hand. Were they here to take her back to the basement cells after all? And would Jed try to stop them?

The men walked toward Marissa, and she felt Jed's tension increase. At the last minute the one with a lieutenant's insignia spoke to Jed.

"The general is having rooms prepared for you."

"Upstairs?" Jed demanded.

"*Sí.* But you're to wait here for a few minutes until the maids can get things ready."

Marissa's relief was like a physical weight being lifted off her shoulders. Thank God she wasn't going back into the dark, dark detention center. For now, anyway.

The guards stepped back into the hall, and she heard them take up positions on either side of the door. For the first time since Jed had appeared in the Land Rover, she was alone with him.

He started to cough, turning away and raising his hand to shield his mouth.

"Are you all right?" she asked.

He cleared his throat. "Yeah. I swallowed wrong or something. Guess…I'm…more nervous than I thought."

The coughing stopped in a few seconds, but Jed's face was flushed. She looked at him anxiously. "You're sure you're okay?"

He nodded.

She grasped his arm, aware that this might be their only chance to exchange vital information. When she started to ask what he had planned, he shook his head quickly. "Now that he's out of the room, there's probably a whole bunch of private comments you want to make about how Miguel's been treating you, but you can bet it will all be recorded."

She drew in a shaky breath. "I wasn't thinking."

"You've had a pretty rough time, honey bee."

The endearment and the gentleness of his voice almost undid her. Her lower lip quivered, and she was suddenly afraid that the tears she'd been struggling to suppress were going to get the better of her.

Jed took her by the shoulders, folding her close. She closed her eyes and rested her head against his chest, struggling to get herself back under control. It wouldn't do either of them any good if she let herself start weeping.

"Better?" he finally asked.

"I—yes."

He pivoted them both so that his back was to the desk. "Stay right here with me."

At first she thought he was telling her not to go to pieces again. He squeezed her elbows, and she looked up. His green eyes bored down into hers as if he were trying to communicate some vital message.

"I'm with you," she tried, hoping the dialogue would lead to something constructive.

He gave her an odd half smile, directing her attention to his mouth. Then his lips drew back slightly so that she could see his teeth. She blinked when she realized he was holding something between them. It was flesh-colored plastic and looked like a large medicine capsule. However, the contents did not appear to be cold medication. Through the translucent sides she could see tiny black printing.

After several seconds, during which he held her gaze, the capsule disappeared back into his mouth. "I've been wanting to give you a real kiss," he said.

Her mouth went dry as she realized exactly what he had in mind. A few moments ago she'd been convinced that some basic part of her had changed. As Jed's grip on her tightened, old fears came zinging back to her. She was alone in this room with a man. He was holding her much too tightly. He could do anything to her he wanted. And she was terrified.

Panicked, she looked toward the door, half wondering what the guards would do if she came charging through. At the same time her hands went up to push against Jed's chest. But she realized he'd been prepared for her reaction. He didn't give her a chance to get away.

"I've got to kiss you, honey. Even if he's getting a kick out of watching."

Her eyes locked with his. He was telling her they were being videotaped as well as recorded. Maybe the general had even arranged this opportunity to see what they'd do the first chance they were alone.

She felt blood roaring in her ears as Jed's mouth slowly lowered to hers. *He'll do it quickly. He won't do anything threatening.*

Even as her conscious mind supplied the reassurance, her body trembled as his lips touched hers. She'd been afraid to let her defenses down with this man for a long,

long time. Afraid of intimacy. But the fear hadn't kept her from secretly dreaming about him.

Overwhelmed, she went very still in his arms. Her only salvation was to let herself imagine what it would be like if he really were her fiancée. The fantasy was so compelling that she grasped it like a lifeline. Then she realized she'd made a mistake—that she'd opened herself to the sensual feelings that had been buzzing between them the whole time they'd been together.

Jed must have sensed the change. "Ah, Marci," he whispered, his mouth brushing seductively back and forth against hers.

Her knees weakened, and her hands slid upward to clutch at the broad shelf of his shoulders. It was either hold on to him or topple over.

"That's right. Open up for me, honey," he whispered, his voice husky.

Every conditioned reflex urged her to wrench herself away. Instead, her lips parted. Because she had no choice. She had to go along with his plan or risk the consequences.

She waited tensely, expecting to feel him push the capsule into her mouth. Instead, his tongue boldly traced the edge of her teeth.

Her first reaction was rigid shock. But he didn't allow her to escape the erotic assault. And like a coin flipping in a game of chance, shock turned to pleasure.

When she sighed involuntarily, he gathered her more firmly in his arms. His tongue breached the barrier of her teeth and began to explore the softness beyond with little teasing strokes. A woman with more experience might have reacted less explosively. But after the strain of staying in control of so many emotions, she was suddenly helpless to repress her response. The gliding of his tongue against her sensitive flesh brought a wave of heat crashing through her body like a tidal wave.

The sensations pooled somewhere in her middle, and Marissa moaned deep in her throat. When she swayed against Jed, he growled something low and unintelligible and cupped her bottom, lifting her on her toes so that her body was more perfectly aligned with his.

The pressure of his erection should have been a threat. Instead, she swayed against him. Even the stubble of his beard rasping against her cheek added to the feeling of intimacy—of need.

She hadn't known it would be like this. So hot. So overwhelming. So empowering. Deep inside herself she sensed that he was as much her captive as she was his.

Breathless, she forgot where they were and what was at stake. The only thing real was Jed and the magic he was working on her senses.

Then she felt something pressing against her teeth. It was too rigid for his tongue.

Her eyes snapped open in confusion. His burning gaze helped guide her back to the known universe.

Events of the past few days flashed through her mind like scenes from a spy movie. The party. The patio. The firing squad. Jed coming to get her out of Sanchez's clutches. Jed had important information for her. It was stuffed into a little carrying case he'd put in his mouth. And he was ready to give it to her.

Marissa nodded fractionally, even as she felt his hands in her hair, steadying her head. When he pushed the capsule forward, she felt it slide between her lips, vividly aware of the intimacy of transferring something from his mouth to hers.

Afraid that she might swallow the container, she tucked

it down beside her lower teeth, the way she'd concealed chewing gun in school when she'd been a kid.

Still confused and shaken, she looked up into Jed's eyes. She expected to see triumph or perhaps even mockery at the way she'd come undone in his arms. She was surprised to encounter emotions that seemed to mirror her own. Or maybe she was only kidding herself.

She wasn't sure how long they stood that way, as if they were caught in a stop-motion picture on a TV monitor.

The spell was broken when the door opened.

"We're to take you upstairs now," the lieutenant said.

It was a relief to break away from Jed, from the intensity of what had transpired between them.

When she saw the guard staring at her flushed cheeks, they grew even hotter. Mercifully, he didn't prolong her embarrassment.

Her legs felt as if they wouldn't hold her up, but somehow she followed the man into the hall. Aware of Jed right behind her, she focused on her feet as she climbed the stairs. The little plastic container in her mouth felt as if it had ballooned to the size of a grapefruit. It was all she could do to keep from probing it with her tongue the way she might worry a broken tooth.

The guard halted before a closed door. She was paying so little attention to her surroundings that she stopped mere inches before crashing into him.

"*El Jefe* will see you at dinner."

Her questioning gaze shot to Jed. "It's okay," he said.

Marissa couldn't manage more than a nod before she stepped into the room. The door was shut and then locked behind her. Eyes closed, she leaned against the thick wood, half fearful and half thankful that she was alone at last.

Her body felt hot and achy in ways it never had before. Her pulse was still racing, her palms were wet. Slowly she rubbed them on the sides of her slacks, barely noticing the pain where the thorn had been.

But she was all too aware of the other unwanted physical sensations. What was she going to do? When she and Jed had been with Sanchez, she'd been playing a part thrust upon her. To save her life. And Jed's. But then the general had left, and Jed had kissed her, and everything had rocketed out of control.

Weak and shaking, she squeezed her eyes closed even tighter. The feelings that kiss had aroused were too threatening for her to examine.

It was easier to focus on Jed's behavior. He could have passed the capsule to her and been done with it quickly. Instead, he'd used the opportunity to kiss her senseless.

Her hands clenched at her sides. She was lucky she hadn't swallowed the damn container. What had been so important that he had to give it to her right then? Was he telling her the escape plan he'd worked out in case *El Jefe* wouldn't release her?

Or were his motives what they seemed? Her emotions did a flip-flop again as she scrambled to recall every scrap of information she had on Jed Prentiss. A few years ago he'd been a crack agent for the Peregrine Connection, that supersecret organization nobody ever talked about. She knew he wasn't with them anymore, and from the little she'd heard she gathered that the separation hadn't been exactly amicable. Had the breakup made him bitter? Did he care whose money he took? A little while ago he'd been talking as if he were working for the Global Bank. But he could be getting double pay for all she knew.

She sighed. She was in one hell of a mess. And she was way too off-balance to decide whom she could trust.

But she did know one thing. It was more important than ever to read the message Jed had passed to her with such relish. She raised her hand to her lips and then thought better of it. If there had been a camera in the general's office, there could well be one in here. Maybe Sanchez was still watching to see what she would do.

For the first time since the door had closed, Marissa took an interest in her surroundings. The furnishings were simple but comfortable, the bed covered in a brightly colored spread that looked as if it had been woven by village women.

Beside the bed was a box of tissues. Faking a sneeze that she hoped was as good as Jed's phony coughing fit, Marissa crossed the room and reached for a tissue. She brought it to her mouth and sneezed the capsule inside. At the same moment she heard the door behind her open. Did Sanchez have a zoom lens on his camera? Had he seen what she'd done and come to collect the evidence?

Chapter Six

Marissa went very still.

"I'm here to help you, *señorita,*" a woman said in Spanish.

Help me escape? Not likely. Marissa thrust the tissue-wrapped capsule into her pocket and turned. The servant she confronted was a plump young woman with the dark hair and large brown eyes of a San Marcos native. She was carrying an armload of clothing.

"My name is Anna. I've brought some things for you to wear. The best we have in the village." She laid her bundle on the bed and picked up one of the dresses. A simple design, it was made of delicately woven local fabric set off by stunning embroidery of birds and flowers.

It was the kind of outfit that would draw envious comments at a Washington garden party. However, Marissa knew that wearing such a dress would put her at a disadvantage with the general. If she was clothed like the local women—who had very little status compared to the men—it would be easier to treat her as an inferior.

"Where are my own things?" she asked.

Anna returned to the hall and brought in the suitcase that had arrived in the jail cell days ago. As Marissa poked through the mess inside, her heart sank. The contents looked as if they had been hastily searched, and only some of the items had been put back. In fact, most of her toilet articles and clothes were missing. If she appeared at dinner wearing any of this stuff, she'd look like a refugee from a Florida hurricane.

"I'll put everything away while you're bathing and washing your hair," the woman said.

"Gracias." Marissa gave her a friendly smile, considering and then discarding the idea of pumping her for information. Probably she didn't know much. And she'd likely be questioned about their conversation. "Do I have time for a siesta?"

"Sí."

"Then why don't you turn down the covers when you finish?"

Marissa took a nightgown off the bed and stepped into the bathroom. Unfortunately, she couldn't be sure she wasn't being observed even here. After a quick glance at the door, she left the tissue with the capsule in her pocket and began to get undressed.

Taking a shower and washing her hair should have felt wonderful after her ordeals in the detention cell and the jungle. But the pleasure was spoiled by her raw nerves. She needed to know Jed's plans. Or what line of bull he was feeding her.

JED TURNED HIS HEAD to stare at the wall to his right, wishing Marci was on the other side and that he could punch his fist through the plaster and make a hole big enough to pull her through. He couldn't stop picturing the dazed look on her face when their kiss had ended. Lord, what a sight. Her lips red and glistening. Her eyes bright. Her cheeks flushed.

Who would have thought Marissa Devereaux was capable of such passion? But when he'd demanded a response, she'd come alive in his arms like a woman suddenly let out into the sunshine after years of confinement in a prison cell.

Of course, she *had* been in a cell. Maybe she'd given up hope of ever getting out of here alive. That could explain it. She was grateful to him for showing up in the nick of time, and she'd given him the down payment on a suitable reward.

Except that it had seemed like more than that. It had seemed as if she'd been responding to him woman to man. And he'd reacted with the same intensity.

He touched his hand to his lips, thinking about the little capsule he'd had so much fun transferring from his mouth to hers. He could have gotten the job done a lot more efficiently. But all the cuddling they'd been doing on Miguel's couch had turned him on. And he hadn't been able to resist the knowledge that Marci had to play along with him or risk getting shot as a spy. Then right in the middle of the kiss he'd realized that he'd lost control of the situation and he'd better call a halt before he forgot what he was doing and swallowed the damn thing.

Striding to the bathroom, he turned on the cold water in the shower and stepped inside. He needed to stop thinking with his hormones. The needle spray cleared his head, and his mind switched gears as he began to lather his chest. He was in as much danger of getting shot for a spy as Marci if Sanchez caught on to their charade. What's more, he couldn't blame the general for being cautious. He *did* have enemies, including the president of the country, who would like nothing better than to strip him of his power.

Jed sighed. He and Sanchez had met when he'd been assigned by the Defense Department to help train the civil guard on the weapons San Marcos had purchased from

U.S. suppliers. He'd known *El Jefe* was ruthless, but he'd followed orders and cozied up to him. Later he'd learned things about the man that had made his blood run cold.

Miguel Sanchez could act like your best buddy one moment and turn into your executioner the next. Sometimes it was a result of his need to demonstrate his power. Sometimes it was simply a political expedient. But whatever was going on now, Sanchez hadn't jumped at the loan offer. Was he having it checked out with Rinaldo before he agreed to anything? Or was there something bigger at stake? He needed to find out from Marci whether she really had discovered anything incriminating in Sanchez's office. But first he had to figure out how to get her alone.

As MARISSA stepped out of the shower, her gaze went to her slacks. They were where she'd left them. After pulling on the nightgown, she casually pulled the tissue with the capsule from the pocket and returned to the room. To her relief, the maid was gone. Slipping into bed, she made an elaborate show of snuggling down under the covers so that the sheet was over her forehead. Then she unwrapped the capsule. It was difficult to open the darn thing without crushing the paper inside.

Long ago when she'd been a school kid defying her father's rules, Marci had read with a flashlight under the covers. She felt like that now as she burrowed more deeply under the sheet and doggedly worked to get the two halves of the capsule apart.

After several frustrating minutes she was able to extract a tightly rolled sheet of ultra-thin paper. It was hard to read the tiny print in the dim light of the little tent she'd created. When she finally got the sense of the message, it was all she could do not to start cursing aloud. Was this some kind of joke?

She scanned the material, her mind automatically lengthening abbreviations.

Jed Prentiss. Born December 17, 1956, Palo Alto, California. Roosevelt High School. University of California at Santa Cruz. Major—political science/Spanish. 5 feet 11 inches; 165 lb. On a dare from Dave Springer, college roommate, had boar's head tattooed on right buttock. Sleeps in the buff.

Marissa made a small choking sound. She didn't give a damn about Jed Prentiss's hidden tattoos or what he wore to bed. Yet she was smart enough to know why he'd supplied her with this material. As his fiancée, she'd be expected to have seen his bare butt—and to know what he wore to bed. Those and all the other details on this list.

Her eyes scanned down the sheet.

Drinks coffee—with milk and sugar. Favorite dessert—none. Would rather have espresso or Irish coffee. Hates eggplant. Favorite singer, Bob Seager.

There was more. Like his brand of toothpaste. His mother's maiden name—Sarah Fielding. His preference in football and baseball teams—the 49ers and the Giants.

It was a minicourse on the life of Jed Prentiss—something she'd never considered studying. Yet she made an attempt to memorize the list.

Somewhere between San Francisco sourdough bread—he loved it—and 157 Wintergreen Street in Laurel, Maryland—where his house was located—she nodded off.

Sometime later, a knock on the door jerked her awake. For a terrified moment she didn't know where she was. Then she heard the maid's voice asking if she was all right.

"Un momento," she called out as she began to scrabble through the bed covers searching for the list. Locating it under the pillow, she breathed a little prayer of thanks and squeezed the thin paper into a ball in her fist.

"Señorita?"

The door opened just as Marissa belatedly remembered she hadn't collected all of the incriminating evidence. There was still the capsule. Cursing herself for letting go of the darn thing, she pretended to straighten the bedding as she searched for the halves of the small plastic container. When she jerked on the spread, one rounded piece leaped up at her like a Mexican jumping bean. As it hit the bed again, she captured it in her free hand.

Anna hurried forward. "You don't have to do that. Let me help you."

"Is it time for dinner already?" she asked in a sleepy voice, scanning the floor beside the bed. No capsule half. If Anna found it, maybe she'd think it had something to do with drugs. Marissa grimaced. Her life was in a sorry state when her choices were being taken for a druggie or a spy.

"Sí."

She worked at putting some enthusiasm in her voice. "Pick out a dress you think the general will like while I wash my face."

Praying the woman would leave the bed alone, Marissa made for the bathroom. Behind the closed door she briefly debated hiding the ball of paper in one of the dressing table drawers so she could study it later. But that was taking too much of a chance. Hoping she would remember most of the information, she flushed the list and the half container down the toilet.

The thought of seeing Sanchez and Jed again made her hand shake as she washed her face and dabbed on a little of the eye shadow that was still in her cosmetic bag. Most of her tortoiseshell pins and combs were missing, so she brushed her hair back from her face and left it to fall loosely down her back.

The men would probably like the effect. For her the flowing hair was simply a visible sign of her loss of control.

So was the dress Anna had selected. As she had feared, it made her look like a village girl on her way to the big city. And the lack of a slip was unfortunate, she decided as she inspected her image in the full-length mirror. She could see her legs much too clearly through the gauzy fabric of the skirt.

With a grimace she rummaged through the closet. But there was nothing else that would do any better. She glanced at Anna again, wishing she was alone so she could look for the other capsule half. But that was impossible. When a guard knocked on the door, she squared her shoulders and ignored his scrutiny as she preceded him down the hall to the first floor.

El Jefe was waiting for her in a small sitting room that was almost as expensively furnished as his office. "You look quite refreshed," he remarked, sweeping his eyes up and down her body as if he could see it perfectly through the thin fabric of the dress.

Hands at her sides, Marissa kept herself from tugging at the shoulders to raise the neckline.

The general was wearing a formal uniform, the rows of medals on his chest another token of his elevated status compared to hers.

Anticipating Jed's imminent arrival, she glanced toward the door.

"I expect you're looking for your fiancé." Sanchez

smiled as he spoke, yet there was an edge in his voice that made Marissa's nerve endings come to attention.

"Yes."

"He'll be along later. You and I got off on the wrong foot, so I invited you down a little early to make amends," he said, playing the part of the gracious host.

I'll bet, Marissa thought, studying him covertly as she took a seat on the couch. "I understand why you have to be suspicious of me," she remarked graciously as her mind flashed on the camera and the film she'd hidden in his toilet tank.

"Please, we won't let any past misunderstandings spoil the evening. What can I get you to drink? Sherry? White zinfandel?"

"Sherry." She kept her gaze trained on his back as he turned to the drink trolley in the corner. Even the way he poured from the cut glass decanter conveyed a posture of command. Yet he wasn't entirely at ease. Why? All sorts of disturbing speculations leaped to mind. Did he know something? Or was this a fishing expedition?

To regain her equilibrium, she tried to focus on the details of the room—like the bust of George Washington in the corner. Was Sanchez arrogant enough to see himself as an equally important military man?

Looking down at the beautifully inlaid table in front of her, she fixed her gaze on a small statue of the Mayan rain god. Too bad it wasn't the god of fools who get themselves into impossible situations. She could have offered up a prayer.

"Tell me, how did you and Jed meet?" Sanchez asked in a conversational tone as he offered her the drink.

So that was his game. He had her alone, and he was going to try to trap her. She took a small sip of sherry, aware that she had to keep her wits about her. "It's nice of you to take an interest in us."

"Jed and I are old friends. But we've lost touch. I'm counting on you to fill me in."

"We were both with the American embassy in Colombia."

"So you're into undercover work," he remarked too casually.

"Oh, no, nothing so glamorous," she answered with a little laugh. "Most State Department employees have enough to do without worrying about undercover assignments."

"Well, Jed's managed. How long ago were you in Colombia?"

"Five years."

"And the two of you have been close all that time?"

In response to the general's line of attack, Marissa felt her stomach tighten. Had he already asked her "fiancé" the same things so that he could compare their answers? Or would that come later? All at once she was glad of the information on the sheet in the capsule. At least she had a fund of personal details she hadn't known a few hours earlier.

She called up a little smile. "We didn't like each other at first," she answered, sticking with a sanitized version of the truth and playing for time. The longer she could stay with vague generalities, the better.

"Oh?"

"We were both too ambitious, I think. And then it was hard for a man like Jed to accept a woman as an equal."

Sanchez nodded, his full attention on her. It was all she could do to keep from wiping her sweaty palms on her skirt.

"But our work kept throwing us together. And gradually

we realized we had a lot in common. We became engaged this year."

Sanchez shook his head. "I can't get over Jed's—how do you Americans put it—making a commitment. Even to someone as lovely as you."

"I like to think I've changed him." Mouthing that line made her stomach knot even tighter, but she kept her voice level.

"Some men do behave themselves when they're engaged. Did he ever tell you about the time we judged a wet T-shirt contest in Cozumel?"

Marissa's hand tightened on the glass of sherry. Sanchez was playing a version of "The Newlywed Game." Only the losing couple wasn't going to get a year's supply of dishwashing detergent as a consolation prize. They were going to be taken out and shot. She sighed and smiled. "I don't know every rowdy incident from his past, but it's no secret that he's enjoyed his bachelorhood."

"And what do you think of that hilarious tattoo on his thigh?"

Her cheeks warmed. "General, really! If you know about his tattoo, you know it isn't on his thigh." She gestured helplessly with her hands. "But I'm the last person you should be talking to about his wild past. What's important to me is that I've got him now, and I've decided it's better not to pry into the things he did before our engagement." The speech sounded convincing to her. She marveled that she hadn't choked on the last word.

Prolonging her agony, Sanchez studied her for silent moments, a smile flickering about his lips. "I apologize for tormenting you, my dear."

"Then let's change the subject."

"Of course. If you'll just satisfy a little more of my curiosity. When did he first kiss you?"

In front of the firing squad. Marissa felt light-headed as she frantically thought of and discarded answers.

"Our first kiss is a little too personal to talk about, don't you think, Miguel?" Jed answered from the doorway. He noted the frustrated look that flashed across *El Jefe*'s face before he managed to conceal the reaction. But Jed knew how to read the signs. The situation was deteriorating.

He opened his arms to Marissa. Rising from the couch, she crossed to him.

"I'm glad you're here, dear heart," she whispered.

"So am I."

He folded her close, feeling the fine tremor of her body as she pressed her cheek against the starched front of his tuxedo shirt. At that moment he wished he'd worn something softer.

"Are they treating you all right? Did you get some rest, honey bee?"

"Yes. And yes."

"Good." He brushed his nose along her hairline, breathing in her clean, fresh scent, realizing such familiar gestures were becoming second nature.

"Mmm. I like what you do for Miguel's shampoo. But ask the maid to bring you some of that gardenia perfume I like."

He saw her swallow, but she didn't pull away. He couldn't stop himself from taking more liberties, nibbling his lips along her cheek and murmuring a low endearment. He knew Sanchez was watching. He might have argued that cuddling like this was an important part of their act. Except that he was rapidly forgetting about the audience. What he wanted was to draw Marci into a dark corner of the hacienda where they could be alone.

"How long were you standing there?" the general asked, reminding him that they were playing a deadly serious game. But that didn't mean he had to turn his fiancée loose.

"Long enough."

He'd been lurking in the doorway for several minutes listening to Miguel give Marci the third degree, and his admiration for her had grown as he'd noted her confident rejoinders. She'd made up some of her answers out of whole cloth. Others had come from the sheets of paper in the capsule. Lord, she was good under pressure. He'd been half tempted to find out what she would say about their first kiss. But he'd been angry at Sanchez for going too far.

He looked down at Marci and grinned. "Miguel loves to brag about that wet T-shirt contest. It's one of the highlights of his international travels."

Sanchez made a dismissive sound.

"He's a man of dramatic contrasts," Jed continued, knowing he was upping the ante by baiting *El Jefe*, but he needed to let off some steam. "It's all right for the guys from San Marcos to sow their wild oats when they're away from home. But out here on his *finca*, he's not letting an engaged couple sleep in the same bedroom."

Marissa made a little choking noise.

"I know things are quite a bit more liberal in the States," Sanchez said. "But in my country, engaged is one thing. Married is quite another."

"Married?" Marissa croaked.

Jed couldn't repress a little grin. "That's one solution to the problem. But I know your sister and the rest of the Light Street gang would never forgive me if I scuttled the big wedding they've been planning."

Marissa stared up at him with a slightly dazed look as if she'd just realized that an engagement was usually a prelude to a wedding ceremony. He pressed his fingers over her wrist, feeling her pulse leap.

Would marrying me be so bad? he wanted to ask. But he couldn't do it in front of Sanchez. Wasn't there anywhere they could risk having a personal conversation?

Even if they found some privacy, minor considerations like her reaction to him would have to take a back seat to the more important issue of how they were going to get out of San Marcos alive.

Still, he was in a reckless mood. "Just think how great making love is going to be when we finally get back together," he whispered, his fingers playing with a strand of hair at her temple.

Marissa swallowed hard.

"See, I'm actually doing you a favor," Sanchez said with a show of good humor.

"Thanks a lot, *amigo*."

The general slapped him on the back. "Now that I've whetted your appetite, why don't we go in to dinner."

Marissa's face was rigid as she turned and stepped rapidly into the hall. Jed wanted to tell her that bantering about women was a good way to distract Miguel, but he had no chance.

The dining room was large, with a table that seated sixteen. Only three places in the center were set with crisp white linen, fine china and gleaming silver.

Sanchez sat across one long end from his guests where he could watch both of them as he kept up the flow of questions through the avocados vinaigrette and the spicy seafood soup. The meal was a strange mixture of the native foods the general liked and the continental cuisine he felt obligated to serve.

The conversation was a mine field, full of traps for the unwary. Marissa was sitting with her left hand clenched in her lap. When Jed reached unobtrusively across to press his fingers over hers, he felt how cold her skin was.

The main course of stewed chicken with black beans was served. Miguel tore into the food, and Jed hoped he was going to concentrate on eating. But after several bites he was at the interrogation again like a dog with a succulent bone. "So your travel agency is located in Baltimore?" he asked Marissa.

"Yes."

"And Jed's still got his apartment in D.C.?"

"No. He moved to Laurel. To be closer to me."

"I've got half my stuff in her apartment, anyway," Jed added. "We'll get a bigger place after we're married. Maybe something like her sister's town house where we can each have our own bathroom, and I won't have to deal with panty hose drying over the shower rod."

Marci's face contorted as she wondered why he was going into so much intimate detail. Then it dawned on her that he was cutting into Sanchez's interrogation time.

They continued to answer questions, each letting the other take the ones that would sound most natural, and Marissa had the exhilarating feeling that she and Jed were working very well as a team. Perhaps they should have tried it before.

"How do you like his gun collection?" the general asked her, raising his voice above the barking of the dogs that had started outside.

Involuntarily, Jed's fingers dug into hers. Gun collecting had never been one of his hobbies.

"He must have it in storage. I haven't seen it," Marissa answered carefully.

Good for you. He gave her a little grin.

"And what—"

The general stopped in midquestion, interrupted by a

slamming door. The noise was followed by a loud voice speaking urgently in Spanish. After several seconds the general got up. *"Un momento, por favor."*

"Certainly," Jed said.

"Stay here."

When the door closed behind him, he and Marissa were alone for the first time in hours.

Marissa could barely repress a scream of frustration. "I can't take much more of this," she blurted.

"I know, honey bee." Jed drew her out of her seat, away from the table and into his arms. She wanted to shout out that he was as much of the problem as Sanchez. She knew she had to keep up the role she'd been assigned, even when it looked as if the audience had disappeared. But if the strain continued like this, she was going to crack.

The noise level in the hall rose.

"Something's going on," Marissa whispered.

"Let's find out what."

"Maybe that's not such a good idea. He told us to stay here."

"I'm as tired as you of playing games." Jed strode to the door and pulled it open.

Peering around Jed, Marissa saw that a group of men had entered the front hall. Thomas Leandro, the socialist university professor, was gesticulating wildly to Sanchez. Behind him stood Pedro Harara, president of the Banco Nacional, and Louis Rinaldo, the minister of development.

The cliché *Latin temperament* leaped into Marissa's mind as she looked at the group that had apparently arrived unannounced. They were some of the leading citizens of San Marcos, and they were all wearing business suits as if they'd gotten up from their desks on short notice and driven directly to the general's *finca*. Yet they looked like an angry lynch mob.

"Where is the woman—Marissa Devereaux—you spirited away?" Leandro demanded. "I hope she's in good health."

"How do you know about that?" *El Jefe* asked, his own voice rising.

"Did you think you could keep it secret? Someone's been asking questions all over Santa Isabella."

Marissa stood transfixed as the front door was thrown open and William Johnson, the mysterious Texan who'd also been at the fateful party, marched into the hall. She didn't know how he fit into all this. But one thing was clear. He felt sure enough of himself with Sanchez to crash the party.

"Well, well. It looks like I've got you by the short and curlies this time. If you think—" He stopped in midsentence when he spotted Jed. "What's this got to do with *him?*" he snapped.

Sanchez turned, finding a focus for his anger in Jed.

There was shocked silence from the group in the hall as they followed his gaze.

"I told you to stay in the dining room," *El Jefe* snapped.

"And I told *you* I'm going to make sure nothing happens to Marissa."

"On that we're in agreement, since I had her brought here for her own protection. It's the only place in San Marcos I could be sure she'd be safe."

Marissa blinked. Had her sense of hearing suddenly failed? Brought here for her own protection? Directly from her prison cell. And then marched out in front of a firing squad. Who did the general think he was kidding?

Sanchez looked as if he were making a considerable effort to control himself as he continued to address Jed. "I'm sorry to cut short our dinner party, but my advisers and I have some internal problems to discuss. You will have to excuse us for the rest of the evening." He made a motion to the guards at the end of the hall and they stepped forward. "Escort my guests to their rooms."

Marissa tried to imagine the expression on Sanchez's face as he turned once again to the men in the hall. Whatever it was, he was back in charge of the situation. Nobody spoke. Nobody moved as the guards ushered her and Jed to the stairs.

Above them in the upper hall, Marissa thought she spotted something white and brown fluttering. She looked up in time to see Clarita sprinting in the opposite direction, her hair streaming out behind her. It was obvious she'd been up there listening to the commotion.

"Please, can you give me a moment with my fiancé?" Marissa asked the guard when he stopped in front of her room.

"No." Opening the door, he ushered her inside, and she was cut off from communication again.

The lock clicked behind her, and she wanted to kick the door in frustration. Instead she acted as if she had nothing better to do than get ready for bed. In the bathroom she changed into a nightgown and washed her face.

Outside on the grounds she could hear the dogs barking. Were more uninvited guests arriving? Or were the Dobermans after some poor animal?

Marissa tried to hang on to her anger. That had worked for her in the past to stave off fear. But tonight her anxiety was too high. She tried another tack. At the dressing table, she began to brush her hair with long, slow strokes the way her mother had taught her so many years ago.

One, two, three. Her concentration was broken at thirty when she heard several sets of heavy footsteps moving back and forth in the hall.

She tensed, listening. It looked as if Leandro, Harara,

Rinaldo and Johnson had all come to the hacienda because they knew she was there. Did they want to rescue her? Or were they simply angry that Sanchez had acted on his own? Who on earth was William Johnson that he'd turn up in the middle of such a scene? And how would Jed's presence figure in?

Marissa set the hairbrush back on the counter, feeling the small amount of dinner she'd managed to eat churning in her stomach. As she returned to the bedroom she acknowledged that she would never get to sleep in this condition. But she didn't want whoever was manning the video cameras to see her pacing back and forth all night, either.

While she'd been in the bathroom, the little maid or someone else had come in and straightened the bed. Chagrined at her lack of awareness, Marissa flashed again on the capsule that was lost somewhere in the covers. She'd better find it before it tripped her up. But how? Maybe she could pretend she didn't like the way the bed had been made.

Crossing the room, she grabbed the covers and flipped them down to the bottom of the bed.

A bloodcurdling scream rose in her throat and burst out as she stared in horror at the black, wicked-looking thing she'd uncovered.

Chapter Seven

The black shape skittered across the taut sheet, the fine hairs covering its body shimmering in the light from the bedside lamp. It was a tarantula about six inches in diameter. It was alive. And its natural habitat was not her bed.

Blood roaring in her ears, Marissa backed away, watching the eight-legged creature move cautiously in the other direction. Probably it was as unhappy to see her as she was to find it under the covers. But that didn't make her feel any safer.

The spider had reached the bottom of the bed when the door burst open and one of the soldiers came dashing in.

"*Señorita*. What is it?" His posture was defensive and his rifle was at the ready.

With a shudder Marissa pointed to the spider.

"Stay back." Moving swiftly across the room to the bed, the guard swung the butt of his rifle against the sheet, coming down on the intruder with a mighty blow.

Sick to her stomach, Marissa looked away, imagining that she could hear the hairy black body exploding under the impact of the assault. From down the hall she could also hear Jed pounding on his door, alternately demanding to be let out of his room and to be told what had happened to her.

A splintering sound made her whirl.

Seconds later Jed careened past the guard, a chair leg held in front of him like a club. A wild and dangerous look was on his face as he glanced around the room and located Marissa. Making directly for her, he took her by the shoulders. "Honey, are you all right? What in the name of holy hell is going on?"

"A—a tarantula." Marissa gestured toward the bed.

He spun and raised the club. When he spotted the spattered blob near the footboard, he cursed. "You were in bed with it? It didn't bite you, did it?" He tossed away the chair leg. It clattered against the wall as he went down on one knee in front of her. Lifting her gown, he ran his hands along her legs, searching for bites.

She braced herself against his shoulders. "I—I was fixing the covers when I found it. Otherwise, I…would have—" The sentence choked off in a little sob.

"Marci. It's all right, Marci." His arms went around her, gathering her close so that his head was pressed to her middle.

Every defense she'd learned over the past few years urged her to pull away, and for the first few seconds she pushed against him. Then as she became aware of his warm breath on her navel and the scratchy feel of his beard against her stomach, rational thought deserted her. In that moment she couldn't remember why he had come into her room in the first place. Her eyelids drifted closed, and her hands tunneled through his hair, gathering him closer against her.

This time when he said her name, she felt the vibration of his lips. Transfixed, she forgot to breathe. For several heartbeats neither of them seemed capable of breaking apart.

Finally he stirred. As his warmth deserted her, she reached for him, but he climbed to his feet and stood in front of her shaking his head as if he were having the same problems as she. But when he anchored her with his gaze, he was all business. "Take your time, but tell me what happened."

Her bottom lip trembled. Too much was happening too fast, she thought for the second time that day. With Jed. With the danger closing in around them.

"Honey, stay with me."

He used the phrase from when he'd been about to show her the capsule. He must have known it would get her attention.

She nodded, struggling for coherence. "Somebody sneaked in here and left that in my bed...."

Jed murmured reassuring words as she stroked his hands across her shoulders. "The bite hurts, but it wouldn't have killed you."

"I know. But the idea of getting in bed with it makes me cringe." Eyes closed again, she pressed her face against his chest. It was then she realized for the first time that he was naked to the waist, and she was in her nightgown. As she stared at the well-developed muscles in his arm, her heart started to pound again.

But she knew she didn't want to untangle herself from the sense of safety his powerful body gave her. She closed her eyes and moved her cheek against his bare chest, feeling the springy hair against her flesh and breathing in the clean scent of his body, wishing with an ache in her heart that everything could be simple and uncomplicated between them. But nothing was simple. Not their personal relationship. Not the perils of Sanchez's *finca*.

Jed continued to gentle her, as if the two of them really did mean something to each other. For a moment she let that fantasy tantalize her again. She hadn't known one person could draw such comfort from the physical presence of another. When she felt his lips brush her hair, she sighed and snuggled closer to him.

"Let's get out of here."

She nodded, longing for him to take her away from this place of fear and confusion.

"You're not supposed to be together." The guard broke through the cocoon Jed had woven around them. "How did you get out of your room?"

"The doors aren't all that solid." He gestured toward the chair leg he'd dropped on the floor.

The man looked incredulous.

Marissa's gaze swung from Jed to the massive wood door of her own chamber. If he'd battered his way through one like that, he must be as strong as a stallion. Or desperate.

"Get the general up here." Without waiting for an answer, Jed crossed to the closet and began to shuffle through the clothes. Pulling a robe off the hanger, he came back and draped it over her shoulders.

"Thanks." She slipped her arms through the sleeves and pulled the belt tight.

"*El Jefe. Pronto,*" Jed prompted, addressing the guard again.

The man shifted from one foot to the other as if he wished someone else had drawn this duty. "*El Jefe* is not supposed to be disturbed."

"Get him. Or I will."

The threat proved to be unnecessary. Sanchez himself appeared in the doorway, his expression dark as he looked from Jed to Marissa and back. She imagined he'd already seen the ruined door. "What's the meaning of this? You're supposed to be in separate rooms while you stay in this house."

"We were until I heard Marissa screaming."

"I demand to know what is going on."

Jed gestured toward the ruined bed. "Look. Somebody has it in for her. By now she could have been curling up to a tarantula. Luckily she stopped to fix the covers."

Sanchez appeared genuinely shocked, but he could have been faking the reaction. "The bite isn't fatal."

"Let's put one on your leg and see how you like it!" Jed growled. Then, making an effort to recover his composure, he spoke in a cooler tone. "Then you don't know anything about this?"

"Certainly not," Sanchez snapped.

"In the barracks sometimes we find tarantulas—and other wildlife," the soldier offered.

"Under the bed covers?" Jed inquired.

He shook his head.

"So who do you suppose put it there?" Jed asked his host. "One of your staff? Or one of your fire-breathing advisers? I suppose they all came up to inspect their own rooms."

"That's right. But none of them would dare try such a trick. Maybe it's just an unfortunate accident."

"Don't tell me you've started believing in coincidences?"

"We will discuss this in the morning."

"I can't sleep in that bed," Marissa choked out. "Not now."

El Jefe looked from her to the ruined sheet, considering. "You can move to another room."

"I'm staying with her," Jed growled.

"I don't think so."

Eyes narrowed, shoulders tense, the two men stood facing each other like gunfighters in old Dodge City. But in this case, only Sanchez had a gun in a holster on his belt.

Marissa saw the fingers of his right hand open and close, and she knew she had to defuse the tension between the two men. "Jed, it's okay," she managed to say. "The rules are different down here. We'll follow them while we're General Sanchez's guests. I don't want to have any more trouble tonight."

Jed nodded tightly. Breaking away from the general, he came back to her and looked down into her eyes. "Are you going to be okay?"

"Yes."

His gaze bored into hers, and she lowered her lashes. It was a futile gesture. She probably wasn't fooling him about her state of mind. She was a nervous wreck, and she wouldn't be okay until she was home. Maybe not then. But she had sense enough to keep her own counsel.

More soldiers were stationed in the hall, several of them excitedly inspecting the ruined door halfway down the corridor. Their buzz of conversation stopped abruptly and they snapped to attention when Sanchez appeared. He had a hurried consultation with a lieutenant before gesturing toward another wing of the house. "There are only two more rooms that are ready for visitors. Jaime will take you." Without further delay he hurried back down the steps.

Marissa spotted two shadowy figures standing in the lower hall craning their necks toward the action like spectators in the cheap seats at a boxing match.

From her vantage point she recognized Leandro's balding head and Harara's squat carriage. The professor caught her inquiring stare and looked guiltily away. Both men disappeared down the hall when they heard Sanchez's footsteps.

Had one of them slipped into her room while she'd been in the bathroom and put the spider in her bed? Not Leandro, certainly. He had been very friendly at the party. And he was reputed to be a pacifist. Of course, Harara was another matter. She'd sensed when they'd first been introduced that he didn't like her. But would he carry his dislike that far? And what about the other men who had arrived tonight? Johnson and Rinaldo. Maybe the perpetrator was deliberately staying out of sight.

She glanced at Jed, wondering if he'd also seen the spectators below. But he was walking with his head bowed. Moments ago his whole body had radiated tension as if he'd been plugged in to a light socket. Now he looked so tired he could hardly put one foot in front of the other.

"Are you all right?" she whispered.

"Yes."

She didn't like the automatic way he answered or the way he turned his face to the side so she couldn't see his eyes. But before they could say any more, she reached her new quarters. The lieutenant stepped between her and Jed, cutting off further communication.

When he opened her door she looked under his arm and saw Jed's guards stop in front of the next doorway. He halted, too, bracing his hand against the wall.

Her chest tightened. She wanted to go to him and find out what was wrong. But when she didn't immediately step into her room, the lieutenant took her by the shoulders and thrust her none too gently through the door.

"Wait."

Ignoring her plea, he shut it behind her with an ominous click. Then she was alone in a pitch-black room. She whirled on thick carpet. There wasn't even a sliver of light coming in from under the door.

"No. Let me out." Raising her fists, Marissa pounded against the rigid barrier. But no one answered, and she stopped after a few moments.

Closing her eyes to shut out the darkness, Marissa pressed her cheek against the smooth wood. Convulsively, her hand fumbled for the knob and twisted one way and then the other. It was a useless exercise. The door was locked. She was trapped in utter blackness. And it had been ten years since she'd felt anything but mindless fear in a dark room.

She understood the symptoms. Abby had explained to her about panic disorder. She knew exactly why this was happening to her. Yet she couldn't stop a fine sheen of perspiration from blooming on her skin. She couldn't stop herself from gasping air into her lungs like a half-drowned swimmer pulled from the bottom of a murky lake. And she couldn't stop the uncontrollable shaking of her body as her ears strained for the sound of someone approaching. Someone who was going to leap on her and—

She gritted her teeth and chopped off the thought. Not now. She wouldn't let this happen.

She *would not* let the old horror take over her mind and soul and make it impossible for her to function like a rational human being. The air around her felt thick and smothering. She wanted to sink to the floor and cover her head protectively with her hands. Instead she focused on taking shallow breaths. Knees locked so she wouldn't topple over, she reached out both hands and began to search along the wall for a light switch or table that might hold a lamp. Perhaps it was only seconds, but it felt like hours before her fingers brushed a switch plate.

Flipping the toggle, Marissa whimpered in relief as

blessed light flooded down from a small chandelier. Leaning against the wall, she waited while her heartbeat returned to normal and the fine tremors stopped racing over her skin.

As she came back to normal, she began to look around the room. It was enough of a surprise that she shook her head in disbelief. While her previous quarters had been comfortable, these accommodations looked like the presidential suite in a five-star hotel. She was standing in a large seating area furnished with velvet-covered couches, Oriental rugs and antique chest and tables. Through a doorway to the right was an even larger bedroom and through that she could see a balcony that looked out over the courtyard.

With a cynical twist of her mouth that only partly hid the fear in her eyes, she considered her surroundings. This room might be more opulent than the last one, but the door was still locked from the outside. That meant Sanchez could come in any time he wanted. Except that it wasn't only the general she had to worry about anymore. An angry group of his advisers had arrived at the hacienda. And someone had tried to…to what? Frighten her out of her mind? Put her out of commission and make it look like an unfortunate accident?

Marissa's skin felt clammy as she considered the possibilities. What was she going to do the next time a plate of food was in front of her? Surely it would be as easy to slip poison into her soup as it had been to slip a tarantula into her bed.

Sinking into one of the chairs, she cradled her head in her hands. She knew she was in danger of losing it—that she was overreacting to the darkness and to the peril all around her. But she simply couldn't help herself. She needed to feel that someone in this place was on her side. No, not just someone. She needed Jed.

As she pictured him, her hand stroked back and forth over the nubby fabric of the bedspread, and she realized she was remembering the feel of Jed's beard against her flesh. She whispered his name aloud as she thought about the way he'd acted at dinner—as if he was as unnerved as she by the questions designed to trip them up. And the way he'd battered down the door at the sound of her scream. It was pretty convincing evidence that he cared about what happened to her. Unless…

She bit back the rest of the thought. She had to hang on to *something* or lose her mind. And whether Jed liked it or not, he was elected.

JED STOOD NEAR THE DOOR holding on to the wall, sucking in air and expelling it too rapidly. He knew he was hyperventilating. It made him light-headed. Yet he was pretty sure that wasn't the only reason he felt as if he were about to topple over.

Fear of what was happening to him clawed at his insides. He tried to find some reserve of physical and mental strength that would pull him out of the torpor into which he was rapidly sinking. But he was too bone weary.

He'd learned his limitations. He knew what could happen to him when he was running on empty. He'd even told Abby Franklin about it. And he knew he never should have gone berserk and battered that door down. Not in the kind of shape he was already in. But a wild panic had seized him when he'd heard Marci scream. He'd imagined one of Miguel's men stealing into her room to have some fun with her. Or worse—to plunge a knife into her heart. He'd had to save her, whatever the cost. So he'd demolished the barrier between them like a bull elephant trying to get to his mate. And now he was in serious trouble.

Unbidden, his gaze flicked to the bed. He'd been trying

to pretend it wasn't there. All at once it was impossible not to stare at the wide, inviting surface. The thing he craved most in the world was to crawl under the covers, close his eyes and give in to blessed sleep. That was all he needed. Just a few hours in the sack and he'd be fine, he told himself. He took an unsteady step toward the bed, then another.

Before he reached it he made a strangled sound deep in his throat and bit down hard on his lower lip. The pain and the coppery taste of blood in his mouth brought back a little of his reasoning ability.

A hollow laugh rumbled in his chest. Who the hell did he think he was kidding? Only himself. It was happening again. The creeping sickness circulating in his bloodstream was taking over his body. And if he lay down it wouldn't be for a mere few hours. It would be more like a day and a half—if he was lucky.

He had to stay awake. Long enough for the terrible craving for sleep to pass. Then he'd be okay. He'd be okay because there was no alternative.

MARISSA SWALLOWED around the lump that had risen in her throat. Since the door had closed behind her, she'd been so focused on her own fears that she'd hardly been thinking about Jed except as her savior. Now that she was a little calmer, she started to consider the way he'd looked just before her view of him had been cut off. He'd gone from violently aggressive to pale and quiet in a matter of minutes.

Her mind made a terrifying leap. My God, had someone been after both of them tonight? Had she gotten the tarantula while Jed had been fed the poison? She might have dismissed the speculation as paranoia. But not in this house where new dangers seemed to spring up around every turn.

Fear clawing at her insides, she shouted Jed's name and pounded on the wall. There was no answer. Either he didn't hear or he couldn't answer. Her pulse was thumping wildly as she looked toward the sliding glass door. Could she get to Jed's room from the balcony?

Midway to the exit she stopped short, wondering if her mind had stopped functioning altogether. The moment she'd walked into her previous quarters she'd assumed she was being watched by a surveillance system.

Brow wrinkled, she tried to think it through, forcing herself to use precious seconds. Sanchez hadn't planned to put her and Jed in these rooms. Unless every bedroom in the whole hacienda was equipped with a video camera, this one could be safe. Still, as she stepped into the tropical night she pulled the drapes closed behind her.

The moon was half full, but it wasn't the only source of illumination. The stars shone down with a brightness that was startling to anyone who lived in a populated area where the ambient light drowned out the natural display. Here in the jungle it was difficult to recognize even the most familiar constellations because there were so many more stars than expected.

Marissa gazed across at the opposite wing of the house. Maybe there was no video camera inside her room, but if she tried to contact Jed, would someone be watching from one of the darkened windows? Would they come sweeping into the room and drag her down to the prison cells? She shuddered, but she didn't return to her room.

Cautiously she made her way to the railing. By leaning far out and peering to the right, she could see into the next room—the one that ought to be Jed's. A lamp was lit, and a surge of relief rose in her chest as she saw him.

Hope leaped in her breast. He was there! On his feet. But her feeling of relief died almost as soon as it was born. Jed was shuffling slowly across the carpet like a man whose feet were encased in cement boots. As she watched, he flopped into a chair by the window, threw his head back and closed his eyes.

In the next moment his head jerked up again and his lids snapped open. He seemed to be looking in her direction. Mouthing his name, she waved her arms in a wide arc. He didn't respond, but perhaps with the light on beside him, he couldn't see her through the glass. Charging back into her room, she looked around for something suitable to throw at the window—something that wouldn't break but that would still be heavy enough to attract attention. The only thing that came to hand was a small metal vase sitting on one of the tables. Bringing it out to the balcony, she judged the distance to Jed's window as she weighed the missile in her palm. Then she pitched it in an underhand throw that landed it against the bottom of the glass.

Her swing was a little too vigorous. But she was lucky the glass hadn't broken. The loud clanging noise of the vase colliding with the glass made her glance around anxiously for a squad of soldiers or a pack of barking dogs. But no one came running to investigate.

Looking back at the window, she expected to see Jed standing with his hands cupped against the glass trying to figure out what was going on. But he was still sitting in the same position in the chair, staring vacantly as if he were oblivious to his surroundings.

The hair on the top of her scalp prickled. If he hadn't heard that clatter, something was seriously wrong.

Marissa stared at the seven feet of dead space that separated her balcony from Jed's. Hitching up her gown, she climbed outside her railing, held on with her left hand and stretched as far as she could with her right foot. But she couldn't touch the other side.

Looking down, she grimaced in frustration. It was only one story to the ground. But the patio below her was cement. If she fell, she could break a bone—or knock herself unconscious. Then the dogs would be on her.

She turned her gaze to Jed again. He was sitting in exactly the same position, apparently unaware of what was happening even though he was staring in her direction. Her throat constricted with apprehension. He needed her. She felt it in her bones. And that knowledge had a curiously steadying effect on her roiling emotions. Since she'd been thrown into one of Sanchez's cells, she'd lost control of her fate. When Jed had appeared out of nowhere she'd been in danger of surrendering to his strength. That role had made her uneasy. Now there was something *she* had to do for *him*, and she wasn't going to let him down.

Turning back toward the house, she inspected the vines growing on the wall. She would have liked a more secure ladder, but they were her only option.

After tying her gown and robe around her hips so her legs would be free, she climbed up on the railing and grabbed a handful of ropelike lengths. Yanking hard, she tested them as best she could, hoping they would support her weight.

Fingers mentally crossed, she transferred her grip to the vine. It still seemed to hold, so she stepped off the railing. Hanging twelve feet in the air, she began to inch cautiously toward the far balcony, feeling her handholds and footholds in the foliage.

When she was halfway across the chasm there was a terrible ripping sound, and then the awful sensation of falling as the vine gave way.

Chapter Eight

Acting purely on instinct, Marissa threw herself to the left, bouncing painfully against the far railing as pieces of vine rained onto her head and shoulders. Luckily her reflexes were good. Somehow in the tangled confusion of greenery she managed to hook her fingers over the metal balustrade to keep from plummeting to the concrete below.

Eyes closed against the debris, she held on for dear life until the sky stopped falling around her. When she was certain it was safe to move, she pulled herself over the railing, then lay sprawled on the balcony surface, breathing hard, surrounded by broken stems and torn leaves. Cautiously she sat up and assessed the damage. Her shoulder throbbed, but moving it didn't cause any additional pain. So it was probably only bruised. In fact, she seemed to be in remarkably good shape, she decided as she brushed plant debris from her clothing. Apparently no one had heard the commotion. On the other hand, anyone walking below who happened to glance up would realize something drastic had happened. But if she was lucky, that wouldn't be a problem until morning.

Never mind how she'd get back to her own room.

Pulling herself up, she brushed the leaves from her robe

and readjusted the front, half expecting Jed to come charging outside to investigate the commotion.

He didn't. As she retied her belt, she peered through the window. He still appeared to be looking in her direction, yet he was sitting in the chair, unmoving, as if he was watching a television screen instead of a death-defying performance on his balcony.

Fear hastening her movements, she yanked open the sliding glass door and stepped inside. "Jed?"

No response.

In half a second she was across the room. Sinking to her knees in front of him, she grasped his large hands in her smaller ones. They were so cold that she sucked in a startled breath. God, he felt as if he'd been in a morgue.

Panic threatened to swamp her, but she forced it down as she studied him more closely, intent on grasping every detail of the situation. He was dressed almost as she'd encountered him last, in the tuxedo pants from this evening. But he'd kicked off his shoes as he'd crossed the room. From the corner of her eye she saw one near the bed. The other was closer to the chair.

His skin was the color of oatmeal. His eyes were still open, but they were unblinking, and they had turned the hue of ice frozen for centuries in an arctic wasteland. Even more alarming, his breathing was so shallow that she wasn't sure she could detect it. Frantically she pressed her hand against his naked chest, burying her palm in the springy hair, feeling for the beat of his heart. She felt no sign of life. That was when gut-wrenching fear really slammed into her. Gasping, she probed harder, her fingers digging into his flesh. The breath left her lungs in a rush when she found a slow but steady beat.

Marissa eased the pressure when she realized that her fingernails were gouging him, although he gave absolutely no sign that he felt the pain. For that matter, he didn't seem aware that she was even in the room.

What in the name of all that was holy could have happened to him so quickly? A half hour ago he'd been ready to duke it out with Sanchez. But something had changed radically. And the only hypothesis that made sense was that her wildest suspicions had been confirmed.

He'd been poisoned. Maybe at dinner. Maybe from food or water in his room. Was Sanchez responsible? Or someone else?

She bit back a frightened sob. Jed's life might depend on getting him to a doctor quickly. But she didn't even know if there was a physician out here in the country—or if he'd be willing to risk getting involved with a patient Sanchez was holding in a locked room.

She hardly knew she was mumbling aloud—half pleas to Jed to come back to her, half pleas to the almighty to bring him back. Opening his knees, she moved between them so that she could get closer as she continued to chafe his cold hands, stroke his bare arms and winnow her fingers through the hair on his chest. Unconsciously she was trying to bring him back to life with her touch. At the same time, some part of her mind realized dimly that she needed the physical contact as much as he.

"I'll get help," she murmured, her lips moving against his cold cheek, her hand cupping possessively around his head. "You'll be okay. You have to be." She started to scramble to her feet when a whisper of sound from his lips made her go very still. Her attention snapped back to his face.

Somehow in her frenzy of touching him and talking to him, a tiny part of the glazed look had lifted from his eyes. He was staring at her, and this time she was sure that he was really seeing her, that he knew who she was. His lips moved, and he seemed to be making a tremendous effort to communicate. What finally came out was a strangled version of her name.

"Mar...ci."

"Oh, Jed, I'm here. Just hang on. I'm going to get a doctor."

The muscles around his mouth contorted into a grimace. "N...o."

She hadn't expected an answer—or an argument from a man in this condition. "I think you've been poisoned," she blurted and then immediately wished she hadn't said so much. She didn't need to add fear to his problems.

He shook his head, the barest movement. She might have missed the gesture if she hadn't been focused on him with every ounce of her concentration.

"I'll be right back."

"Stay...." He gasped in air and expelled it in a series of disjointed syllables. "Happ...ens...to...me." It sounded as if he were dredging up each word from the depths of his soul, letter by painful letter, and she had the feeling he was determined to make the explanation or die.

She clenched her hands in frustration. It was hard to understand his slurred speech—and equally hard to judge if he really knew what he was saying or if he was hallucinating.

Torn between going for help and listening to what he was trying to say, she angled her head so she could get a closer look at him. As she searched his face, she saw that his eyes were piercing, almost pleading for her aid.

"What are you talking about?" she whispered.

"Happ...ened...before...." His tongue flicked against his lips. "Wat...er."

Marci glanced toward the door and back to Jed again.

His hands tightened on hers, the pressure weak but urgent. "Help...."

Torn in two, she tried to decide what to do. She was taking a terrible risk, but his wishes were so strong that she couldn't ignore them. Rising, she sprinted to the bathroom. When she returned with a glass of water, he still hadn't moved, but she could see that his eyes were tracking her, and her heart surged as she realized the improvement in only a few minutes. If he'd been poisoned, wouldn't he be getting worse—not better?

She knelt beside him again, supporting his head with one arm and lifting the glass to his lips with the other. He spilled a little as he drank thirstily, and she wiped her hand against his chin, vividly conscious of the intimacy of helping him with something so basic.

When half the water was gone, he closed his eyes and sighed deeply. She brushed the damp hair back from his forehead. His color was pinker, his breathing more regular. Pressing her hand against his chest, she decided that even his skin temperature seemed closer to normal. Silently she offered a little prayer of thanks.

He was watching her closely. All at once she didn't feel comfortable with her hand plastered against his naked chest. Not when he was staring at her with such intensity. Trying to look matter-of-fact, she lifted her palm away and took his wrist, probing the pulse point. It took a few seconds to feel anything, because the beat was still alarmingly slow. "Are you feeling better?"

"Pain."

She was immediately alert. "What hurts?"

"Noth...ing." She saw his Adam's apple bob. "Need...hit...me."

"What?" She gasped, tipping her head to the side, won-

dering if she'd heard right and, if she had, whether his
mind was coming up with nonsense.

"Need...stimu...la...tion...wake...up...." In his present
condition, saying more still seemed to be too much effort.

"Jed, I can't hit you."

"Have...to...."

The urgency in his voice tore at her heart. She felt as if
she had stumbled into a world where black and white had
somehow gotten reversed and she was being asked the
unthinkable.

"Pain."

The desperation in Jed's voice made her pull back her
arm and drive her fist against his shoulder. It wasn't much
of a blow. She simply couldn't make herself hit him with
much force.

"Harder."

"I'm sorry. I can't."

His eyes searched hers. "Then...other...."

She leaned forward, her ear turned toward his lips to
catch his whispered words.

"Other ... stim ... u ... la ... tion ... wake ... me ...up...."

There was a long, pregnant silence in the room.

"What should I do?" Even as she asked, she saw the
way his gaze had focused on her lips. He didn't have to
spell out what kind of stimulation could affect him as
strongly as pain. She could figure that out for herself.
When she'd first come into the room and knelt beside him,
he'd been cold as ice and barely breathing. Instinctively
she'd started to stroke and touch him. The physical contact
had made a tremendous difference. He'd come back to life
enough to communicate with her. Now she had to bring
him all the way back. If she couldn't hurt him, she'd have
to please him. With intimacy. Touching.

She couldn't meet his eyes. Feeling as if a giant knot were twisting in her middle, she raised her eyes to his. Even a few days ago she might have suspected that he'd somehow rigged this performance to see how far she would go. Tonight she sensed how much he needed her.

And the realization was like a power trip.

Moving around to the front of the chair, she came up on her knees so that her mouth was level with his. She felt his breath, felt his tension as he waited for her kiss.

Like Sleeping Beauty, she thought. Only in reverse.

Could she heal him? And perhaps herself? With something so simple yet so profound as a kiss? For one dizzying moment she felt as paralyzed as he. Then she leaned forward and brushed her lips against his as if sealing her fate—and his.

Marissa wasn't sure what she had anticipated. In the back of her mind she half expected that his arms would suddenly snap up and trap her so that any choice she had was taken away. But his large hands remained where they were, palms turned downward, fingers slightly curled, lying on the arms of the chair.

She was testing the waters as she turned one of his hands over, stroking his fingertips gently and then pressing her palm flat against his. When she felt a slight answering pressure, she let out the breath she'd been holding.

"Don't...stop...please."

It gave her an unaccustomed feeling of potency to know that she could bring him back to life. With a sense of awe, she touched his cheek with her fingertips, dragging them up and down, enjoying the way the scratchy endings of his beard moved under her touch—astonished at how much pleasure the simple contact gave her.

He didn't move, but his total attention was focused on her. She kept her gaze on him as she swept her hair over her shoulders and out of the way. She thought she could see the green of his irises deepen when she reached to stroke the arches of his brows, brushing the hairs in the wrong direction and then smoothing them back into place.

He made a sound deep in his throat, a sound that urged her lips back to his.

The first touch made her sigh. She was quickly caught up in the delight of rubbing her lips back and forth against his once more, teasing him—and herself. She'd never thought she'd have the nervé to play with a man this way. Certainly not *this* man. Part of her was overwhelmed. Part was honest enough to admit how much she was enjoying the heady sensation of power and pleasure. .

She cupped Jed's face in her hands; then, with her tongue, she traced the curve of his lips, feeling his shivering reaction all the way to her toes.

"Do you like that?" she asked in wonder, marveling that she could make him tremble.

His answer was a rough growl. For the first time since the contact had begun, he moved, opening his mouth silently, asking her to deepen the kiss.

"Jed." She spoke his name against his lips, nibbling, tasting, testing as she felt something hot and sensuous unfurl within her. He wasn't the only one coming alive. Sensual feelings spiraled through her, making her cry out.

The desire for more was a force she was powerless to resist. Her tongue stroked the insides of his lips and along the edges of his teeth, and she marvelled at the contrast of textures—velvety soft, hard and rigid. The exploration brought her to a new level of sensuality. But it wasn't enough. Caught up in the heady sensations, she wanted—needed—more. She heard herself make a strangled little sound as she sealed her mouth to his, swaying forward so that the upper half of her body was pressed against him.

Marissa wasn't sure when Jed's tongue began to move against hers, wasn't sure when his hands came up to stroke across her back and then tangle in her hair. She was so totally caught up in the encounter that she didn't even know which of them had pulled the robe off her shoulders so that only the thin barrier of her gown separated his heated flesh from hers. But one of them must have dispatched the garment because she was suddenly vividly aware of her breasts moving against his naked chest, her nipples tingling with pleasure at the contact with his thatch of springy blond hair.

Tiny shudders of sensation racked her body, making her inner muscles clench. She hadn't known desire could be this overwhelming, this frantic, this insistent. Had she really denied herself this pleasure for so long?

She was still kneeling on the floor in front of him.

"Marci. Honey." He gathered her up in his arms, pulling her half onto his lap. She sprawled across him, her middle pressed to his. He murmured endearments as his lips nibbled a trail down her neck, then to the V between her breasts.

His hot tongue against her sensitized flesh made her gasp. With his face he nudged aside the top of her gown, his mouth moving back and forth, tantalizing first one breast and then the other. When his mouth found one hardened nipple, she cried out and arched against him, dazed by the pleasure of it. And shocked to the core.

Somewhere along the line the rules had changed. She was no longer the one in charge. She was still hot and wanting. But now a voice inside her head was talking to her, warning her about the monster she'd unleashed.

She thrust it aside, choosing to remain captive in the web of sensuality that bound her to Jed. She wanted him. Wanted him to take her where she'd been afraid to venture.

If she could only go ahead and let that happen, it would work out all right. She'd come this far. She could go the rest of the way because it was Jed who was kissing her and touching her, and making her feel so needy. But she didn't have to be frightened; she was safe with him. Then he moved, holding her as he lowered her backward. All at once he was coming down heavily on top of her on the rug. She was trapped. And the fear she'd been so sure she had overcome came surging back in full force.

When she began to struggle, his hands held her so that she couldn't move. With a panicked sob she pushed against him.

"Jed. No. Please."

He was still weak. And she was infused with the strength of near hysteria. Desperately she wiggled away. When he reached for her again, she managed to keep several inches of heated space separating her body and his.

Her breath came in jagged little gasps. So did his.

He looked confused. "Marci, I thought you wanted this."

With shaking hands she pulled her bodice back into place. Then she found her robe where it had fallen on the floor, hauled it over her shoulders and drew the front closed. Pretending that the fabric could protect her from what she was feeling. Mortification. Sexual frustration.

She wanted to curl into a ball and hide her face from him. She wanted to run from the room. Somehow she managed to stay there, facing him.

"What's wrong?"

"We can't. You can't…" She heard the turmoil in her own voice and struggled for calm. Her emotions were too raw for her to explain her panic attack.

"Wrong."

"Jed…a little while ago I thought you were dying. That's how this started. You asked me to—to—"

His face hardened. "I see. You were on a mission of mercy, and it got out of hand."

"No. I mean—" She ran a trembling hand through her hair, wondering what to say.

He leaned back against the bottom of the armchair, drawing in large drafts of air, and she knew he wasn't going to force himself on her.

Half guilty, half relieved, she continued. "I was so frightened when I came in and found you like that. What happened to you?"

"You don't need to know."

She pinned him with her gaze, thankful for the change of subject. "Don't I? Jed, how do you think I got into your room?"

"I—" He stopped and looked toward the window as if he were dredging up a distant memory. "You came across from your balcony to mine," he said slowly. "The vines broke, and you fell. You could have killed yourself.

"You mean you saw me? But you were just sitting there like a statue."

His face was grim. "I remember it—sort of like a dream. I couldn't move." As if in denial he flexed his arms.

"I thought you were in a coma or something. I thought that you'd been poisoned."

"I was." His voice was low and raspy. His eyes told her that he wished he hadn't shared the information.

She felt goose bumps rise on her arms. "By Sanchez? Tonight?"

"No. Years ago. On an assignment in Royal Verde." His voice sounded like ground glass.

"What…what happened?"

"I'll tell you about it when we have more time. All you need to know is that you can't count on me in an emergency because I'm likely to go tharn on you," he said bitterly. "You know what that means?"

"Yes." He'd used a word Richard Adams had made up in *Watership Down*. It referred to the way his rabbit characters froze in place when faced with danger.

She scooted across the rug and took his hand. "You're not like that."

He grimaced. "Oh, yeah? I thought I just gave you a graphic demonstration. I was sitting in the chair watching you almost kill yourself, and there wasn't a damn thing I could do about it. The stuff that does it to me is still in my system," he snapped. "It always will be."

"I don't understand. You were fine until tonight."

"Usually I'm normal. But when I'm overtired and under a lot of stress, my body reacts by shutting down," he said harshly, as if he were revealing that he'd let himself become addicted to drugs.

She tried to get through to him with the steady pressure of her hand over his, wishing he would turn his palm up. But he seemed to be simply enduring her touch. "It's not your fault."

"But it's my *problem*. It limits my ability to do my job."

"Is this thing why you had to quit the Peregrine Connection?" she blurted.

He snatched his hand away. "How do you know about that?"

"You hear things."

"That's just great! What else is grist for the rumor mill?"

"Nothing," Marissa managed.

Still, anger simmered in Jed's eyes as he looked away,

and she wished she hadn't asked the question. Or maybe she'd done it on purpose, to punish him because he'd made her lose control. Only she knew the accusation was a lie. Losing control had been *her* problem.

"Jed, I'm sorry," she whispered. "I know—"

"How I feel?" he cut in. "Were you really going to use that line? Somehow I seriously doubt that you know how I feel." Pushing himself up, he swayed on unsteady legs.

She scrambled off the rug and reached a steadying arm toward him, but the mortification in his eyes made her hand drop back to her side.

"I'll be okay in a minute." After taking several deep breaths he made his way to the window where he stood looking out into the night.

Marissa stared at his rigid shoulders, sharing more of his pain than he could imagine. With all her heart she wanted to go to him, comfort him. And make amends for pushing him away when her passion had led him to believe she wanted him. She especially wanted to make amends for that. She *had* wanted him. Only she hadn't had the guts to go through with it. Because she was still fighting her own demons.

Would it make him feel better if he found out how closely she could identify with him? How much they were alike? All at once she wanted to tell him about the unspeakable thing that had happened to *her*. For the first time in years she was willing—no, anxious—to talk about her own worst nightmare. No matter what the personal risks.

Scrambling up, she crossed the space between them. "Jed, I—"

He turned, and she saw that he looked amazingly like his old self. "I'm feeling a lot better."

"I see that." She also saw that a mask had dropped

over his face. He'd hated admitting weakness to her, and he was dealing with it the only way he could.

"Thank you for helping me." He might have been thanking her for helping him fix a flat tire for all the emotion he put into the acknowledgment.

"I was frightened for you. I wanted—"

"To wake me up."

"It was a lot more than that." She gulped. Unless she explained what had happened to her, she'd lost him.

However, he continued as if she hadn't spoken. "I guess I should have told you about my little infirmity before I asked you to marry me, honey bee," he said tightly, his gaze sweeping the room before boring into hers.

"Oh." She realized with a start that she'd been so focused on herself and Jed that she hadn't remembered the house rules. There was always the possibility that the room was bugged, and someone might be listening very avidly to what they were saying. She and Jed were supposed to know each other intimately. In fact, their lives might depend on maintaining that fiction.

She was pretty sure he hadn't been thinking about their deception a few moments ago. But as he'd regained his strength, his mind had snapped back into focus.

Her own thoughts raced over the minutes they'd just spent together, trying to examine what they'd said from the point of view of someone glued to a microphone. It might sound as if they weren't communicating too well. But at least neither of them had talked about anything incriminating—with regard to the two big issues at stake, her search of Sanchez's office and their bogus engagement.

And what about the way they'd abruptly broken off lovemaking? She flushed, but her thought processes churned on. It was logical that she might have stopped things because she was worried about Jed's health. Logical, too, that he might not have shared every unpleasant episode from his past.

From his point of view, the worst part of the exchange was that he'd told her an important secret about himself— something that threatened his masculine ego. Something he wouldn't want the general or anyone else to know. In return she'd nearly made a confession that would have handed *El Jefe* the key he needed to break her. Thank God Jed had stopped her.

"What are we going to do?" she whispered.

He fixed her with a wry look. "For starters, unwind in a nice hot shower together."

"What?" Marissa's voice cracked on the syllable. Had she heard that right?

"Now that I finally have you where I want you," he added, then slowly and distinctly mouthed, "Where we can talk." He watched her intently to make sure she'd understood.

Reluctantly she nodded. He was right. The only way they were going to be sure they couldn't be overheard was if some heavy background noise drowned out the sound of their voices. But did it have to be a shower? In desperation she looked around the room. If there had been a radio or a television set, she would have turned it on full blast. But neither device had been provided.

Jed started toward the bathroom, his steps a good bit surer than they had been a few minutes ago. Marissa stared at the broad expanse of his naked back, profoundly relieved that he was feeling better, yet at the same time nervous. He was taking charge again whether she liked it or not.

On legs that felt like someone else's limbs she followed, wondering where she'd find the nerve to go through with what he was suggesting.

The bathroom was large and luxurious, but when Jed closed the door it seemed to shrink to a tiny cell.

Jed turned on the taps full force. His next step would be to disrobe. It was a sure bet that he wouldn't get in the shower with his pants on.

Marissa clenched her hands at her sides and somehow kept herself from backing out of the room. If she'd only been smart enough not to get caught in Sanchez's office in the first place. But here they were in enemy territory with very few options—and it was her fault. Without giving herself time to think about what she was doing, she snatched off her robe and let it drop to the floor.

Jed pivoted back, towering over her, his eyes darkening as they swept over her translucent gown. When they lingered on her bodice, she felt her nipples contract.

She swayed toward him, the flame ignited by their passion still glowing inside her. Then she stopped herself with a hand on the edge of the sink.

He gave her a half smile, slightly mocking, a little sad, mostly reassuring. "We both know there's unfinished business between us."

She moistened dry lips. "Jed, I'm having trouble handling this."

He pitched his voice well below the sound of the pounding water. "You want me."

"We have to talk about us."

He sighed. "When we get out of here. Right now, you don't have to go any further with this shower deal if you don't want to."

"What?"

He stepped closer and lifted her palm to his lips. Transfixed, she felt his gentle kiss. Somehow it steadied her nerves. She hadn't thought he'd be capable of gentleness after what had happened. But he was full of surprises. She knew she had only begun to learn what made Jed Prentiss tick, and she wanted to find out more.

Taking her by the shoulder, he dipped his mouth near her ear. "My educated guess is that our friend doesn't have a video camera in here. Just audio, if that. It ought to be as safe to talk like this as it is under the running water. For a few minutes, anyway."

She swallowed hard, thankful that he was letting her off the hook. "Thank you."

His next words made her head snap up.

"The first thing I have to know is if you trust me."

It was an honest question. She gave him an honest answer. "I wasn't sure at first. I thought you and Sanchez might have cooked up some kind of deal to get me to talk."

"And now?"

"I know you're on my side." When they got out of San Marcos there was a lot more she planned to say. But it would have to wait.

"That's something, anyway. Because we've got to rely on each other to get out of here."

"Yes."

They stripped the conversation to its bare essentials, a hurried exchange of information in staccato bursts of speech.

"Was it your idea to pretend that we were engaged?" she asked.

"Jason came up with the basic plan. Abby refined it," he replied.

"She would. What happens now?"

"I was hoping Miguel would buy the distraught-fiancé act. Now I'm not so sure. Maybe Harara will help us."

"He hates American women."

"He owes me a favor."

"What if he's afraid of Sanchez?"

Jed looked frustrated.

"Maybe there's something we can use. Or maybe it's too dangerous. When I was in his office, I found something."

"Good." His hands gripped her shoulders.

"It's hidden—" Marissa stopped abruptly when she heard a noise in the bedroom.

Jed cursed under his breath. With instant awareness and lightning speed he reached for Marissa and pulled her into his arms. Lowering his mouth to hers, he gave her a hard kiss that she knew would leave her lips reddened.

Seconds later the door burst open, exposing them to hostile eyes.

Chapter Nine

Marissa clung to Jed for stability, gasping as his lips moved over hers like a passionate lover with nothing more urgent on his mind than making the most of a clandestine tryst. However, there was no way she could respond to him as her ears strained to catch the first words from whoever had burst into the room. She could only stand where she was, holding on to Jed, and let him take charge of the performance.

"That's enough," a harsh voice commanded.

Taking his time, Jed slowly lifted his head and turned toward the intruder in the doorway.

Miguel Sanchez glared at them, his gaze flicking to Marissa's reddened lips and then insinuatingly down the length of her gown. "You know this is against the rules."

"Miguel, don't you think this moral mania of yours has gone far enough?" Jed asked mildly. "Since when do you come barging in to your guests' bedrooms?"

The general's eyes glittered dangerously as he regarded them. It had to be after two in the morning, but he was still wearing the dress uniform he'd donned for dinner. Now it was rumpled, and patches of sweat showed under his arms. "Bedrooms. Separate bedrooms."

"See, I told you they were together." The high-pitched

female voice in back of him stabbed through Marissa. Craning her neck, she drew in a startled breath as she caught sight of Clarita. She blinked. The teenager was dolled up as if she were on her way to a nightclub. Heavy shadow set off her dark eyes, her lips were a red slash and her dress was a low-cut gown that showed off too much of her creamy breasts. Her heavy perfume hung in the air, while she stood rubbing her hands as if she were lathering them with soap.

"I said you couldn't trust the woman to follow your orders. I said she was out to make trouble. But you never listen to me. You're one of the ones against me. Like her." There were more accusations. Clarita's words came out in a torrent like a fountain under sudden pressure.

Marissa expected Sanchez to stop her quickly. Instead he looked angry and frustrated.

Marissa stared at Clarita, trying to take the whole thing in, trying to reconcile the various impressions she'd formed of the girl. Her behavior was erratic, hostile, unbalanced, Marissa realized. For a long moment Clarita stared back, her eyes glittering with a hysterical light. As quickly as the storm of words had risen, it subsided, and quite suddenly she shrank against the wall, looking down at her feet.

Jed had angled his body so that Marissa was slightly behind him. When he spoke, it was to Clarita. "Little one, we mean you no harm. Why are you spying on us?"

She shook her dark hair so that it fell in soft waves over her shoulders. "To prove I was right. And don't call me by baby names. I'm hardly a child anymore."

"I see that," he muttered, as if he were having trouble relating this person to the girl he used to know. "But that doesn't mean we have to stop being friends."

"I thought we were," she snapped. "Until I found out you were against me."

"Now what in the name of the blessed virgin is going on?" The question came from the hallway. They all turned toward the bedroom as Pedro Harara, clad in a red silk robe, strode through the door. Moments later he was joined by the other three men who had arrived unexpectedly that evening. Johnson looked as if he'd hastily pulled on his pants and shirt. Leandro and Rinaldo were in nightclothes. But only Leandro looked as if he'd actually been asleep.

There were several seconds of dead silence while the professor nervously finger-combed his hair over his bald spot.

Then Sanchez laughed and held out his arm dismissively as if he'd been interrupted scolding two naughty children. "You know how it is when visitors from a more permissive society come here. They have trouble conforming to our quaint, old-fashioned ways. I've explained the rules to Jed and Marissa more than once. In this house we set an example for the youth of San Marcos. Engaged couples must sleep in their own rooms. But these two keep finding ingenious ways to get together."

"I know what you mean. I had the same problem with my daughter," Rinaldo said. "I was afraid she was going to disgrace the family name with a tell-tale bulge at the front of her wedding dress."

"How did you handle it?"

He gave a little cough. "Expediently. I moved up the wedding date."

"Ah." Sanchez's face took on a contemplative look. "Now there's a good idea," he murmured, his manner becoming expansive as the idea took hold. "If these love-birds can wait one more night, we'll hold a wedding ceremony here tomorrow. Then I can stop playing *dueña* and get back to more important business.''

Marissa's mouth dropped open. Had she heard him right? ''A...wedding?'' she croaked.

''Yes. It's short notice, but my people will love the excuse for a fiesta.'' Sanchez grew more animated as he got down to the particulars. ''First thing in the morning I'll contact the village priest and the woman who sees to the bride's instruction. We have our own traditions here that go back centuries. You'll find they add to the sense of ceremony.''

The more details he added, the more Marissa felt her throat constrict. This wasn't happening. This man wasn't planning her wedding and intending to carry out the plans tomorrow. Yet he was. Somehow she dredged up a coherent objection. ''We can't get married in San Marcos. My...my sister has everything planned at home.''

''I know Jed mentioned your friends back in Baltimore. If they're disappointed, you can have a second ceremony when you get back.'' Sanchez grinned conspiratorially. ''You can even keep this one secret, if you like.''

Perhaps the general had more to say. But Marissa heard nothing besides the roaring in her ears. Married to Jed. Impossible. If she'd thought she'd be forced into this position, she would have— What? She had no answer. And she'd never felt less in control of her destiny.

She wanted to bolt from the room. Perhaps Jed had read her mind because he kept a hand on her shoulder. His grip wasn't tight, but somehow it held her in place. She felt as if she was going to pass out. Miraculously, she stayed on her feet.

For the second time that evening Jed must have helped her on with her robe, because she found herself wearing it. Dazed, she followed the general back to her room, and moments later she was alone. Without regard to who might be looking, she sank onto the bed, cupped her face in her hands and rocked back and forth, feeling sick and terrified. And desperate.

"WHAT THE HELL ARE YOU trying to pull?" Jed growled as he strode into Sanchez's office. He'd stopped to put on a shirt and shoes that didn't go with the tuxedo pants he was still wearing. At least his bedroom door hadn't been locked, undoubtedly because Miguel was trying to make it look as if he and Marci were guests instead of prisoners. Thank God for small favors.

"I'm convinced you care for Señorita Devereaux. As much as rascals like you or I can care for a woman," *El Jefe* answered.

"I don't need you to run my love life."

"It's a bit more than that, *amigo.*"

Jed took a deep breath. He was angry with himself and angry with Sanchez. But he'd better stop showing it. This was the first private conversation he'd had with the general since he'd charged onto the field and snatched Marci from the firing squad. Since then, Sanchez had had a chance to think things through and decide how he was going to proceed. But he was also under pressure from the contingent who had arrived this evening. "Why don't you fill me in?" he asked, hoping his elevated heart rate didn't filter into his voice.

Sanchez shrugged and spread his hands in a palms-up gesture. "We keep coming back to the basic fact that your fiancée got herself invited to a reception at my house, then slipped out and stole into my office. I have no way of knowing if her story about the door being unlocked is true—or if she broke in. Nor do I know what she might have tampered with before the guard found her."

"She didn't tamper with anything!" Jed retorted, his voice imbued with righteous indignation.

"How can you be sure?" Sanchez drawled. "How do I know you weren't exchanging information instead of kisses a little while ago?"

"You saw what we were doing."

Sanchez gave him a considering look. "I saw what you wanted me to see. I noticed you were running the shower so no one could hear what you were saying."

"Wouldn't you, under the circumstances? But you're determined to put your own interpretation on everything we do."

"On the contrary, I'm doing my utmost to get the two of you out of San Marcos without looking like I'm going soft."

"I'm listening."

"Why do you think Harara and the others came charging out here tonight?"

"I can make some educated guesses about your political advisers. I don't know how Johnson fits into the picture."

"I don't owe you an explanation. But I'll give you the executive summary. Johnson is an arms dealer. What we're negotiating is perfectly legal. However, he's giving me a very special price, and he wants to make certain that the details of the transaction stay private so other clients don't start demanding the same terms."

"All right, I'll buy that," Jed replied. "But I suspect your compatriots have more official motives. They found out you were holding Marci, and they want to make sure you don't do anything that will jeopardize relations with the U.S."

"That's a fair assessment of Rinaldo's position," Sanchez conceded. "He grew up grubbing for money, and he thinks your six million dollars for economic development is a good deal. Leandro is here to monitor the situation for President Palmeriz, although he's pretending he has my best interests at heart. Harara wants me to get rid of Señorita Devereaux to make sure national security hasn't been breached.''

''You're lying.''

''Of course he'll deny it, if you ask.''

''So what do Marci and I have to do, storm your arsenal and shoot our way out of here?''

Smiling, the general shook his head. ''Nothing so drastic, old friend. Calm down and think this through like a male chauvinist citizen of San Marcos. Rinaldo gave me the idea. But he's right. Remember how things work down here.''

Jed listened intently.

''I wasn't lying when I said this is a country with old-fashioned values. Including our attitude toward the fair sex. Women here don't have equal status. Very few dress up in suits and high heels and go to the office. A good wife stays home and obeys her husband. And if he orders her to keep her mouth shut about confidential government information she might have seen, she does what he says.''

Jed's eyes narrowed as he spoke slowly. ''You're saying our getting married will satisfy your requirements? That once Marci and I tie the knot, she's safe. And we can go home.''

''Yes,'' Sanchez replied. ''You can leave the day after the ceremony, when I know you've consummated the marriage.''

''It's that simple?''

''There's one other stipulation.''

''Which is?'' Jed asked cautiously.

Sanchez paused a moment, and the intensity of his dark, speculative gaze made Jed want to lower his eyes. Ingrained training and long years of experience kept him from moving, but it couldn't keep sweat from forming in the palms of his hands.

"We were friends once," Sanchez began. His tone, full of warmth and sentiment, made Jed even more nervous. What did the old devil want? "Maybe we're not exactly *simpático* anymore," the general continued. "But I still know you're a man of honor. So I want you to give me your word that my private business stays private. In other words, you guarantee that if your wife did see something she shouldn't that she'll keep it between the two of you."

"You trust me to do that?" At least Miguel hadn't asked for proof that it was going to be a real wedding night. Jed didn't honestly know if he could insure that.

The general's gaze was steady. "It's either trust you or kill you."

"I appreciate the frankness—and the vote of confidence."

"I must have your word of honor."

Jed had come downstairs ready to promise the moon if that was what it would take to get Marci out of here. Yet he executed a quick mental tap dance before he answered. If Sanchez were an honorable man, he'd have to deal with him honorably. But he knew of too many occasions when the general had broken his solemn oath. Still, Jed would do his best to keep Marci quiet—unless she'd found something that was too monstrous to suppress. "I give you my word that your private business remains private," Jed replied.

The general pulled a small knife from his drawer. "Do you remember the solemn blood ceremony we used to use in the old days when the men graduated from boot camp? I think that would be a fitting way to seal our bargain. With a mingling of blood. Give me your hand."

Jed felt a knot twist in his stomach. "I didn't do it then. I can't do it now."

Sanchez looked up sharply. "You can't validate your oath?"

Jed swallowed hard. For a second time tonight he was going to have to reveal the weakness that had made a shambles of his career. "I have a sickness in my blood."

The knife jumped in Sanchez's hand. "*Dios.* You're not HIV positive?"

"Not that. It's something else. A very exotic tropical disease I picked up in the Caribbean," he explained, telling Miguel a small part of the truth. "Apparently there's no cure. The pattern is like malaria. The symptoms come back to me from time to time."

El Jefe looked at him speculatively. "What are they?"

Jed kept his gaze steady. "Worse than gout. But leave me a bit of dignity."

"I'm sorry. It's hard for someone like you or me to admit any weakness."

"I've learned to live with it."

"Is it the reason you started thinking about marriage?"

Jed shrugged. "Maybe I'm tired of being alone—of not having anyone who's there for me." He hadn't been sure what he was going to say, but he realized he'd come pretty close to the truth.

"I think I have a better understanding of your behavior." Sanchez held out his hand. "We'll shake on the deal."

They clasped hands.

"Thank you," Jed said with genuine feeling. "Marci means a lot to me." Again he silently acknowledged how true that was and how much he wished that things were different, that the two of them really could make a life together.

But he couldn't worry about the future now. Although Sanchez had made him an offer he couldn't refuse, he knew the man too well to simply relax and take their bargain at face value. For all he knew, Miguel's current decision to trust him could turn into tomorrow's decision to kill him.

THE BIRDS SINGING in the foliage outside her window woke Marissa. She hadn't planned to sleep. In fact, she'd lain in the dark making wild, impractical plans to escape. At one point she'd wondered if braving the dogs was better than braving her wedding night. But sometime in the early-morning hours fatigue had overcome her, and she'd dozed off. Now it must be about six-thirty, the time when the birds began their raucous chorus, she thought as she threw off the covers with a shaky hand and crossed to the window. The morning was misty, but the haze would burn off. It would be a beautiful day for a wedding.

Oh, God. Once again the sick, trapped feeling threatened to sweep away reason. Crossing to the closet, she yanked out a dress the staff had moved from the other room. As she was pulling down the skirt, there was a knock on the door. Without waiting for an invitation, Anna fluttered in.

"Good, you're already up. I heard they gave you this beautiful room," she gushed, talking a mile a minute as she went about straightening the bed. "Everybody's excited about the wedding and the fiesta. But there's so much to do. It's lucky we were working on a wedding gown for Carmelita. But she's not getting married for two weeks, so we'll have time to finish another one for her."

So it wasn't all a nightmare. It was real.

"And you have to go and see Madre Flora right after breakfast." Anna flushed.

"Mother Flora?"

"*Sí*. We have our own ways here, traditions that go back before the Spanish arrived. Madre Flora is in charge of the women's marriage instruction and the special rituals before the vows." She giggled. "I went to her when I got married last year, and she told me so many things. It made all the difference with Carlo—when he—" She broke off, blushing again. "But I think you already know about…about what to expect on your wedding night."

Marissa sucked in a sharp breath.

Anna was in too much of a dither to notice. "This is so exciting. The last woman from the city who got married here was *El Jefe*'s wife. And I was only a little girl, so I don't remember much. But people still talk about it."

Marissa was only half listening to the excited prattle. "I want to see my fiancé." Jed would get her out of this. He had to!

Anna shook her head. "Don't you women from the city know anything? It's bad luck to see him before the ceremony on your wedding day."

Marissa ducked into the bathroom. She tried to focus on salvation as she washed her face and brushed her teeth. But it was hard to keep from dissolving in a pool of tears.

For ten years she'd made sure she was in control of her life. But in a few short, horrifying days she'd been rendered totally helpless. Totally at the mercy of events that were rushing forward, carrying her along. It was like being on a rudderless ship speeding down a fast-flowing river. And coming from around the next bend, she could hear the roar of a tremendous waterfall. No way to stop the boat from plunging over. Impossible to dispel the growing fear that she would be destroyed by the rocks below.

But she couldn't simply bail out. Not and leave Jed on board. Which was why she urgently needed to talk to him. If she did marry him, he'd have to know—

She chopped off the thought with a bone-deep shudder. As she stepped out into the hall, she looked toward Jed's door. It was closed, and she wondered if he could possibly be sleeping.

"This way," Anna urged.

Marissa resisted for a moment. Then it occurred to her that Jed might already be downstairs, so she hurried after the maid. But when she arrived on the patio she didn't find him.

Her eyes flicked toward the doorway on the other side of the open space. Perhaps she would have bolted if a guard hadn't been standing in the shadows. Resigned, she looked around and spotted two of last night's visitors, Rinaldo and Harara. They were walking toward a lavish buffet set along one wall, but they stopped in midstride and looked at her with undisguised interest. Rinaldo, at least, seemed to be in a good mood, as if he heartily approved of the day's events. Harara couldn't hide his disdain.

The amicable one waved her a greeting. "Did you sleep well?"

Marissa made a tremendous effort to pull herself together. She might be half-sick with worry, but she wasn't going to let them see she was anything more than a nervous bride. She flashed a rueful smile. "It's a little hard to sleep when you're so excited. And the change of plans is a bit unnerving."

"Well, you'll be glad you did it. If a man and a woman are in love, then they should get married. And you've got perfect weather for a wedding," Rinaldo continued, unaware that every word he spoke was making her cringe.

Harara turned to the table and began filling his plate with chunks of melon. "Let's hope you have sense enough to listen to your husband," he muttered.

"What?"

Before he could elaborate, a high-pitched shriek rang out from somewhere above them.

Marissa froze. So did the two other guests on the patio. In contrast, the servants went about their business as if nothing out of the ordinary had occurred.

The wail came again—from somewhere on the second floor across from Marissa's room. The sound choked off in midcry as if a hand had clamped over an open mouth.

Marissa craned her neck toward the windows, trying to determine the exact location of the sound. "Does someone need help?" she asked the uniformed attendant who was straightening up the buffet.

"The women will take care of it."

"Of what?"

"A man was hurt this morning out in the fields. His wife is one of the maids, and I think she must have learned of the accident," he said.

It struck Marissa that there was something odd about the explanation, as if the servant had memorized it, as if he'd already repeated it many times before. She studied his face, but he didn't meet her eyes.

"I hope we haven't disturbed your wedding-day breakfast," he said, looking genuinely distressed. "Can I help you fill a plate?"

Marissa glanced once more toward the second floor, almost certain that something wasn't right. But in this house she was also sure there was nothing she could do.

Snatching a plate, she pivoted toward the buffet. The men stepped aside as she approached the table, and she stared at the sumptuous spread, wondering what would go down past the lump in her throat. Coffee? Dry toast? Melon? The scrambled eggs and the quesadillas would be impossible, but she took some anyway for appearance's sake.

Once seated, she took small sips of coffee and nibbled on a dry roll, but she did little more than push the rest of her meal around the plate.

It was almost a relief when Anna returned with a middle-aged woman and came directly to her table.

"It's normal to be nervous on your wedding day," Anna declared as she eyed Marissa's almost untouched breakfast. "It's time for your appointment."

Marissa could see the men at the nearby table listening and exchanging grins—as if they knew something she didn't.

Anna gave them a sideways look. "There's a lot to do to get ready. Rosita and I will take you."

"Oh." Marissa pushed back her chair and tried to look confident.

As they exited, Rosita walked in front of Marissa. Anna was directly in the back so that they formed a little parade. She felt as if she was a prisoner again and that all the men, guests and staff alike, were watching the procession with interest.

The soldiers were a bit more subtle in their scrutiny, but she felt them following her down the hall with their eyes. After she and the two women passed one group of sentries, Marissa thought she heard a low-pitched exchange of suggestive remarks. She felt the back of her neck heat, but she kept her eyes forward. No one stopped her and her escorts when they left through a door in the rear of the hacienda.

As they moved away from the buildings that made up the compound, Marissa felt her nerves jump. She was being led off into an isolated area of the jungle. For all she knew this could be a plot of Sanchez's that Jed knew nothing about. She slowed her steps. "Where are we going?"

Rosita turned and gave her a look that was half stern,

half compassionate. "You come from far away, but you must honor our customs while you are here. Anna told you about the wedding instructions all of our women receive. This is a solemn occasion. Do not speak again. You should approach Madre Flora with reverence. And she will decide whether the wedding will proceed."

"You mean—"

"Silence."

Marissa nodded tightly. It sounded as if this was some kind of test. Maybe, if she flunked, she could get out of marrying Jed. Her heart started to race. Was it really that simple? Did the wise woman of the village have the power to decide that the match wasn't suitable?

The escorts kept walking at a brisk pace. Soon they were in the cool shade of towering trees and giant ferns where shafts of light filtered through the leaves. Above her, parrots called out, and a family of spider monkeys chattered as if they resented the human intrusion. The trail was narrow but well-worn, and it seemed to lead Marissa into another, more primitive world. She knew instinctively that hundreds of women before her had taken this same path on their wedding days. This journey might be new to her, but it was steeped in tradition.

Torn between nervousness and awe, she wanted to ask more questions. But she was sure she wouldn't get any answers from her guides.

They crossed over a fast-running stream on a wooden bridge with carved female statues like sentries on the front posts. Marissa wanted to stop and have a better look, but the women urged her on, past mahogany trees and Spanish cedars, the group's progress heralded by the drumming of a red-crested woodpecker.

Beyond the bridge the trail widened. After what seemed like at least a half-mile tramp through the forest, Rosita stopped by a giant kapok tree whose massive gray green trunk and branches were decorated with bromeliads and trailing pink orchids. Breaking off one of the orchids, she turned to Marissa and tucked it into the hair over her ear. "There. Madre Flora likes it when a bride approaches her with a flower in her hair. Since you don't know the custom, I've done it for you."

"Umm," was all Marissa could manage through suddenly parched lips.

The woman took her arm and led her around a curve in the trail where she found herself facing an ancient-looking wall made of massive stones covered with green moss. There was a doorway to one side, its shape that of the flattened corbel arch the Mayans had used.

She hadn't had any idea there were Mayan ruins on Sanchez's *finca*. But she was sure he wouldn't advertise the fact, since he wouldn't want archaeologists mucking about on his property and getting in the way of his military exercises. On the other hand, as she looked at the wall, she decided that ruin wasn't exactly the right word. This construction was in better shape than the site the American team was excavating down the road.

A macaw screeched in a nearby tree and took flight. The woman gestured toward the archway. "You must go in alone."

With her mouth so dry she felt she might never swallow again, Marissa shuffled forward. Caught and held by a sense of unreality, she hardly dared to imagine what was on the other side of the wall. When she stepped through the doorway, she had to stop and give her eyes time to adjust from the filtered light of the jungle to blazing sun. She was in a large paved courtyard bounded on one side by a truncated pyramid, its steps climbing to a flat platform just below the tops of the tallest trees. Around the other sides of the courtyard were low buildings made of the same stone as the wall and topped with thatched roofs.

Carefully tended beds of flowers and shrubs bordered the walls, and Marissa had the strange fantasy that if she closed her eyes and opened them again she might find the place bustling with dozens of women in ancient Mayan costume.

The plaza was completely silent. Yet she sensed that she wasn't alone. A thatched, open-air structure on her far right gave protection from the tropical sun. As she peered into the shadows she saw that someone was sitting on a low stone bench cushioned with colorful native rugs.

The figure raised a hand, beckoning her to come forward. She wanted to turn and run. Instead a greater force drew her farther into the plaza, as if a string were attached to the middle of her chest, pulling her forward. When she stepped under the canopy she found herself facing a tiny woman who she guessed had to be the fabled Madre Flora. At first glance the old woman hardly looked impressive. Her shoulders were hunched, and the hands clasped in her lap resembled dry sticks. Her white hair was braided and piled on her head, and the brown skin of her face was as wrinkled and cracked as a dry creek bed.

She gestured to a pillow at her feet. "Sit with me, *hija.* We will get to know each other a little."

Marissa sat, feeling the scratchy fabric against her legs. Pulling her skirt close, she clasped her hands over her knees to keep them from trembling. For what seemed like minutes, she and the old woman regarded each other. Marissa saw wisdom and contentment in her black eyes and years of hard living in her face. She swallowed painfully, wondering what her own countenance revealed. Amazingly, she felt her panic subsiding under the old woman's steady gaze. Simply sitting with Madre Flora was having a calming effect on her, almost as if those black eyes had put her under a spell.

"Thank you for honoring me with this visit," the *madre* finally said in Spanish.

"I don't think I had a choice," Marissa answered in the same language.

"There are always choices in this life, *hija*."

"Not when *El Jefe* holds power over you," Marissa answered with a little shake of her head. Immediately she wondered if it was wise to say something so revealing.

The old woman peered at her, the look in her eyes becoming almost amused. "You are worried someone might be listening."

"Yes."

"None would dare. Not even *El Jefe*. What passes between us will stay private. As for choices, you made the decision that brought you to his *finca*."

Marissa shrugged and looked toward one of the flower beds. What was the use of trying to explain about working for the U.S. State Department to an Indian woman who had lived all her life in this place?"

"Why did you ask me here?"

"To help you discover the truth. Do you love this man you are to take as *sposo*—as a husband?" Madre Flora asked suddenly.

Caught completely off guard, Marissa blurted, "I truly don't know. I wish…" She wasn't able to finish the sentence. *Did* she wish she loved Jed? Could she admit that to herself? Or did she wish he had made some kind of unspoken commitment to her? Would that make her feel safe with him tonight?

"The women say you have already been intimate with him."

"That's a lie!"

"Ay. But you know something of his lovemaking."

"I know that when he kisses me and touches me, it feels...wonderful. I didn't know being with a man could be...like that," she admitted with awe in her voice. She felt heat spread across her cheeks as she realized how much she'd revealed. She hadn't thought the interview would start like this. She hadn't dreamed she'd feel compelled—driven—to confront the very issues she'd been avoiding for so long.

The old woman's face was unreadable. Marissa wanted to look away, to hide her raw emotions. But she couldn't; she was held captive by the *madre*'s wise, assessing gaze.

"Slowly we are getting at the truth," Madre Flora said.

"Are we?"

"Mmm. I sense your fear, *hija*. You are afraid of allowing him to be close to you."

Marissa swallowed.

"You're not sure you want to marry this man. But you've learned that you are drawn to him—sexually. You have admitted that much to yourself."

Marissa gave the barest nod.

"A man and a woman giving each other pleasure in their marriage bed is one of the great joys of this life," the old woman continued. "Things go more smoothly when the bride knows what to expect on her wedding night. Do I need to tell you how it is done—the joining of the flesh?"

Marissa flushed more deeply and shook her head.

There were several moments of silence. "Making love is an important part of marriage, but there is much more to linking your destiny with a man's. Each of you has obligations to the other. What are the qualities that make Jed Prentiss a good husband in your eyes?"

Marissa thought about Jed and smiled. "He goes after

what he wants—and usually gets it. He's intimidating. Very strong.'' She swallowed and went on. ''But down deep he's a good man. He has a code of honor. He's shown me he cares about me. He's trusted me with knowing his secret weakness. And I don't think he would hurt me,'' she added. She hadn't realized she knew so much about Jed. But it was all true.

''Those are good things. But will he provide a good living for you and the children you have together? Will he make a good father?''

Marissa had barely thought beyond tonight. But she didn't have to struggle for an answer to the question. ''I can provide my own living. I've done that for years.''

''A good father is important to a child's success in life.''

''That's not essential,'' Marissa argued. ''If the child is strong she can overcome her home life.''

''You are more independent than the women from the village. That is good and bad for you.''

Marissa hesitated, then admitted, ''I've had to be independent. I've learned to take care of myself.''

''I can see that. And more. You have been hurt in the past.''

Marissa's head jerked up.

''By two men, I think. Your father and another.''

''How…how do you know that?''

''By what you told me about your home,'' Madre Flora said, her voice gentle. ''By your fear of intimacy—and of strong men.''

Silence settled over the sunlit courtyard. Marissa struggled to draw in a steady breath. Her father…and Lowell Dougan. She'd avoided even thinking his name for years. He was just a shadow. The man in her past who had hurt her. But in Madre Flora's presence, hiding anything, even from oneself, she was learning, was impossible. "I didn't tell you any of that." Marissa spoke defensively.

The old woman smiled kindly. "When a woman comes to me for this talk, she gives away a great deal by the way she answers my questions. And even more—by the things she chooses not to say. You have come a long way by yourself in this life. You have proven you have great strength. But I think you are ready to take the risk of giving your love and your trust to Jed Prentiss."

Marissa realized her hands were clasped in a death grip. "I want to," she whispered, hearing the truth in her own voice. "But I don't know if I can."

The old woman laid a gnarled hand on Marissa's shoulder. "Have faith in yourself and in Jed Prentiss. He is very different from the other one."

"I know that," Marissa answered. "But it's so hard to let myself be...vulnerable."

Madre Flora nodded. "The gods have been kind to you in this. They have sent him to you at the right time. You are ready for him—for love—if you let yourself be."

More than anything, Marissa wanted to believe the old sage. She'd thought that submitting to this outlandish interview might be a way of getting out of the marriage ceremony, that Madre Flora would issue a fiat even Sanchez couldn't ignore. But things had changed as they'd sat here talking. Her hopes and fears had crystallized. And she knew she was stronger than she imagined. What if somehow it could actually work out with Jed? What if theirs could be a real marriage? She'd been attracted to him for years, but she'd never dared to imagine anything as awesome—or as final—as marriage. Yet what if Madre Flora was right?

Suddenly, almost mystically, as if conjured by the

madre from whatever magic lingered here in this ancient hallowed place, a spark of hope flowed to life in her heart.

Hope. It was a feeling she hadn't experienced in a long, long time.

Chapter Ten

As Jed automatically lifted his coffee cup and took a sip, his thoughts were entirely of Marissa. She'd looked so damn frightened last night. Was playing at marriage with him for a couple of days really such an awful prospect?

He'd planned to find out if she was still so upset this morning. But the servant Miguel had assigned to him had kept him in his room inspecting the clothes he was going to wear at the ceremony, and he'd finally realized he was being delayed on purpose. Probably so that the bride and groom wouldn't meet at breakfast, he decided.

When he'd come out onto the patio she was nowhere about. But Thomas Leandro and William Johnson had been deep in conversation, the arms dealer's Texas twang contrasting strangely with the professor's cultured Latin American accent. He'd thought about trying to start a casual conversation designed to shake them down for information. Then Pedro Harara had pulled up a chair, and Jed's anger had soared. That little pip-squeak was the one who wanted Marci out of the way. Jed had wanted to drag the bastard out of the room, shove his shoulders against a wall and make him understand the flaws in his logic. But strong-arm tactics weren't exactly appropriate behavior for a man on his wedding day. And there was always the possibility that Sanchez had lied about the man's motives. So Jed had clamped his hands around his cup and eavesdropped with distaste as Harara had started expounding on his favorite topic—international finance, a subject he could stick with for hours. Amusement and relief had broken through Jed's anger as he'd watched the listeners' eyes glaze over. Harara might have his opinions, but as far as political influence went, he was lower than the spots on a snake's ass, thank God.

Shifting his chair so he had a little privacy, Jed tried to swallow some breakfast while he thought about the strange turn events had taken since he'd arrived at the hacienda.

Was Miguel going to produce a marriage license before the ceremony? Were he and Marci really going to be saying their vows in front of a crowd of people? And then what? It wasn't forever, of course. They might be marrying in haste, but they'd have plenty of leisure to undo the damage when they got home.

Yet that still left their wedding night. Maybe he should tell his bride that Miguel wasn't going to let her off the estate unless he was sure they'd consummated the marriage.

He smiled, enjoying the prospect. It wasn't as if they were starting from scratch. They'd gotten to know each other quite well last night. She'd revived him pretty quickly with her comforting little kisses and her hands stroking his body. After that it had taken all his willpower to sit quietly in that chair and let her turn up the heat. When he'd finally gone from passive enjoyment to active participation, he'd felt her passion rise. It was only after he'd gone into overdrive and pushed her down on the rug that she'd frozen up on him.

He thought about that. And about the way she'd been responding to him—up to a certain point. Then, in his mind's eye, he saw the mask of fear that had shrouded her face when he'd started to lose control and get aggressive.

As he remembered the haunted look in her eyes and the way she'd struggled from his grasp, his fingers clenched the fork he was holding. Damn. Why hadn't he figured it out before? The signs were there for anyone with half a brain to read. Anyone sensitive enough to understand what was going on. Some creep had gotten rough with her in the past. He'd bet his life on it. Now she was afraid of letting herself be defenseless again. That's why she'd kept herself so aloof. Not because she was cold. But because she was scared.

How scared, he wondered. How rough had the nameless bastard been with her? Jed grimaced, unwilling to follow that line of reasoning to its logical conclusion. He'd rather think about the kind of approach that would make her feel comfortable. They might not be making lifetime vows to each other at the ceremony, but he cared about her. And she was attracted to him. Hell, it was more than that. She cared, too. Or she wouldn't have come swinging across from her balcony to his, like Tarzan's mate, when she thought he needed help. Then she would have done a better job of socking him instead of choosing the other alternative. But she was the one who'd made the decision to fight ice with fire.

He swallowed a frustrated sigh. Too bad they weren't going to get off to a very promising start this evening. If he remembered his backwoods San Marcos customs, the two of them were going to be teased unmercifully by a drunken crowd and locked in a bedroom together. He'd done it to other guys when he'd been training Miguel's troops, never dreaming it would happen to him. The prospect was a little daunting. On the other hand, it did have its upside, he admitted as he stretched out his legs under the table. Marci would be clinging to him for protection. Comfort would naturally lead to mutual enjoyment. And they'd both end up having a wonderful time while he showed her how rewarding making love could be.

From the corner of his eye he saw Johnson slide him a glance and then fiddle with his Stetson and look away when he saw he'd been caught.

Funny, he'd have thought Leandro—the San Marcos native—would be the one with the anticipatory glint in his eye. But maybe over their eggs and quesadillas the professor had filled in the arms merchant on the local customs.

Brisk footsteps made him look to see who had entered the patio. It was Sanchez.

He looked pleased with himself as he approached the table. "You've got a beautiful day for a wedding."

"The ancient gods must be smiling on me. By the way, what time is the ceremony?"

"At six. Followed by what you'll doubtless think is an endless wedding supper. Then you're spending the night at that little cottage I use for guests when the main house is full. Nice and private."

"Yeah."

El Jefe grinned and pitched his voice low so that the other guests couldn't hear. "Come with me. I want to show you something."

"What?"

"You'll love it. But I can't explain until we're alone."

Jed followed, wondering if Sanchez was going to let him test the springs on the wedding bed. Or maybe he had a two-hundred-dollar bottle of champagne he'd been saving for a special occasion?

"What's the big mystery?" he asked as they walked through the hall toward the back of the hacienda.

"Something quite special." *El Jefe* paused by the guardhouse and picked up a machete. "You know how women are. They think they can keep secrets from their lords and masters. But we've got the drop on them." He led Jed out the back door of the main house and down a path that disappeared into the jungle.

"According to my sentries, the women came and got the bride about an hour and a half ago. I figure it ought to be about time for the good part," *El Jefe* said in a raspy whisper. "Come on. But keep your voice down."

Before they reached the trees, Miguel angled off to the right. Several hundred yards farther on he paused for a moment and then selected an entrance into the underbrush, where he hacked away at several branches that were partially blocking the path. Jed followed and found himself on a narrow, barely discernible trail. He cocked his head to one side and looked inquiringly at *El Jefe*. "Are you going to come clean with me?"

"Come clean. That's good! The local customs here go back before the Spanish conquest—to ancient times when the Indians worshiped pagan gods. The women have some very interesting rituals to get the bride ready for the groom."

"Oh?"

"You can have a nice view of the proceedings. It's one of the special pleasures of getting married out here in the boonies. But if you're too much of a prude, you can skip the fun and have a siesta."

Jed's mouth was suddenly dry. "Suppose I take you up on the offer?"

His friend slapped him on the shoulder and handed over the machete. "I thought you'd be interested. With a little hacking you'll be able to follow this trail. In about half a mile you'll come to the wall of an ancient Mayan temple. Go around it to the side where there's a steep hill. It's actually the back of a pyramid. If you climb it and go into the enclosed platform on top, you can see down into the ritual baths.''

THREE WOMEN CLAD in short halter dresses and heavy gold necklaces and earrings came out of the building at the back of the courtyard. Marissa had never seen any of them before. In fact, she had the strange sensation that they could have stepped directly from an illustration carved into the temple wall.

"Come,'' one of them said.

"But—''

"There is nothing to fear. Here we serve the ancient ways. We must prepare you for your bridegroom in the manner handed down from mother to daughter through the centuries. The rituals will fill you with joy and anticipation for your marriage.''

Before Marissa could protest further, they surrounded her and led her toward the building. The doorway looked dark and forbidding, and she would have held back if she could. But they pressed her relentlessly forward. When she stepped inside, she found it was pleasantly illuminated by shafts of bright light slanting at intervals through the thatched roof. She was aware of Madre Flora somewhere in back of her, silent, watching.

"Oh!'' As her eyes adjusted to the light she saw that the walls were painted with vibrant murals. Some were jungle scenes. Others depicted the interiors of stone buildings richly decorated with plush draperies, soft mats and comfortable pillows.

Marissa flushed when she realized that among the greenery and opulent cushions were naked men and women kissing, touching, making love.

"What is this place?"

"The temple of the women," one of them murmured as if that explained everything.

A heavy, perfumed scent hung in the air, and Marissa saw smoke wafting from a metal burner at the side of the room. The women led her toward it.

"No, wait!" No one answered. Instead they pressed on her shoulders, gently forcing her to kneel with her face in the choking smoke.

Panic seized Marissa. She held her breath as long as she could, trying to struggle away from the hands that clamped her in place. But she couldn't get away. Finally she was forced to take a breath.

She heard someone chanting words in a language she couldn't understand and the tones of strange musical instruments coming from another group of costumed women in the corner of the room. The ones at her side kept her kneeling before the burner, and it was impossible not to draw more and more of the heavy incense into her lungs.

Gradually her senses merged with the music and the chanted words swirling around her. She felt transported to another time, another place, where all the civilized conventions of her world had not yet been invented, and ancient gods held sway. Her eyes would no longer keep their focus, and she rocked back on her knees.

"Good. You are ready to go on," Madre Flora pronounced.

The other women helped her up, supporting her languid body.

"What are you doing to me?" She'd thought she'd shouted the question. Yet no one acted as if they'd heard her.

Hands were on her clothing, lifting her dress over her

head. Then her underwear was efficiently stripped from her body so that she stood before them naked as the day she was born.

JED MADE HIS WAY along the trail, stopping every few feet to hack at some plant that had grown up in his path. One thing about the jungle, the greenery grew so fast it required constant effort to keep a trail open. He kept his ears tuned to his surroundings and his eyes on the underbrush, alert for hidden dangers from men or wildlife.

On the face of it, this was a pretty crazy thing to be doing. Yet Miguel had intrigued him with his allusions to ancient traditions. What were the women doing? Practicing fertility rituals? Anointing the bride with aphrodisiac herbs?

As he hacked his way past another ironwood seedling, guilt nagged at the back of his mind. Whatever was going on this morning, he shouldn't be spying on Marci. But the invitation was simply too tempting to resist—and a lot more appealing than sitting around the hacienda biting his nails until the ceremony. Besides, hadn't Miguel told him that all the grooms did it? Why should he deny himself the privilege just because he was a visitor?

However, he was beginning to wonder if his host was playing a practical joke on him when he finally saw the wall of the temple Miguel had spoken about. Hands on hips, he surveyed the massive barrier. He'd been to the *finca* dozens of times when he was training troops, and he hadn't known this place existed. If you hadn't heard about ruins buried in the jungle, you certainly wouldn't realize you were looking at a pyramid, he decided as he looked up at the hill rising at a steep angle from the jungle floor. It was covered with everything from vines and ferns to small trees.

The place reminded him of Tikal, the ancient Mayan site he'd visited in Guatemala where a highly sophisticated civilization had flourished while Europe was in the Dark Ages. Abandoned and swallowed completely by the fast-growing tropical vegetation, the city wasn't rediscovered until the mid-eighteen hundreds. Archaeologists had uncovered a number of the temples, but sometimes they restored only the front or the top, leaving the rest as they'd found it. Like this one, Jed thought, where all he could see was the covered platform at the crown.

He reached for a convenient root and pulled himself up, bracing his foot as he stretched for the next handhold. It was a hard climb. He hoped Miguel wasn't putting him on, and that it was going to be worth the effort. Finally he reached the stone platform beneath the treetops and he stopped for a few minutes to catch his breath.

In front of him was a small building about eight feet square, overshadowed by the tops of the trees. Stepping inside, he shaded his eyes from the sun. Probably the structure had once been topped by a roof, but it had long since disappeared.

Narrow windows slashed through the wall opposite the door. Making his way across, he peered downward. To the left and right, the view was obscured by trees. Directly in front of him was a cleared area with what looked like a wide circular well in the center. What he saw about thirty feet below him made the air whoosh out of his lungs.

"YOU ARE VERY BEAUTIFUL. You will please your husband with your body," one of the women murmured in Spanish as she spread Marissa's hair like a curtain of gold around her shoulders.

Marissa wasn't capable of framing an answer. The smoke had taken the edge off her panic and pulled her into the rhythm of the pagan ceremony. She'd lost all will to resist. When her three attendants led her up a flight of steps in the back of the building, she followed.

They were all chanting softly and rhythmically in a language she didn't understand, their voices rising and falling with the music that followed them into a sunlit courtyard slightly smaller than the one where she'd talked with Madre Flora.

They helped her over a low, circular stone wall, and she gasped as she stepped into the cold water up to her knees. It raised goose bumps on her arms and made her nipples tighten to hard pebbles.

Still singing the primitive melody, the women scooped the water up in clay pitchers decorated with more pictures of men and women together and began to pour the water over her shoulders. She closed her eyes as she felt it cascade over her breasts and hips and belly. It was easy to imagine Jed's fingers on her body in place of the water— caressing her in all the places that longed for his attentions. Dimly in the corner of her mind that was still in touch with her modern sensibilities she wondered if the heat of her body was raising the temperature of the water.

FOR LONG MOMENTS at a time Jed forgot how to breathe as he watched Marci standing in the tub, naked and beautiful and regal as any Mayan princess who'd ever lived. She was like those royal women of centuries past who had stood in the sacred pool below, the sun cascading down over her, drenching her body in gold.

He'd never dreamed he'd see such a gorgeous sight. He looked at the hair falling around her shoulders like spun gold and longed to run his greedy fingers through the riches. Her eyes were shut. Her face radiated a strange, almost mystical expression that held him for long moments. Then his enraptured gaze moved a few inches lower to her beautifully rounded breasts, their erect nipples an enchanting deep coral color.

His fingers flexed as he thought about what it would be like to cup her softness and then stroke those hardened tips until she moaned with pleasure. He could almost feel her twisting against him, begging for his mouth to take the place of his hands. In his most private fantasies he had never imagined anything so erotic—Marci standing there in all her glory, eyes closed, skin glowing pink as water sluiced down her body.

His own body tightened painfully, and his fingers clamped onto the window ledge in a death grip. If he didn't look away, he was in danger of going off like a rocket. Still, he was powerless to resist the sight of his bride—and at that moment he reveled in thinking of her in those terms—as she was prepared for their wedding. Prepared for *him*. His chest rose and fell rapidly in unconscious rhythm with hers as he took in every precious detail, following the rivulets of water downward, watching them trace the indentation of her waist and slide lower, weaving through the curly triangle of hair at the top of her legs and then down her rounded thighs.

The women chanted as they worked, and Marissa swayed slightly to the sound, making him ache to come crashing down there and snatch her away. One of the attendants began to wash her long golden hair, and she threw her head back so that her breasts thrust upward, toward him, as if she were offering herself to his hands.

He stifled a groan. At that moment another one of the peasant women looked up, her gaze focusing unerringly on the narrow windows where he hid. Instinctively he jumped back, wondering if he'd made a noise that could be heard in the courtyard. But he knew he'd swallowed the groan and that it was unlikely the women would hear anything besides their own chanting.

When he cautiously looked again, the curious one had switched her attention back to Marci. But the woman had known he was there; Jed was certain of it. Suddenly, in the sort of intuitive flash that had often saved his life, he saw the truth. This whole thing was a setup. And he'd better figure out why he was there.

He wrenched himself away from the seductive view, feeling as if he were going against an elemental force that tugged at every cell in his body. Drawing in a shuddering breath, he struggled to pull his mind back to sanity.

He commanded his brain to work. Commanded himself to think the situation through. Okay, so what did it mean that the women knew he had come to watch this erotic little ceremony? Maybe they always knew they were putting on a performance for the men, and it gave them a secret sense of power. He could understand that—particularly in a society where the women made very few of the rules. But how did that apply to *him*, personally? Since he and Marci were both outsiders.

He felt the hair at the back of his neck prickle. What if Sanchez was taking advantage of a tantalizing local custom to make sure the bridegroom was fully occupied for a couple of hours? While the general— While he what?

Jed's thoughts spun back to the previous evening's conversation. Last night Sanchez had said he had to either trust him or kill him. And he'd jumped at the offer of *El Jefe*'s help. He'd wanted to believe that the general was going to come through for him. Perhaps because they'd once been friends.

He'd like to argue himself into sticking with that comforting scenario. But now he realized he'd let himself be lulled into a dangerous assumption.

If only for his own peace of mind, he'd better find out what was happening back at the ranch. More to the point, from this moment on, he'd better start acting as if he were a moving target. Ducking low, he retraced his steps across the enclosure and descended as quickly as he could.

When he got to the bottom he paused to survey the immediate area, wishing he was armed with a gun instead of a machete. Then he started up the overgrown trail at a cautious trot, his eyes still scanning the underbrush while his mind raced.

He tried to recall everything he'd learned about Miguel Sanchez's tactics when he was on the attack. Basically, the general had two modes of operation. When he was sure he could get away with it, he was quick and ruthless. A prime example was the way he'd marched Marci in front of the firing squad. On the other hand, if too many witnesses were present, he reverted to elegantly subtle plans that placed the blame squarely on someone else—like opposition terrorists. He never put himself in unnecessary danger. Which meant he wasn't going to send an assassination team with machine guns into the wedding chapel or the reception area.

So where would the smart money place their bets, Jed wondered. It didn't take long to figure out.

His face hardened. The honeymoon cottage Miguel had mentioned. It was perfect. He and Marci would be alone. No one else would be around to get hurt—or to witness the murders. Afterward, there would be a thorough investigation. A suspect would be identified and probably shot as he was being arrested.

The more he thought about it the more certain he was. Because another key facet of Miguel's twisted personality shone through clearly in the plan. *El Jefe* was going to give his friend a last glorious night with his bride before he blew him away.

Jed made it to the edge of the trees in fifteen minutes and stood staring at the expanse of sunlit field ahead. Every nerve in his body screamed for him to cross the open space at a dead run. But he knew a casual stroll would look a lot less as though he'd cottoned on to Miguel's plans.

He used the enforced five-minute walk to mentally review what he knew about the layout of the *finca*. The barracks for the soldiers, garages for their vehicles and armory were separated from the general's house, although there was a small ready room where the troops assigned to the complex could relax. On the way to the ruins he'd noticed, not far from the hacienda, some newer structures that had gone up since he'd been here last. Sanchez wouldn't store ammunition so close to his living quarters. But what did he consider important enough to keep within sight of his office?

Sneaking a look would be a good idea, Jed decided. But it wasn't his top priority. First on his list was a visit to the ready room. Switching directions, he headed for the small facility.

As he sauntered inside, he saw four bored guards slouched in front of an oscillating fan waiting for their turn at the sentry stations. When they saw him, they snapped into models of military posture.

"At ease," he said in Spanish.

They looked doubtful, and he gestured toward the chairs. "Sit back down. Please. I came to ask some advice—man to man."

The corporal raised an inquiring eyebrow. He'd been at the *finca* when Jed had visited before, and they knew each other slightly.

"About a suitable gesture of respect for the troops and the villagers on my wedding day."

That got their attention.

He leaned comfortably against the cabinet near the door. Extra side arms were stored inside—unless Miguel had made some changes. "I'd like to buy drinks for everyone. As much as they want."

All four faces grinned back at him. "You'd earn our eternal gratitude, Señor Prentiss," one of the men said.

"So what's the beverage of choice?" He knew that both potent dark rum and beer were produced in the province. "Come on, help me out. I'm serious. I want your advice. This is the only wedding I'm ever going to have, and I'd like to do things right."

"Beer would be fine," a corporal answered. "But—"

"But we'd rather have rum," a young recruit allowed.

"Sure thing," Jed agreed. "Get some of both. Is there somewhere on the *finca* where I can swing the deal?"

"We'd be glad to take care of it for you," the corporal offered.

"I'd be grateful." He got out his wallet and peeled off the equivalent of three hundred dollars—about twenty bills—knowing that would buy a heck of a lot of joy juice. In fact, there would be enough cash left over to split among these guys, and no one could accuse Señor Prentiss of giving them a bribe.

He laid the money on the edge of the desk, then cursed as the breeze from the fan picked it up and scattered it like dry leaves in a hurricane. While the men scrambled to retrieve the flying bills, he reached into the gun cabinet and wrapped his fingers around the handle of a service revolver. It was under his shirt and in the waistband of his trousers before they had finished picking up the loot.

He shook his head in disgust. "Sorry, this wedding thing has got me pulling all kinds of dumb stunts."

The corporal shoved the cash into a pants pocket. "No problem, Señor Prentiss. I understand how it is when you tie the knot."

Jed took a step farther into the room, cleared his throat and lowered his voice. "Look, like I said I'm, uh, a little nervous about tonight, you know. I don't want to screw up, if you get my drift."

"*Sí,*" the corporal answered.

The others nodded knowingly, some struggling to repress grins.

"I've been to weddings down here, so I realize there's going to be a lot of rowdy stuff going on until we're alone. Maybe even afterward."

The grins widened.

"My bride's never seen anything like it. I think it's going to make her pretty nervous. So once we're alone together, I'd like to keep it that way. Could you do me a favor and make sure no one comes around to rattle the windows or set off a firecracker once we're in bed?"

"You've got it."

"Thanks. Just until midnight. Things ought to calm down by then."

Jed left, then looked up in surprise as the corporal followed him out and accompanied him down the path. Damn. This was a hell of a time to pick up an escort.

They were about twenty-five yards from the guardhouse when the corporal glanced around and cleared his throat. "Perhaps I should keep my mouth shut, but I like you, and you were generous with us."

Jed felt a stab of guilt. He'd been expedient.

"There's something else you should know. If you want a piece of advice."

Jed swung toward him. "Shoot."

The man looked uncomfortable. "Clarita could make trouble for you tonight."

The warning didn't come as a complete surprise. In fact, it fit right in with the girl's recent hostility toward him and Marci. "When she was younger, we used to be friends," Jed said cautiously. "Now she's doing all kinds of crazy stuff. It looks like she's jealous of Marci."

"Crazy stuff. *Sí*. She's not playing with a full deck. And *El Jefe* doesn't want to believe anything's wrong with her. So he just lets it continue, and everybody has to pretend nothing strange is going on. Like that screaming fit of hers this morning when one of the women was helping her pick out a dress for the ceremony. You heard it?"

Jed nodded. He'd used the word *crazy* because he hadn't known how else to put it. The corporal was telling him that the girl was mentally unbalanced—and everyone on the *finca* talked about it behind her father's back. The revelation explained a lot, he realized as he thought back over the girl's behavior. It also saddened him.

"It's been going on for about a year," the corporal continued. "She seemed to change overnight. She can be dangerous if she takes a dislike to you. Like last night when that tarantula turned up in your fiancée's bed. Everybody's betting it was her."

Jed swore under his breath. "I appreciate your clueing me in."

"Don't tell *El Jefe* you heard anything from me."

"Of course not. But she needs help."

"It's safer not to get involved." The man finished and quickly returned the way he'd come.

Jed mulled over the new information. Clarita was a loose cannon. But she wasn't his most pressing problem. When he was well out of sight of prying eyes, he ducked under the branches of a date palm and checked his weapon. Well, now he knew he had six bullets.

For an unguarded moment he thought about slipping into Miguel's office, pulling the piece and taking *El Jefe* hostage. The plan had a lot of macho appeal. But there were too many unknowns to try anything so brazen. Including his own ability to stay on his feet for the hours required to get them off the *finca* and onto an airplane out of this damned country. He grimaced. Suppose in the middle of the hostage scene he had an attack and conked out the way he had yesterday evening? So much for macho appeal.

Marci was another problem. His insides clenched when he pictured her standing in that tub. She'd looked sexy as hell, but she'd also looked pretty spacey. Chances were good she'd been given some native drug. Which made sense, because he couldn't imagine her holding still for that little bathing ceremony otherwise. He'd have to wait until she was back in commission and at his side before he risked any power plays.

Once more he affected a casual stroll as he crossed the grounds in back of the hacienda. The closer he got to the guest bungalow, the more convinced he was that he'd guessed right about Miguel's plans. The place was isolated. And it was also away from the main flow of activity. Perfect for a honeymoon couple who wanted to be alone. And with a wild party in full swing at the big house, nobody would discover that the newlyweds had been knocked off by invading terrorists until the next day when they didn't appear for lunch.

He was about to pull open the door of the cottage when a noise from inside warned him to retreat. He wasn't a moment too soon. As he slid around the side of the building, the door opened and a man stepped into the sunlight.

"Son of a bitch," Jed muttered under his breath.

Chapter Eleven

William Johnson stood on the brick steps, a satisfied smirk on his long face and what looked like a small toolbox swinging from his right hand. He glanced around to see if anyone had noted his departure from the cottage. Satisfied that he was alone, he tipped his Stetson to a jaunty angle and headed off at a brisk walk toward the hacienda.

As the Texan departed, Jed followed the toolbox with narrowed eyes. Somehow he doubted that the man had been fixing a leaky toilet. His first impulse was to jab his recently acquired pistol into the middle of Johnson's back and make him talk. But then he might not get the straight dope on what he and Miguel were up to. Instead he stayed where he was until he was satisfied that the man wasn't coming back. His face was impassive, but his heart was slamming against the inside of his chest when he finally slipped through the front door and stood waiting for his eyes to adjust to the interior light.

The two-room bungalow was as plush as the quarters where he'd slept last night, with a few additional lavish touches, like an executive-size hot tub in an orchid-filled greenhouse off the bathroom, and a fully stocked bar in the sitting area. Just perfect for a quiet honeymoon. So what little marital aid had the arms dealer added to the premises?

MARISSA NESTLED more comfortably into the soft environment surrounding her. It was warm and billowy. The most luxurious spot she'd ever slept in, and her unconscious mind translated it into another place. In preparation for her wedding, she'd been bathed and perfumed and dressed in a loose-fitting robe. Now she was with Jed in a wonderfully plush, wide bed. They were snuggled together kissing, touching—making each other happy, with the perfect freedom she'd craved for so long.

What had she been so afraid of? Making love with Jed was everything she'd longed for it to be. Sweet and sensual and thrilling. Except that outside someone was operating mining equipment, and the low buzz of machinery kept intruding on her sense of privacy.

She tried to press her ears into the pillows to blot out the annoying intrusion. But the sound wouldn't go away. As she woke up and the dream let go of her mind, she realized that what she was hearing was the low murmur of women's voices. Had they followed her and Jed to the bedroom?

Marissa stirred restlessly. No. She was still in the temple where they'd brought her right after breakfast. Making love with Jed was only a dream.

Disappointment surged through her. Dreaming of Jed was warm and satisfying—and safe. Reality was still frightening.

Her eyelids fluttered, but she didn't fully open them. Her mind was still fuzzy from the drug they'd made her breathe. Knowing she was slow on the uptake, she gave herself a few moments to orient herself. Then suddenly something the women said caught her attention.

They were speaking in low, idiomatic Spanish that was almost too quick for her to understand in her present muzzy state. But she marshaled her attention to grasp the flow of words. They'd mentioned a name, but she'd missed it, and she sensed it was important. Lying very still, she strained to figure out who they were discussing so avidly. It had to be a man.

"Come on, how do you know so much about him, Bonita?"

"Can you keep a secret?"

"I swear it."

"Well, *El Jefe* sent me to his bed the last time he was here."

The other woman sucked in a sharp breath. "I had heard of such things at the hacienda. My husband would never allow that."

So much for the general's moral code, Marissa thought. It sounded as if he only invoked it for his convenience.

Bonita made a clicking sound with her tongue. "My husband thinks *El Jefe* will give him a soft job if he lends out his wife to important visitors."

"How was it?" The question was asked with a mixture of envy and distaste. "Are the gringos good lovers?"

"Well, Carmen, the truth is, he was too fast."

Carmen laughed.

"That's one secret he'd want me to keep. The other is that he's not a gringo."

"*Un momento.* I thought he was from Texas."

Marissa's half-functioning mind scrambled to process that revelation. *Texas.* It took a minute for her fogged brain to figure out that they were talking about William Johnson.

"That's just a story he tells, like the one about supplying guns for the troops," Bonita explained airily. "So nobody knows he came to bring the special mining equipment."

Marissa strained her ears. She'd had no idea what Johnson did. Guns? Mining equipment? They must have mentioned it earlier in the conversation. That's why she'd put mining equipment into her dream.

And it fit in with something that had happened earlier—Sanchez's odd reaction when Jed had offered to arrange a government loan to develop the copper mines in Junipero Province. Did he already have Johnson for a private backer? More to the point, did they have some kind of illegal deal to keep the proceeds out of the government coffers?

"That fake Texan is a powerful man. Sometimes I think *El Jefe* is worried about what he's going to do."

"*El Jefe* has power! Everyone is afraid of him," Carmen protested.

"Here on the *finca,* yes. And in Santa Isabella."

Marissa sat up as she strained to hear the conversation better.

The women turned to her. They were part of the trio who had bathed her. The third was no longer there. "We didn't know you were awake."

Marissa stretched and shook her head. The cobwebs were clearing. "What was that smoke you made me breathe?"

"It comes from a special plant we use for sacred ceremonies. It helps you relax. Don't you feel wonderful now?"

She nodded a fraction. She wouldn't have taken the drug if she'd been offered a choice, and she felt the edge of anger at being forced. But she kept it in check.

"Who were you talking about just now?" she asked.

Bonita looked like a schoolgirl who'd been caught smoking in the bathroom by one of the nuns. "Oh, that's not important."

"It's Señor Johnson, isn't it?"

Bonita flushed.

"He's a mining engineer?"

"I'm sorry we woke you up. We shouldn't have been talking," Carmen said quickly.

"I won't tell anyone if you give me a little information."

Carmen shot Bonita an angry look. "See, you've gotten us in trouble with your big mouth."

"You were the one asking all the questions!"

"I—"

"It's all right," Marissa interjected. "I promise I won't get you in trouble. But my...fiancé has been working as a mining engineer since he left the military," she improvised. "He was hoping to work with *El Jefe* on a project in Junipero Province."

"That's where Señor Johnson goes when he comes here," Carmen answered. "I know because my brother is one of the pilots who flies him."

"So perhaps it would be better for my fiancé if he developed a project elsewhere in San Marcos," Marissa murmured.

"You'll be his wife soon," Bonita answered. "Really, it's time to start getting ready for the wedding ceremony."

Marissa felt her stomach knot. She'd been happy to think about something besides the wedding. "I didn't know it was so late."

"Madre Flora said to let you sleep until four. But now we have to hurry and do up your hair so you can get dressed."

Marissa swung her legs over the side of the low bed. She expected to be light-headed when she stood. In fact, she felt so wonderfully refreshed that it was hard to focus on any of the things that should be worrying her.

The woman went behind a screen in the corner of the room and brought out a lacy white gown with a high waist, a modest neckline and a flowing skirt.

Marissa unconsciously touched her tongue to her dry lips as her fingers stroked the beautiful fabric. Her wedding dress. It was really going to happen. If she'd said the right things this morning, she could have convinced Madre Flora that the ceremony should be canceled. But deep in her heart, Marissa admitted, she wanted to go ahead with it. Conviction, however, did not entirely prevent her insides from quaking.

As SHE STEPPED into the sunlight, Marissa clasped her bouquet of pink-tinged orchids in a death grip. It was the only way she could keep her hands from trembling. Blood pounded in her ears so that she could hardly hear what was going on around her. The sound of an organ playing the "Wedding March" seemed to come from far away. Masses of flowers decorated the patio. A sea of faces turned expectantly toward her. They seemed to swim in her vision. But she saw the pairs of armed sentries well enough, standing at attention at each entrance. An honor guard? Or insurance against the bride escaping?

Swaying on unsteady legs, she scanned the crowd for the one man who mattered.

Jed. She needed to see him waiting for her at the altar.

Then she caught a glimpse of him and felt some of the terrible knot inside her loosen. He was standing next to Sanchez, in front of the priest, looking devastatingly handsome in a white dinner jacket. Behind them were the high-ranking officers from the *finca*, the men who had arrived yesterday, Rinaldo, Leandro, Harara and Johnson, and at least fifty other dignitaries. Leandro smiled at her, and Rinaldo nodded. Harara looked as if he were trying to put the best face possible on a bad situation. Clarita was over to one side, her expression blank.

Marissa viewed the scene like someone trembling at the edge of a fantasy. How else could she explain the gauntlet stretching in front of her? It might be made of flowers and people dressed in party clothes, but it had been created to test her courage. She swallowed hard and took a step forward and then another, slowly closing the distance between her and Jed—trying to focus on him and only him.

The expression on his face, as she drew near enough to see him clearly, made her heart skip a beat, then begin to pound so hard it felt as though it would break through the wall of her chest. He was looking at her as if she were the center of his universe. Never, in her wildest imaginings, had she pictured a man ever looking at her like that.

Her chest tightened painfully as she came down the aisle toward him. She wished with all her heart that this was real—a real wedding that marked the beginning of a real marriage. Wished that he'd *chosen* to take her for his wife, not that he'd been coerced into it.

Yet even as Marissa acknowledged that heartfelt longing, she knew a wedding between her and Jed would have been impossible under normal circumstances. They were here only because she'd been caught in Sanchez's office. And Jed had volunteered to rescue her by pretending to be her fiancé.

Did he truly care what happened to her? Or was she simply an assignment?

Her heart lurched inside her chest. Then she thought about the way he'd been with her since he'd arrived. He'd kissed her like a man who cared. He'd broken down a door to get to her when he thought she was in trouble. He *had to* feel something stronger than duty.

What would happen tonight? Their wedding night. Did

she have the guts to make it into something real? A moment in time she could cherish long after this sham of a marriage had ended.

Marissa felt light-headed by the time she reached Jed's side. He gave her a confidential smile. She managed the ghost of a smile in return, and suddenly things came a little better into focus.

Someone lifted the bouquet from her hands. Someone folded back her veil. Then she felt Jed's strong fingers close around hers.

"You look beautiful," he whispered huskily.

"So do you."

His soft laugh zinged along her nerve endings. "Nobody ever said that to me before."

She didn't dare look at him again. She simply stood clutching his hand and listening to the priest's words of welcome to the wedding guests, then his little speech about the solemn obligations and responsibilities of marriage.

As she listened, another emotion bubbled up inside her. Oh, God, could she really go through with a religious ceremony? Until this moment she hadn't considered the idea of exchanging holy vows of love and commitment—on making sacred promises that were supposed to last "until death do you part."

For a panicked moment Marissa wanted to turn and run. She kept herself standing in front of the crowd of onlookers by pressing her shoulder to Jed's arm. Somehow she made the right responses. Thank heaven she managed to kneel and stand again without getting her legs tangled in her dress. And when Anna produced a ring at the right moment and pressed it into her hand, she didn't drop it.

The priest's voice and Jed's reassuring presence beside her carried her along. But she was so dazed that she didn't realize the ceremony was over until Jed turned her gently toward him and covered her lips with his.

The kiss was as sweet and sentimental as a lacy valentine.

"Mrs. Prentiss. At last," he murmured as he lifted his head and looked down at her.

His eyes were a clear sea green. And she knew that whatever happened later, she would remember the look in them until her dying day.

"Congratulations to both of you," Sanchez said.

Jed turned, and Marissa saw tension knot the muscles in his shoulders. Then he grinned and stuck out his hand. The two men shook.

She and Jed moved to the other end of the patio and stood under a canopy made by one of the balconies. A line formed, and well-wishers came to them, smiling and offering congratulations. Marissa knew very few of them, which added to her sense of unreality.

It was a relief to greet Professor Leandro. "See, it's all for the best," he said as he kissed her soundly on the cheek. Stepping back, he brushed several strands of wispy hair out of his face. "You get a wonderful wedding reception at the general's expense."

Next in line was William Johnson. The man who was supposed to be from Texas kissed her, holding her too tightly and sliding his lips from her cheek to her mouth. She pushed away, remembering the things she now knew about him that she needed to tell Jed. But this was hardly the moment.

Her new husband gave the man an angry look. "Don't take liberties with the bride."

"Just a friendly buss, old son." Johnson strolled away.

For a moment Jed's eyes drilled into his shoulder blades. Then he pulled his attention back to the next well-wisher.

A band began to play a lively folk tune. Marissa saw waiters circulating around the patio with trays of champagne flutes. It was twilight, and colored lanterns were switched on overhead, casting a magical glow over the patio.

Back to fantasyland again, Marissa thought. This was a wedding reception. Her wedding reception! She had to keep reminding herself of that.

The band leader doffed his sombrero and urged Señor and Señora Prentiss to honor them with the first dance. As if he'd done it a hundred times before, Jed took her in his arms and began to lead her around the area that had been cleared for a dance floor.

They'd taken only a few steps when the sound of multiple explosions made her go rigid. Seconds later she tried to drag Jed off the patio and into the protection of the building.

"Easy." He held his ground and grasped her forearms.

"Somebody's shooting. Get down," she gasped, even as she wondered why the crowd around them was laughing instead of running for cover.

"No. It's just some of the villagers setting off firecrackers. They love an excuse to let off steam. Let's hope they keep the pyrotechnics outside."

She nodded and made an effort to relax. He knew the customs here. She didn't. But then, she'd been at a disadvantage from the start.

Somewhere off to her left she heard a high-pitched, uncontrollable spasm of giggles. Without looking she knew who it was. Clarita.

Out of the corner of her eye she watched Sanchez advance swiftly on his daughter. Taking her by the arm, he ushered her off the patio and into the house.

Jed watched them leave with a sad expression on his

face. Then he pulled Marissa back into his arms and settled his cheek against her hair. "You're doing great," he murmured.

She moved her mouth next to his ear. "I found out some things this afternoon."

He turned his face, as if kissing her cheek. "Me, too."

She caught a mingled anger and frustration in his voice. Then he gave a little shrug, telling her that there was nothing they could do right now besides go with the flow. When he pulled her closer, she sighed and closed her eyes. He was right—they were stuck in this crowd until custom dictated they could escape.

She held on to him, letting him guide her around the floor in a slow dance, his legs brushing hers sensually with every step. She knew scores of eyes were avidly watching the bride and groom take their first dance as man and wife. And it was best to look as if they were totally wrapped up in each other, she rationalized as she let the enjoyment of being close to Jed blot out her uncertainties and then the people around them.

The moment she stopped trying to keep tight control over her mind, the dreamlike thoughts she'd had in the bath came back to her. Jed's hands moving erotically over her naked skin, heating her from the outside in. Was the drug she'd breathed still lingering in her system, affecting her? Feeling light-headed, she pressed her face into his shoulder. He pulled her closer, the heat of his body enveloping her, his hands moving up and down her back, playing with the column of tiny buttons that held her dress closed. She knew he was turned on, too. His lips brushed the hair at her temple. He murmured something low and sexy that made her wish the wedding guests would all vanish.

She didn't realize the music had stopped until a chorus of wolf whistles brought her back to reality.

The general was grinning as he moved to the center of the floor. "I hate to interrupt you lovebirds, but it's time for dinner."

Everyone except her and Jed laughed uproariously.

Blushing hotly, Marissa and Jed followed Sanchez into a ballroom filled with beautifully set tables. Huge arrangements of tropical flowers formed the centerpieces. Around the walls, trellises of bougainvillea turned the room into an outdoor bower. For the first time it occurred to her that this reception must be costing the general a fortune.

"This is lovely. But how did you arrange it on such short notice?" she marveled.

"I'd move heaven and earth for you, my dear. You know that. I've had my people working all night," he answered with a grand gesture, as if the sentiment were real and the expense were nothing to him. Maybe it was, if he had an illegal source of income, Marissa mused.

She and Jed were seated in the center of a long table near the wall, with the honored guests on either side of them. But not Clarita. Apparently Sanchez had banished his daughter from the festivities.

It was strange to sit there watching people eating and drinking and enjoying themselves, Marissa reflected several hours later. Her own stomach was so tied in knots that she could do little more than politely taste the food.

She was married to Jed. All during dinner he'd kept touching her and drawing her close, and she'd felt the erotic surge building between them like a power plant on overload. Later that night they were going to be alone in a room together. And, as her husband, he'd have the right to do anything he wanted to her body.

She stole a glance at him where he stood, laughing and

joking at the bar with several of the guards. He seemed to
be having a much better time than she was. Whenever
someone asked her to dance, he went over to have a drink
with the men.

He came back to her walking unsteadily with a glazed
look in his eyes. She shuddered as the realization hit her
that he was getting drunk. She'd planned that when they
got to the honeymoon cottage they could sit down quietly
and talk. That she could tell him why she was afraid of
intimacy and why she needed him to take things slowly
with her. But what if he was too out of control to listen?
Would he just go ahead—

Marissa's skin turned cold as Jed sat down and draped
his arm around her.

"You'd think things would start to wind down soon,"
he muttered.

"Jed, please don't drink any more."

"Aw, honey bee, don't spoil my fun."

"Please—"

William Johnson approached the table, and Jed's smile
faded. The Texan had also been imbibing steadily through-
out the evening. His face was flushed, and his lips quirked
into a leer as he saw the groom check his watch, something
he'd been doing all evening.

"It's getting late. Already one o'clock. I guess you're
anxious to spirit the bride to your honeymoon cottage."

Marissa sensed Jed's sudden tension. Johnson had made
him angry in the receiving line. Now he was rubbing him
the wrong way again. Under the table she latched onto her
husband's hand and squeezed it hard, hoping she could
have some effect on his behavior. The last thing she
wanted was a scene.

Just then the clock in the hall began to strike—twelve
bongs in all.

"I guess you're wrong about the time," she said lightly.

The Texan appeared puzzled, then he cursed under his breath. "I forgot it's an hour later in Santa Isabella."

That was true, Marissa recalled for the first time since she'd arrived at the *finca*. They were far enough west to be on the other side of a time zone.

She felt Jed's fingers dig into her palm.

Her head swung toward him. "It's okay. The time doesn't matter."

"I'm afraid it's critical," he hissed as the Texan turned away to face the crowd.

"Are you worried that you're getting overtired again?" She stopped abruptly, knowing he wouldn't want her to mention his illness in public. "Didn't you take a nap this afternoon?"

He glared at her, and she knew by the instant clarity and glittering anger in his eyes that he hadn't been drinking as much as she thought—as much as he *wanted* people to think. "Oh, I did all the right stuff," he said, then darted a quick glance at Johnson, who was waving everyone over and shouting for *silencio*.

When people turned in his direction, he pointed to Jed and Marissa. "Let's get to the real fun of the evening. Let's put the bride and groom to bed."

Marissa went cold and stiff. Now what? Ignoring her reaction, Jed slid his arm around her and nibbled his way across her cheek until his mouth reached her ear. He might look like a man anticipating a steamy wedding night, but the message he delivered was harsh and grating. "Let's hope it doesn't take too long. Because if we end up in that honeymoon cottage after one in the morning, we're going to be very dead."

Chapter Twelve

There were enthusiastic shouts around the room. All at once the crowd had only one purpose.

"Bed!"

"Put them to bed!"

As the band struck up a raucous tune, Marissa tried to focus on Jed. Had she heard him correctly? "What?"

"I hope to hell it's not going to be too long before we're finally alone," was all he said by way of clarification, and she realized he couldn't explain anything to her now. But the look in his eyes assured her that he hadn't been playing some kind of practical joke.

"Get the donkeys!" several people called.

"Start the procession!"

"Strip them first," a drunken voice chimed in—adding to the general amusement of the onlookers.

Looking thoroughly pleased with himself, Johnson turned and winked at Marissa. "Don't you just love these quaint local customs?"

Wide-eyed, she sought to disappear behind Jed. He wrapped his arms protectively around her. "Would they really strip us?" she asked above the clamor.

"I saw it happen once. Let's hope we've got diplomatic immunity."

"Oh, God."

A drunk-looking man staggered toward them with a glass of rum in one hand and a machete in the other. Two others grabbed him and pushed him out of the way. He landed on his rump, the liquor sloshing down the front of his shirt.

"Please, can't you just let us go?" Marissa asked a woman standing close by.

She shrugged. "The men want to have their fun."

Several villagers led two donkeys into the hall. Both animals wore sombreros and halters decorated with flowers. Tin cans were tied to their tails, and bands of bells circled their legs. They made a terrible racket as they moved across the tile floor.

Marissa stared at the beasts in astonishment. If they'd been part of a holiday parade, she would have laughed. As it was, she found nothing about the scene amusing.

Fighting panic, she scanned the room for a way out. Before she could take a step, eager hands lifted her into the sidesaddle on the back of one donkey. She'd never ridden in that position; it felt terribly unstable, and she held on for dear life as the onlookers clapped and stamped their feet. Pretending to be a bit unsteady, Jed climbed onto the other beast before anyone could help him.

Laughing and calling boisterously to each other, the wedding guests began to parade the two of them around the room with Marissa in the lead. Merrymakers surged around her, clapping, laughing and making remarks about what the groom was going to do soon and how the bride was going to respond.

Jed had said they didn't have much time. This had to stop. But how?

As they made the first circuit of the room, Marissa racked her brain for some way to end the ordeal. The man guiding her donkey was none too steady on his feet and kept veering toward the flowered trellises that had been set up around the walls.

He was going to knock one down if he didn't watch out, Marissa thought. Then inspiration struck. Hoping Jed was watching what she was doing, she angled a foot outward and hooked the toe of her shoe through a gap in the latticework. As the donkey moved past the flower-covered screen, it wavered dangerously and began to topple toward her.

Marissa screamed as if she were both surprised and terrified, lifting her arms above her head to ward off the blow. Jed slid from his own animal and sprang forward. Just as the trellis was about to strike him on the shoulders, he gave a tremendous push, so that it landed with a crash on the tile floor.

The music stopped. The crowd went utterly silent at the unexpected turn of events.

Jed stared back at the faces that had gone from gleeful to grave in the blink of an eye—his countenance dark and dangerous. "Thank you for a wonderful party. But I think my bride and I have had enough fun for one evening," he said as he helped her down from her donkey. "Please feel free to continue the festivities without us." His tone was even, but his body language telegraphed the message that the teasing was over for tonight.

Nobody said anything.

He inclined his head and waited for several more seconds. Then, taking Marissa's arm, he led her out of the reception room and down the hall toward the back of the hacienda. Some of the crowd followed, but they were more subdued now.

"Good going," he said as they emerged into the darkness.

"I didn't know if it would be enough."

Marissa saw that the path to the honeymoon cottage had been marked with a line of lanterns. As they reached the door, Jed stopped and spoke to several men who were standing at attention near the door. "Thanks for keeping watch. I don't think we'll be needing you now."

"Don't you want us to make sure nobody comes around?"

"I appreciate your help. But go in and join the party now. Have yourselves a good time."

The door closed behind them. Mercifully, they had escaped from their tormentors. But now what?

Marissa's eyes were large and round as she stared uncertainly at Jed, smoldering sensuality mingling with layers of uncertainty. He'd said they couldn't stay here. She still had no idea what was going on.

"Alone at last." He gave her a sardonic smile, and her heart rose to block her windpipe.

He took her icy hand. "Come see the surprise I've got."

She looked at him questioningly when he led her to the bar. Kneeling, he removed the panel under the sink and pointed inside. Marissa stared in horror. Wedged between the water pipes was a bomb. The clock on the timer said one-thirty.

"When Johnson came over to us, I realized he was mixed up about the time difference. But that's okay, because it got us out of the party early," Jed commented, his careful choice of words telling her that they still couldn't count on a private conversation.

"Johnson?" Marissa repeated, her eyes fixed on the bomb.

Jed nodded.

The clock said the device was going to go off in half an hour—if Johnson hadn't made some other miscalculation. Pieces of the puzzle were starting to fall into place. The man had a mining deal going with Sanchez, and it looked as if he was willing to kill to get rid of the competition. But did Sanchez know?

"He wanted to give us a real send-off," Jed agreed. He rolled his eyes. Marissa looked at him in frustration. Exchanging information was still impossible.

"So now that we're alone, Mrs. Prentiss, why don't you slip into something more comfortable?"

Totally confused by the abrupt change of subject, she frowned. But her confusion became understanding as Jed pulled a pair of men's slacks, a shirt and sandals from behind one of the sofa cushions. It looked like the outfits the villagers wore. Travel clothes, she realized. He had obviously stashed them here earlier in the day.

Jed looked from the bomb to the line of small buttons down her back. "Let me help you off with your dress."

Marissa nodded wordlessly, and he came up behind her, his hands brushing aside the wisps of hair that had escaped from her French twist.

She stood very still, the touch of his fingers on her hair and neck sending little zings along her nerve endings.

A moment ago he'd been all business. When his fingers came in contact with her skin, everything changed. He drew in a shaky breath as he buried his nose in her hair. Then his lips grazed her neck. "Like silk," he murmured.

Transfixed, Marissa moved her head against his face. She'd been dreading this kind of intimacy, yet her responses to this man held her captive.

For several heartbeats Jed seemed to forget what he was supposed to be doing. Finally he began to unfasten the buttons at the back of her dress.

She tried to stand very still as she felt the fabric slowly open, exposing the skin of her back to his view. Little shivers raced along her skin as he touched her—not only with his fingers. He followed the progress of the buttons with his lips, sensually kissing the flesh that he revealed. When he slipped the dress from her shoulders, he made no move to pick up the peasant outfit she was supposed to put on.

"Jed?"

He bent to capture her earlobe in his teeth, nibbling with controlled pressure that made her dizzy.

"Jed…" His name sighed out again.

"Your skin is so soft. And you smell so good." He drew in a ragged breath as he nuzzled his cheek and nose against her back. His fingers stroked up and down underneath one of her bra straps.

Her own breath was coming in little gasps. In some part of her mind she knew that the seconds were ticking by—each one moving them closer to terrible danger. She knew they had to get out of this room. But she wasn't capable of moving at this moment. He tugged her dress lower. It would have puddled around her feet if there had been an inch of space between her body and his. "Ah, Marci, I've been looking at you all evening, thinking about undressing you like this. This is our wedding night." He pressed her hips back against his, and she knew unmistakably he was ready to make love to her.

"Yes," she breathed as her body responded to his words, to his touch. She had never felt more aroused—perhaps because some part of her still recognized that she was safe. He wasn't going to take her into the bedroom. He couldn't. Or could he?

"I've got to touch you. Just touch you."

He wasn't asking for permission. He simply took what he wanted. His hands came up to clasp her breasts, kneading them gently through the silky fabric of her bra, making her gasp with pleasure. Involuntarily she closed her eyes and arched backward against him. He found her nipples, drawing small circles around them with his fingertips until they hardened to tight peaks of sensation. She pressed into his hands, whimpering deep in her throat.

"You want me."

She had no thought of denying the truth of his statement. "Yes."

His teeth and lips played with her neck and the sensitive curve of her ear. Starved for more direct contact, she tried to twist around so that she could kiss him. But he held her fast. His hands stroked down her front, pushing the dress out of the way. It slid to the floor, and he slipped his fingers under the edges of her panties.

Her body jerked as he touched her intimately, holding her captive. All thought was driven from her mind but the need to get closer still.

Then Jed's muttered curse brought back a measure of sanity. "We're playing with dynamite here."

This time her little whimper was equal parts fear and arousal as her gaze shot to the bomb. She would have toppled backward if he'd stepped away from her. Instead he reached for the shirt on the couch and helped her slip her arms through the sleeves. He left the buttons for her.

Marissa took gasping little breaths as she closed the front, then stepped into the trousers he was holding out. They were too long, and he knelt to roll up the cuffs, making an obvious attempt not to brush her ankles.

While she shoved her feet into the sandals and tucked her hair under the brim of her hat, he quickly shucked off his dinner jacket, dress pants and shirt and donned an outfit similar to hers—only his looked rumpled, as if he'd already been wearing it. Then he bent and lifted up another

cushion. Her eyes widened when she saw he was holding
a revolver.

"Where did you get that?" she asked, forgetting for a
moment that someone might be listening.

"I won't tell if you don't," he answered as he tucked
the weapon into his waistband. Then he slung a knapsack
over his shoulder.

When they stepped into the tropical night, she let out a
long sigh. It was a relief to be away from the room with
the bomb, but she didn't know much about dynamite. How
far from the house would they have to go to be safe from
the blast?

Jed took her hand. In the light from the myriad stars
and the almost full moon, they began to move rapidly
away from the cottage. From destruction.

Marissa glanced back at the little cottage. It stood alone,
apart from other buildings, which made it the perfect place
for Johnson's scheme. The blast would damage nothing
else on the *finca*.

As they reached the edge of the plantings that provided
privacy, Jed stopped under a date palm to reconnoiter. Marissa could see that when they crossed the open area they'd
be completely exposed. But there was no other way to
escape.

They stepped onto the grass, heading toward the nearest
clump of foliage. Before they'd gotten more than a few
yards the sound of footsteps crunching on the gravel path
made them both stop abruptly. Jed's fingers clamped down
on Marissa's. They were trapped. And running for the
nearest clump of trees would only give them away.

Her body went cold all over as she felt his free hand
silently pull the gun from his trousers. Then two dark
shapes came into view. It looked like a couple of men from
the village heading home after the festivities. They were

staggering. Please God, let them be too drunk to notice what was around them, Marissa prayed.

"Come on," Jed whispered. "Act like you belong here, and they won't pay any attention."

She'd forgotten she was dressed like a man. That nobody would take her for the bride unless they saw her face. With her heart in her throat she started walking again, putting one foot in front of the other as the pair lurched away at an angle across the clearing.

She half expected them to turn and clamp a hand on her shoulder. Miraculously, she and Jed reached the nearest knot of trees without incident. After that, to her relief, it was possible to zigzag their way across the *finca* without being exposed for more than a few seconds.

Then, in the distance, she could hear the dogs barking, and for a panicked few seconds she imagined a pack of Dobermans looming out of the darkness.

Jed must have had the same thought, because she felt him tense. Then he relaxed. "Don't worry about them. There are too many people on the grounds tonight. And the general won't want his guests getting torn up."

Marissa took what comfort she could in the reassurance as Jed led her toward a low building that looked like a warehouse made of corrugated steel with a long bank of garage doors.

"Wait here," he whispered.

"Why are we stopping?"

"Call it curiosity."

She doubted mere curiosity would delay Jed at a time like this. Stepping into the shadows, she watched him disappear around the side of the building. Several seconds later Marissa heard a groan and felt her heart lurch. Sprinting around the corner, she found an armed sentry lying on the ground by a small door. Jed handed her the man's machine gun and tucked his own pistol back in his waistband.

"Sorry I had to do that," he muttered.

"He'll report it when he wakes up."

"Yeah. But he didn't see me. So he can't tell Sanchez who it was."

Marissa served as lookout while Jed took a small tool kit from his knapsack and tackled the padlock on the door. He had it open in a matter of moments.

Inside it was pitch-dark. But Jed must have spent the afternoon getting ready for this, because he'd brought along a flashlight. Marissa held it as he tied up the soldier; all the while she felt her tension balloon. She wanted to leave the *finca* as quickly as possible, and she had to remind herself that Jed wouldn't be stopping in this place if it wasn't important.

"Now let's find out what my great and good friend's got under lock and key," he said. Taking the flashlight from Marissa, he began to play the beam over some large pieces of machinery. "Either he's going in for road building and housing projects in a big way or—"

"I vote for mining equipment," she said in a low voice that matched Jed's.

"Oh, yeah?"

"When they thought I was asleep this afternoon, two of the women were talking about Johnson." She felt her cheeks heat as she recalled the circumstances and was glad the flashlight beam wasn't trained on her face. "Apparently he's a mining engineer who comes here all the time. And he's not from Texas."

"Sanchez told me he's an arms dealer."

"Because it's a plausible explanation for their relationship. And one you'd believe," Marissa supplied. "But the women who were discussing him didn't have an ax to grind. Try this scenario. What if Johnson and your friend have some kind of private deal to develop the copper deposits in Junipero Province? They cut the government out and take all the profits.''

Jed's eyes narrowed as he considered the theory. "That would explain why he didn't jump at the loan offer to the Ministry of Development.''

The beam stopped as it hit a gigantic circular pan that must have been fifteen or sixteen feet in diameter. "Wait a minute.'' He stepped closer and whistled. "Well, I'll be damned. Did the women mention copper mining?''

"Not specifically.''

"Well, I think there's a better reason why he wants to keep the Ministry of Development out of Junipero Province. He and Johnson aren't mining copper. They're mining diamonds.''

Marissa's eyes widened. "Diamonds? What makes you think so?''

"Ninety-five percent of the world's output still comes from South Africa. But diamonds are in Brazil, Venezuela and Guyana. So why not in the unexplored jungle of San Marcos?''

Jed stepped closer to one of the metallic circles and played the light along the edge. "Here's the manufacturer's name. It's a firm in Cape Town. You've heard about miners panning for gold—separating the ore from the gravel in streambeds by washing it in pans. The gold stays on the bottom because it's denser than the gravel. Well, the same principle is used with diamonds. Only the pans are gigantic.''

"You're positive this stuff couldn't be for copper?''

"No. I could give you a lot of technical details about copper refining, but all you have to know is that it's an entirely different process.''

Marissa nodded.

Jed looked at his watch. "Let's get out of here. The explosion is going to give us the perfect cover to get off the *finca*."

"How much time do we have?"

"A little less than eight minutes."

"Oh!"

They left the guard tied up in the building and retraced part of their route, angling off to the right and ending up at a wire fence that should have been electrified. Apparently Jed had disabled the mechanism, because his hand didn't sizzle when he lifted it up and helped her down into a deep concrete draining ditch about fifty yards from the honeymoon cottage. At this time of year the ditch was bone-dry.

The overhang of a little platform sheltered them from view. It also hid a motorcycle leaning against the wall of the conduit.

"You've been busy," Marissa commented.

"Yeah. I pulled a straw hat down over my face and went native. With all the hoopla of the wedding preparations, nobody was doing their usual jobs."

Jed had picked a perfect place to watch the fireworks. They were out of sight and protected from the explosion, but they had an unobstructed view of the little house.

"Only three minutes now," Jed whispered, slipping his arm around Marissa and drawing her close. She leaned against him in the dark, feeling tension build inside her that was not only from the anticipated explosion. There were still so many things she wanted to talk about with Jed, yet everything would have to wait.

"Two minutes."

Marissa strained to see the cottage through the darkness. Silently she began to count off the seconds. When she'd reached thirty, she saw a figure approaching the back door. It was a woman walking stealthily and carrying a basket. As she paused and looked around to see if anyone was watching her, Marissa felt her breath still. "Good heavens, it's Clarita!"

Jed groaned. "Damn her."

Clarita took several steps closer to the cottage. In a panic, thinking of nothing but the danger to the girl, Marissa pulled herself up to the rim of the ditch and started to scramble forward.

Chapter Thirteen

Jed moved faster than Marissa, clamping his hand over her arm so hard that she gasped.

"Please. I've got to stop her."

"Are you as cracked as she is?"

"What?"

"You can't go out there now. The place is going to blow at any second. I won't let you kill yourself trying—" Jed stopped abruptly and raised his voice. Speaking in Spanish, he shouted, "Halt. Or I'll shoot."

He sounded just like one of the guards. Clarita whirled toward the command.

"Back up, *señorita*," Jed added.

The girl raised her chin haughtily. "Do you know whom you're addressing? When I tell *El Jefe* of your presumption, he will—"

The end of her sentence was cut off by a blast that sounded like a volcanic eruption and felt like a ten-ton airplane slamming into the earth.

As the ground shook, Jed pulled Marissa down, shielding her body with his. The last thing she saw was the walls and roof of the cottage flying outward. Then debris began to rain down.

Jed didn't wait for the dust to settle. "We're in the clear. Come on."

Marissa stayed where she was, straining her eyes to see through the dust. "We can't leave Clarita. She may be hurt."

"People are coming. They'll take care of her."

Marissa realized Jed was right. After several seconds of stunned silence, guards began shouting and hurrying toward the blast area from all directions. Reluctantly she let Jed lead her away.

Bending low, he grabbed the handlebars of the motorcycle and began to walk it down the ditch.

"Not yet."

He stopped and shrugged. They both listened to the noise and confusion as the soldiers tried to make sense of what had happened.

"*Madre de Dios!* Señor Jed," someone shouted. "Where are you? Are you all right?"

"Nobody could survive that."

"Here's a woman."

"Was she inside?"

"I don't know."

"By all the saints. It's *El Jefe*'s daughter."

"See. They found her," Jed whispered.

"All right." Marissa nodded in the dark and followed Jed.

"What did you mean when you asked if I was as crazy as she?" Marissa asked in a low voice.

"She's having mental problems. Everybody on the *finca* knows it, but Sanchez won't get her any help."

Marissa sighed. "That explains a lot of her strange behavior."

"I hope this changes Sanchez's mind."

As they moved down the ditch, the noise and disarray

behind them faded to a distant babble of voices. About a quarter mile from the blast site Jed started the machine and climbed on. Marissa perched on the seat behind him and circled his waist with her arms. She leaned her head on his shoulder as they moved slowly down the pavement, still with the lamp off. But there was enough light from the moon and brilliant canopy of stars to navigate.

She pressed her cheek to his shoulder and hung on to his powerful body, letting the vibrations of the engine lull her. It was hard to believe they were really getting away from Sanchez.

When the motorcycle slowed, her head jerked up. A chain-link fence blocked the ditch.

"Now what?"

"Not to worry. Can you hold this thing for a minute?"

"Yes."

He dismounted and walked to the fence. Grasping the center of the links, he pulled, and they parted like the Red Sea opening for the Israelites.

He grinned back at her. "Superman!"

"You cut it this afternoon."

"Right."

He came back and guided the machine through the opening. As Marissa followed him outside the fence, she felt as if a hundred-pound weight had been lifted from her shoulders.

"Thank you," she breathed.

Jed propped the bike against the fence. They each took a step forward. Then she was in his arms, and he was crushing her to him. Their lips came together in a long, searing kiss that was broken only when they both had to come up for air.

"Oh, Jed, Jed. You got me out of there. You saved my life. I owe you so much."

"You don't owe me anything."

It wasn't exactly the declaration Marissa wanted to hear. But she knew he wasn't a man who articulated his feelings easily. She gestured toward the cut fence and the motorcycle. "You must have been running around all day getting things set up. If you want, I can drive and you can rest."

"You don't have to coddle me. I'm fine!"

She realized she'd said the wrong thing again and hastened to repair the damage. "Jed, it's been pretty hard for me to stand by like a helpless female and let you run the rescue operation."

He nodded. "Yeah, I understand. But I didn't exactly do it by myself. If you hadn't played the part I tossed at you, we never would have made it."

"That's true."

"So you can leave the driving to me. I'm probably a lot more experienced on a motorcycle than you are."

She climbed in back of him again, and they started off once more at a slow speed, still with the lights off.

"I've got a boat waiting for us at a little town called Zapaca. We can be out of San Marcos in another four hours," he told her.

She shook her head. "We can't. We have to go back to Santa Isabella."

"Impossible. When Sanchez doesn't find any bodies in that cottage, he's going to come looking for us."

"You think he gave the instructions to Johnson?"

Jed nodded grimly.

"All the more reason why I want to get the goods on him."

"You know as well as I do that the next time somebody looks, that diamond mining equipment will have disappeared from those warehouses."

"Of course. But there's another way. I assume you know Victor Kirkland at the State Department sent me down here?"

"On a damn fool mission."

"You were here for the same thing," she challenged.

"I didn't get caught with my hand in the cookie jar."

So they were back where they'd started at the cocktail party—wary opponents.

"I would have been okay," Marissa said, "if somebody hadn't given me away."

"It wasn't me!"

"I know," she said softly. She felt the muscles in his shoulders clench. "Maybe Johnson saw me leave the party. Maybe it was Clarita who called the guards. But that's not the important thing now."

"I'm listening. You've got sixty seconds to convince me we should risk our lives by staying in a country where the head of the army can execute a U.S. citizen without a trial."

She began to speak quickly. "Before I got caught, I photographed some documents that were in code. I couldn't read them, but I assumed they were Sanchez's plans for overthrowing President Palmeriz—because he thinks the army is stronger than the democratic government. That's what Victor sent me down here to scope out. Now it looks like Sanchez is going to use the money from the diamond-mining operation to finance a coup. After I breached his security, he probably moved the documents to a safer location. But we can still get the film. I sealed my camera in a plastic bag and stuck it in his toilet tank. If he'd found it, I'd already be dead."

Jed swore. "I suppose it's in the private bathroom off his office."

"Nobody will be expecting us to break in there. They'll expect us to clear out as fast as we can."

He didn't answer one way or the other.

She felt her tension mount. "So where are we going?" she asked after five minutes of silence.

"To the coast."

"I'm not leaving San Marcos. I'll get the film myself."

"Honey bee, you'll only get caught again, and this whole sideshow will have been a waste."

A sideshow. Was that what he called it? Anger surged inside her. But she knew her reaction was reflexive. For once, she swallowed her pride. "You're right. I'm not being rational," she admitted. "I'm angry about what that bastard did to me—to us—and I want to get back at him in spades. But more than that, I want to come home feeling that I accomplished my mission. I don't want to be talked about for the rest of my life as the bumbling idiot who had to be rescued. But I need your help to pull this off."

She'd laid herself bare, and she waited anxiously for his answer. Although he shifted in his seat, he was silent again for several miles.

Afraid he wasn't going to respond, she had no option but to sit behind him, holding on tightly as he swerved around a tree limb that had fallen into the drainage ditch. When he finally began to speak, his voice was gruff. "I understand how you feel."

"I hoped you would."

"But it's not a simple case of my changing plans. Maybe you'd better hear the whole story of what happened to me in Royal Verde."

"You don't owe me any more explanation than you already gave me."

"I want you to know where I'm coming from, as the touchy-feely types put it." She felt him suck in a long draft of air and let it out slowly, a man working up to some sort of shameful confession. "I was on assignment trying to pinpoint the source of a very nasty street drug. I'd zeroed in on a local mental hospital where some strange stuff was going on—like voodoo ceremonies with human sacrifice."

Marissa sucked in a sharp breath. "How did they get away with that?"

"The director of the place would remind you of Sanchez. He was a law unto himself on his own estate. Unfortunately I picked voodoo night to reconnoiter, got shot out of a tree with a blowgun and ended up locked in the asylum's disturbed ward. The director tried to get me to talk—using a variety of interesting methods. When that didn't work, he decided that I, along with a female agent they captured later, were going to be the next sacrificial victims."

"No!"

"They starved me for a few days to make me weak. Then they brought us to the ceremonial ground, made us drink a vile concoction and tied us to stakes."

Marissa pressed her face against his shoulder, not sure she wanted to hear the rest, but he plowed on. Marissa guessed that the concealing darkness, and the fact that his back was to her, made it easier to talk.

"I wouldn't be alive at all," Jed continued, "if the voodoo priestess hadn't decided to double-cross her partner. I found out later that she put some kind of organic compound on the knife she plunged into our chests. Along with the stuff we drank before the ritual, it sent us into a state of suspended animation, so everybody thought we were dead. And the team that had come down to clean up the flap on Royal Verde was able to get us out of there."

"Oh, Jed, it must have been awful."

"Well, when the priestess plunged the knife into my body, I went out like a light."

Marissa winced.

"After they revived us, I thought I was back to normal. I even joked about being a zombie. But it turned out not to be very funny. It wasn't until months later that I discovered there's a virus in my blood. Too much stress and fatigue trigger the sleeping sickness you saw the other night. The doctors tell me there's no medical treatment. I've just got to live with it." He swiveled his head partly around. "So you're pushing your luck if you're counting on me to help you get in and out of Sanchez's office. I may let you down when you need me the most."

"Don't call yourself a zombie."

"And what would you call it?" he asked bitterly as he focused on the pavement ahead of him once more. "For my next career I can be exhibit A in that voodoo museum in New Orleans."

Marissa clasped her hands more tightly around his middle and moved her cheek against his neck, longing to talk face-to-face, to make him understand that the confession didn't change the way she felt about him. "What happened isn't your fault."

"I shouldn't have gotten caught."

"Neither should I!"

"That's different."

"How?"

He was silent for several moments. Then he sighed. "Okay. I guess I know how you're feeling about this assignment. If you trust me and you want me to take you back to Santa Isabella, I'll do it."

"Thank you."

"Hold the thanks until we're in the clear."

Marissa closed her eyes and clung to him. He'd been

achingly honest with her, and she wanted to be the same with him. But unlike Jed, she didn't feel comfortable having a personal discussion straddling a motorbike. She wanted more time and a better place, where she could watch his face as she spoke. Yet the pressure to confess her own deficiency was like a balloon expanding inside her chest. Trying to ignore it, she leaned into him, hoping he'd know by the way she held him that she trusted him completely.

The machine plowed on through the night. When Jed reached the end of the ditch, he consulted the odometer and a map from his knapsack. Turning left, he bumped across a stretch of open field to the road—where he turned on the light and sped up.

They'd gone only a few miles when he cursed and slammed on the brakes.

Marissa tensed.

"We've got company." He gestured down the blacktop.

She expected to confront one of Sanchez's men. Instead she made a little exclamation when she saw orange fur and black spots. A jaguar! It was sprawled on the pavement only a few yards from where Jed had stopped. The big cat lifted its head, regarding them as if they were intruders in its private bedroom.

"They like the heat the road absorbs during the day," Jed explained.

"I know."

He eased the machine gun off the saddle carrier and handed it to Marissa. "They don't attack people unless they're very hungry."

"Right."

"But keep an eye on him."

Hoping the weapon was just a precaution, she trained it on the animal as Jed revved the engine. The cat watched them warily for several more seconds, its body poised to spring.

Marissa held the gun steady. To her relief, the animal leaped up and trotted into the underbrush.

The next few miles passed without incident. When they came to a road that branched off to the right, Jed consulted the map and the odometer again and turned right.

"Where are you going?"

"I didn't know what the situation would be when I came back from Baltimore, so I arranged for several safe houses where we could hole up if we needed to. One isn't far from here. I rented it in the name of the Audubon Society—for some bird-watchers who are supposed to be coming down to San Marcos in a couple of weeks."

"We'll be safe there?"

"I can't give you an ironclad guarantee. But we'll be as safe as anywhere in the country."

For all her bravado, the thought of falling into Sanchez's clutches again made her shudder. She knew Jed was giving her a chance to change her mind about staying. But she clamped her teeth together and didn't voice any more objections.

As Jed sped on, Marissa realized how wrung out she was. She'd been mentally prepared for a long ride, but the reality was taking its toll. Slumping against him, she closed her eyes as the bike bumped down a gravel road. When they jolted to a halt, she realized to her astonishment that she'd actually fallen asleep. Blinking, she saw they were in front of a native dwelling with a thatched roof and walls of bamboo poles. Dismounting, she staggered over to the rows of vertical posts and braced herself with her hand.

"Are you okay?"

"Just stiff." She made an effort to straighten while Jed pulled out a set of keys. After a couple of tries he unlocked the padlock on the door and shone the light around the interior.

"All clear."

Handing Marissa the light, he retrieved the motorbike and brought it inside with them. She played the beam around the small room, revealing a bed, a rickety table and a pile of supplies. It was about as basic as one of *El Jefe*'s cells.

"Not very plush, I'm afraid," Jed admitted. "But I think we're safe."

"I assume the bathroom's out back."

"Yeah. There aren't any three-star hotels out here."

"I wasn't complaining."

He led the way to the minimal facilities. "Ladies first."

She wished he wasn't standing right on the other side of the door, but she knew he wasn't going to leave her alone in this part of the jungle tonight—or any other night.

After they'd returned to the house she watched him move efficiently around the small room, locking the door behind them and lighting an oil lamp.

When she heard the lock snap, she felt her throat go dry.

Stop it! she shouted inside her head. *This is Jed. He's not going to hurt you.*

He broke the seal on a bottle of water. Marissa took several swallows to moisten her dry mouth. It was tempting to draw into herself—to lie down, roll away from him and pretend all she wanted to do was sleep. But she wasn't going to take the coward's way out. She'd psyched herself up to talk to him, and every moment she waited increased the tight feeling in her chest.

She watched Jed set down his pack and stretch, drawing her attention to his powerful muscles. "We've got field rations if you want something."

"I'm not hungry."

There was nowhere to sit besides a double bed with rope springs attached to the wooden frame. Marissa stared at it for several seconds before gingerly lowering her body onto it.

Jed hesitated, then joined her. As the weight shifted on the thin mattress, she struggled to breathe without giving away her nervousness. But she couldn't stop herself from twisting her stiff fingers around a strand of her hair.

"We'll probably both feel better after a good night's sleep," Jed said noncommittally, and she knew she wasn't fooling him.

The pressure inside her chest made her words come out high and shaky. "After we finish the conversation."

"Which conversation?"

Knowing she was stepping into a mine field, she plowed on. "You said you understood how I felt about getting caught by Sanchez. I wanted to tell you I understood about the…the zombie stuff."

He moved away from her, propping his back against the wall and pinning her with his gaze. "I don't need empathy right now. I need sleep."

Marissa ignored the sarcasm in his voice. "You feel like somebody stepped into your life and took away your power to make your own decisions. You feel angry because your choices are limited. You don't feel quite whole. In fact, used and degraded are better descriptions. And you keep cursing yourself for a fool because you've let that one unfortunate incident rule everything you do." She blurted out the phrases that had been running around and around in her head for the past few hours.

Jed's eyes glittered in the lamplight. "What are you trying to do?" he demanded. "Expose every raw nerve in my body just so you can prove a point?"

Her heart was threatening to pound its way up her throat.

"I'm trying to show you that I get it—better than almost anyone else would."

He remained silent, a wary but curious look coming over his handsome features.

She gazed down at her hands clasped tightly in her lap. The knuckles were white. She'd deliberately forced this confrontation, and she'd told herself she wanted to look him in the eye. Yet suddenly she couldn't quite meet his gaze. "What you went through," she began, then paused to draw a steadying breath and start again. "What you went through comes pretty close to the experience of being raped."

The devastated look on his face almost undid her.

"No," he whispered. "No."

She nodded, determined to make him understand how it was for her. "For ten years I've known I wanted the same things a normal woman wants. Being alone made me so sad. But the fear was stronger. I couldn't get close to any man—because one of them won my trust and then tore my heart out. So I made myself tough and cold and unapproachable." She swallowed hard. "Then I met someone I liked. Someone who turned me on. Someone I wanted to be…close to. But that scared me so badly I worked overtime to make sure he kept his distance. And if you haven't figured it out, I'm talking about you."

She'd said it. Not the worst, perhaps. But enough. There was complete silence for several seconds, and she cringed inside, hardly able to believe she'd been that honest. Now what would he think of her?

"Marci?" He closed the space between them, taking her by the shoulders—gently, oh, so gently. Slowly, as if he were afraid she'd bolt, he pulled her into his arms. For a moment she held herself rigid. Then she gave up and went limp against him. She'd told him her deep dark secret, and

he had taken her in his arms. That was miracle enough.
But all at once it seemed possible that the rest of it was
going to be okay, too.

As his hands stroked her hair, her back, the knot of
tension in her chest began to loosen. "Honey, I figured
out some guy must have been rough with you. I didn't
know you were raped."

"Oh, Jed, all these years I've worked so hard to fool
you. To keep you from thinking of me as a woman."

He uttered a single short laugh. "I thought of you as a
woman, all right."

Compulsively, she continued. "You're so masculine.
Aggressive. Intimidating. You take what you want. And I
was afraid of that. Then you came down here pretending
we were engaged, and you stood all my rules on their
heads. Jed, when you kissed me that first time, it was like
fireworks going off."

"Yes."

"Afterward, I was quaking inside. But I knew that if I
let you or Sanchez see how scared I was, I'd get us both
killed."

"I kept pushing you," he muttered. "Seeing how far I
could get you to go."

"Why?"

"You're not the only one who's been attracted for years.
I guess I liked having you in a position where you couldn't
back off." He laughed. "That's the macho answer. And
it's part of the truth. The other part is that once I kissed
you, I could hardly remember my own name."

"Oh, Jed."

He turned her to him and started to kiss her. Then he
pulled back as if he'd put his face too close to an open
flame.

She felt her world shatter. "I've dumped a lot of heavy

stuff on you," she murmured. "I understand if you can't deal with it."

When she started to turn away so he couldn't see the tears in her eyes, he took her fiercely by the arms. "Honey, don't ever make the mistake of thinking I don't want you. Or that I don't care. I'm trying my damnedest to get this right."

"I—"

He touched her quivering lips with his finger. "There are things I need to know. Like, how do you feel now? Are you still afraid of me? And how close do you want me to get? Tonight."

She raised her head and looked at him, feeling as if time were standing still, waiting for her answer. Here it was, at last. Was she going to continue being a coward? Or could she finally, here and now, reclaim her life? "I'm still afraid," she said, her voice shaking as much as her body. "And at the same time, I feel like I'll die if I can't make love with you."

His knuckles grazed her cheek. "Have you made love since…I mean…since it happened?"

"No," she whispered. "But when you kissed me and touched me, it made me so hot and shaky that I felt like I was going to jump out of my skin." She nestled against him, daring to let the warm feeling steal over her once more. It was wonderful to finally be honest with him— with herself. To let him know what she wanted. She could do this. It was going to be all right.

He chuckled. "I understand the feeling."

"But…but…I have to explain something to you first," she said, breaking past shyness. "Remember that night in your room when you tried to…to push me down onto the rug. I…"

"That scared you," he finished.

"Yes. Your weight on top of me. So maybe we can't… I mean…could we…?"

"I think we can work around that. If you're sure it's what you want to do. Or we can, you know, take it slow, get to know each other better."

"I don't want to take it slow. This is…" She hesitated, raising her face to his. "Jed, this is our wedding night."

She'd thought she had everything figured out. She'd thought she could simply have what she wanted, now that she'd bared her soul. In the next moment, to her astonishment, she burst into tears.

Chapter Fourteen

"Marci, honey?"

Marissa tried to answer but found she was incapable of speaking around the sobs that racked her body. All she could do was cling to Jed as she fought to get control of herself.

"It's okay. It's okay," he murmured, along with other soothing words she only half heard.

By slow degrees she managed to subdue the storm of tears. Jed held her, continuing his gentle reassurance until she was calmer. When he brought a tissue out of the knapsack, she blew her nose.

"Honey, we don't have to—"

"Don't you understand? I want you so much I feel like I'm going to burn up from the inside out!" she cut in fiercely. "I thought...I could...we could..."

He waited patiently, not pushing her into difficult explanations.

She gulped in a lungful of air. "I told you, I want to be normal."

"You are!"

"I don't think this is going to work unless I tell you what happened. I need you to understand why tonight is so threatening to me."

"Okay," he said softly.

She held the edge of the mattress in a death grip, her fingers so rigid that she wondered vaguely if she'd ever pry them open again. "Did you ever see that movie *Cape Fear,* where a man who was sent to prison terrorizes his lawyer's family—especially the wife and daughter?"

Jed nodded.

"I've seen it a dozen times. Maybe to convince myself I'm not the only fool who could be taken in by a smooth-talking stranger."

"Don't call yourself a fool," he said harshly.

"Okay. Sure. I was eighteen, in my first year of college at the University of Maryland. There was this guy named Lowell Dougan. He started a conversation with me in the library. I was pretty shy. But I was happy to finally be on my own, away from my father. Lowell was so charming and funny that he got me to go out to dinner with him that night. After that he sort of…swept me off my feet." She sighed, trying once more to come to terms with what had happened. "I was pretty naive. My father had hardly let me date in high school. So I didn't know much about men. Lowell flattered me. Made me feel special. Convinced me we were madly in love with each other and that we should get married. Probably you're thinking I was pretty stupid."

"No. It sounds like you were lonely—and susceptible."

"I was. Lowell kept sidestepping any questions I had about his family or his background. I didn't know he'd been in the army and been court-martialed and spent four years at Leavenworth Penitentiary. I didn't know my father had started the court-martial proceedings because he'd caught Lowell hitting on female GIs. I didn't know he was being so nice to me to get back at Colonel Devereaux."

"Because he deliberately hid all that from you."

"But I should have had more sense than to run off and

marry him!'' she protested. ''On our wed-wedding night I found out that what he really wanted was revenge.''

Jed cursed vehemently.

''He kept me captive in a motel room for two days—raping me and…other things. He'd leave me there tied up in the dark for hours, wondering when he was going to come back. Then he'd leap into the room and—and—'' She didn't want to tell him any more.

Jed's eyes blazed. He pounded his fist against the wall. ''I'll kill the bastard!''

''You can't. He shot himself. At least he didn't make me watch. He left me tied up until the maid found me in the morning.''

Jed held her tightly. ''Oh, Marci. Oh, Lord.''

''My sister Cassie doesn't know because she was away at the University of Virginia. My father told me it was my fault. For years I believed him.''

''No!''

''Abby Franklin's been helping me deal with it. She's a psychologist in the building where I work. She's been great.''

''I know. Remember, she helped refine the rescue plan.'' He swallowed. ''Before I left, I had a session with Abby. I told her about what happened on Royal Verde and asked her if I was up to this rescue mission. She told me she thought you and I would be good for each other.''

Marissa laughed. ''I made the mistake of talking to her about you. She's been after me for six months to stop acting like a coward.''

''You're not! A coward wouldn't have raided Miguel's office.''

''No. It had to be someone with nothing left to lose.'' Marissa looked down at her hands. She'd thought she was past the hard part. But there was one more confession she felt compelled to make. "I didn't want to tell you about Lowell—about him specifically. I didn't want you to be thinking about what he did to me when we make love," she whispered.

"The only thing I'm going to think about is how much I like being close to you."

"Oh, Jed." Her eyes misted. Blinking back the tears, she moved closer to him quickly and slipped her arms around his neck. When she felt more in control, she whispered, "I've waited a long time for this."

"So have I. But we don't have to rush. Maybe it would be better to hold off until another night. One that's not so…loaded."

"No. I've got a chance to replace that other wedding night with this one. That's the only way I'm going to wipe out the horror of what happened." She stopped as another thought struck her. "I'm sorry. I just realized I'm putting a lot of pressure on you. More than I have any right to. I know it's not a real marriage. But—"

"It's as real as we want to make it."

Her eyes shone as she gazed at him. He gave her a little smile and glanced around the confines of the shack. "I just wish I could check us into the Ritz, instead of this hovel."

"It's not on Sanchez's estate, and that's the only thing that matters."

He looked at her with such tenderness that she dared to let hope bloom. Perhaps that was the moment she knew for sure that she had fallen in love with him. Her heart swelled with gladness. She wanted to tell him how she felt. Yet she didn't want to put any more pressure on him. She couldn't be certain what would happen when they returned to civilization, but she would take whatever he offered tonight.

He gathered her close and covered her lips with his,

kissing her at first with leashed passion. As she made her eager response known, he deepened the kiss, and she realized she was playing in the big leagues.

"Jed, I don't have much experience with this sort of thing," she whispered.

"Then we're both in the same boat."

"Oh, come on!"

He gave her a rueful little grin. "Sure, I've had my share of fun. The difference is, I've never been with anyone who was so sure of herself in every situation except in bed. And I've never been with anyone who turned me on so much that she made my hands shake. But, honey, I want to do this right. I want this to be as perfect for you as I can make it."

His words brought a warm flush to her skin. "I want to please you, too," she whispered. "I want that so much."

"You do."

"What if I can't—"

"We're not setting goals. We're just doing things together that feel good to both of us. The only rule is that if you're uncomfortable with something, you tell me."

He paused to prop up several pillows along the wall so he could sit comfortably against them, his legs stretched out and crossed at the ankles. He looked completely at ease, and when he held out his hand to her, she nestled beside him. He gave her a lazy kiss that started with her mouth and ended with his lips and tongue exploring her neck. It was warm and sweet and very arousing. When he'd finished, she found that he'd angled her body around so that she was facing him, her breasts inches from his chest. "*Now* I've got you where I want you."

Still a little nervous, she hesitatingly returned the smile. This was all so new. But she felt a fierce trust gathering inside her.

He carefully pulled out the last of her tortoiseshell pins and combed her hair around her shoulders, burying his nose in the golden strands and turning his head so that he could nibble on her ear. "You smell so good. But you taste even better."

There were things she'd been wanting to do, too. Tentatively, she touched her tongue to the edge of his jaw. "You're bristly."

"Maybe I should use some of that bottled water to shave."

"Don't. I like you the way you are."

"Then we're on the same wavelength."

He kept the pace slow and light, getting a little more intimate with each kiss. Finally he unbuttoned the top of her shirt and nibbled along her collarbone and down to the tops of her breasts.

She whimpered, amazed that anything could feel so good. So erotic.

"Okay?"

"I'm burning up."

"Well, we're probably both a little overdressed."

Marissa giggled, silently admitting that she was still a bit on edge.

Jed pulled off his shirt and tossed it on the floor, and she knew he was waiting to see if she was comfortable with that. Catching her lower lip between her teeth, she flattened her hand against his chest.

"You have a sexy chest."

"Not as sexy as yours."

"I don't know about that." She traced the contours of his muscles and slid her fingers through his springy hair, enjoying the freedom to touch him. While she did, he slowly unbuttoned her shirt but didn't take it off. Instead, he unsnapped his trousers, worked them over his hips and kicked them out of the way.

Her gaze dropped to his briefs. She swallowed as she zeroed in on the bulge that proclaimed his arousal.

He waited several seconds, then crooked a finger under her chin, forcing her eyes to meet his. "Honey, being with you like this turns me on. I can't hide that. I wouldn't want to. I want you to know what you do to me."

"What if you lose control?" she blurted. "What if—"

"Do you trust me?"

"More than anyone else in the world."

"Well, any time you want me to stop, all you have to do is tell me. And I will. No matter what we're doing. Okay?"

She nodded. This was the moment of truth. The moment she well and truly put herself into his hands. Perhaps because she wanted to prove something to herself, she undid her trousers and skinned them down her legs. It didn't take a lot of exertion, but she was breathing hard and her heart was pounding when she finished.

Jed stroked his hand along her calf. "You've got gorgeous legs." After a long kiss, he pulled her onto his lap facing him, guiding her knees to either side of his hips so she was straddling him.

The pose was so blatantly erotic that Marissa's legs stiffened. Then she gradually relaxed, lowering her body until she was pressed intimately to him, their flesh separated by only a couple of layers of underclothes.

"Mmm. That feels wonderful," he rumbled as he dropped butterfly kisses over her neck and shoulders.

"Yes." The position might have frightened her, except that she was the one on top—with the freedom to bail out if she wanted.

Jed kept his arms at his sides as if he understood that

she needed to feel unfettered. He nibbled at her jawline, her neck. Then, using his mouth, he skimmed back her shirt as his fingers played with the fabric at the top of her bra. She held her breath as he dipped inside. Trembled as her skin prickled and her nipples hardened.

More. She wanted more.

Maybe she'd said it aloud. Because he dipped lower with little strokes that were like heat lightning crackling over her nerve endings.

She made small, incoherent noises in her throat, unsure of what to ask for. "Jed, Jed. That's so good."

"Oh, yes."

Somehow her shirt disappeared. Then her bra. She cried out again and again as he caressed her breasts, lifting and squeezing them gently. Every time he came back to the centers, she felt as if tiny explosions were going off inside her body.

"Oh...oh..." The waves of sensation brought incoherent syllables to her lips. An ache started deep inside her. An ache that made her instinctively rock her hips against him.

"That's it, honey," he crooned. "That's it. Do what feels good."

"What?" she gasped.

"Anything you like."

She moved frantically against him, knowing her body needed *something*—that it was reaching desperately for *something*. If she didn't find it, she would go mad.

Then as he sucked one nipple into his mouth and tugged at the other with his thumb and finger, she felt a knot of tension inside her break apart. It was as though a gateway of bliss had opened up. She rocked and pressed against him, crying out as a burst of sensation took her, making her feel as if she were flying, spinning, shattering.

He held her, kissed her, murmured words of praise as

she came back to something approaching normal. Only normal had changed. She would never be the same again.

"I—I—is that what it's supposed to be like?" she gasped, little aftershocks of pleasure rippling through her.

"I don't know. We'll have to try it again and make comparisons."

"We." Her cheeks grew rosy. "I think it was just me."

He laughed a little shakily. "How's that for iron control?"

"Jed—"

"All in good time."

"But you—"

"I wanted you to find out what that felt like."

She closed her eyes and moved her cheek against his, still caught up in the miracle of her body's response. "You're making this seem easy. You're making me wonder why I was ever afraid of you."

"Good."

She turned her head and their lips met, caught, sealed with heat. He led her back along the path she'd just taken, and she was astonished at how quickly her passion built again. He caressed her breasts the way he had before, making her whimper with the pleasure of his touch.

"Jed, I want—I need—"

"Yes. Raise up a little, so I can..."

She did, and he helped her off with her panties, his fingers stroking the warm, wet place that she understood was the seat of her sexual sensations. Then his briefs were gone, too. And there were only the two of them—naked on the bed.

His eyes met hers, mistaking her uncertainty for fear.

"It's okay. We can stop right here if you want."

"I don't want to stop. I just don't know what to do."

"What do you want to do?"

"I want you inside me." The words came out as a wispy gasp.

Without any hesitation he guided her hips down once more, watching her face as the tip of his erection touched her.

She had thought she'd be afraid when the ultimate moment came. Instead she felt a terrible urgency to join her body with his. Plunging downward, she gave a little cry as she felt his heat and hardness press into her.

"Are you all right?"

"Yes. Oh, yes."

He let out a long, luxurious sigh.

She kissed his neck, his jaw, his mouth. "Jed, I want this to be...good...for you."

"It's wonderful for me."

She pressed her forehead against his.

"But you're going to have to do most of the work. Except for this part, and this," he whispered as his hands found her breasts again and his lips nibbled at hers.

This time she understood what to do. This time she knew how to move against him. How to court the sensations that were building once again to a peak.

She heard his breath coming in great gasps. Felt his body shake and his hips strain upward against hers as low, sexy words tumbled from his lips. She moved faster and faster, exulting in the pleasure and in the knowledge that she was taking him with her.

"I can't—" He called out her name. His body jerked against hers, inside hers, sending her over the edge once more into that world of pure sensation. Only this time he was with her. She was giving pleasure, not just receiving it. And his gratification multiplied her joy a thousandfold.

SOME TIME LATER she was aware that her cheeks were wet. He kissed the tracks of moisture.

"Oh, Jed, I didn't know it could be like that. Thank you."

"Anytime."

She curled against him, her head on his shoulder.

His fingers combed through her hair, and he stirred. "Marci?"

"Umm?"

"I'm not sure I can sleep like this. Is it okay to lie down?"

She laughed softly. "I think I'm past worrying about that."

He took her down to the surface of the bed, kissing her tenderly, murmuring gentle words. She was exhausted and exalted. Triumphant in the knowledge that she'd conquered the fear that had ravaged her for so long. "We ought to have done this a long time ago."

"We'll just have to make up for lost time. But not now. I don't know about you, but I'm beat."

"Pleasantly fatigued."

He settled them under the covers, and she snuggled against him, feeling safe for the first time in days.

A LOUD CHATTERING in the trees woke Marissa just after dawn. For a moment she was disoriented as she stared at the misty light seeping through the cracks in the bamboo walls. Then she sensed the warmth of Jed's body next to hers, and a feeling of well-being stole over her as she remembered the incredible journey he'd led her on, right in this bed.

"I'd like to take a shot at those damn monkeys," he muttered, burying his face in her neck and pulling her closer.

"The birds will start up soon." She closed her eyes and snuggled against him, marveling at the wonder of waking up next to him. To the man she loved. She longed to make that declaration aloud. But she wasn't going to do it until they were safe and could think about the future.

His lips and teeth played with her ear. "We can't travel until it's dark again. So we can stay in bed all day if we want to."

She felt a warm glow spread across her skin. "I'd like that. But…"

He raised his head so he could look down at her. "Are you okay?"

"Wonderful," she answered softly. His lips traveled across her cheek to her mouth. "I just need to make a quick trip to the facilities."

He started to get up.

She gently pushed him back. "You relax. I'll be fine by myself."

In the act of pulling back the light covers, she realized she was naked. And that she didn't know where her clothes had landed the night before. And that Jed was lying on his side with a grin playing around his lips—watching her.

Her shirt was hanging off the end of the bed. Quickly she snatched it up and buttoned the front. Feeling a bit more secure, she risked a sideways glance at Jed as she made a search for her pants. They were half under the edge of the covers. "Enjoying yourself?"

"It's a very pretty view. Almost as good as—" He stopped abruptly.

"As what?"

Looking like a schoolboy who'd been caught spying on the girls' locker room, he sat up. "As the bathing ceremony."

She stared at him, her face growing hot. "You saw that?"

"Part of it."

"Oh, God!"

He knit his hands together. "I knew I was going to feel like a sneak until I fessed up. There's a place at the top of the pyramid where the guys watch their brides. Sanchez sent me over there to get me out of the way while Johnson put the bomb in our honeymoon cottage."

Marissa made a strangled exclamation.

"One of the women looked up at me for an instant and clued me in. I started wondering what Sanchez was up to, and I knew I had to get back to the hacienda." He swallowed. "But it wasn't easy tearing my eyes away from you standing there in all your glory."

"You saw—"

"Come here." His voice was rough.

Uncertainly she crossed to the bed and let him draw her down into his embrace.

His lips nuzzled her hairline. "You're embarrassed."

"Wouldn't you be?"

"Sure."

"You didn't hear what I talked about with Madre Flora, did you?"

"No. That must have been before I arrived."

She relaxed a fraction.

"There are lots of ancient customs that modern man dismisses as primitive. But sometimes it's a good idea to go back to our roots."

"Are you quoting Sociology 101?"

He laughed. "No. The way I look at it, you and I were lucky to get a chance to participate."

"Maybe," she allowed, her voice soft as she thought about the soul-searching interview with the wise woman.

Madre Flora had helped her sort out her feelings about Jed.
But she wasn't ready to talk about that conversation with
him yet.

"So do you want me to come help you bathe?"

"No!" She wasn't ready for that, either.

"Then hurry back."

He was still watching her as she found her slacks and
shoes and started toward the door.

"Take the revolver. And watch out for wildlife."

Marissa nodded. If she'd been a little more clearheaded,
she would have thought of the weapon herself.

"There's a barrel of water in a screened area outside.
Soap and towels are in the supply boxes."

"Thanks."

Finally equipped, she stepped out the door and closed it
behind her. The early morning was cool and foggy, typical
of the jungle. In a few hours the sun would burn off the
mist, and the heat would start to build up.

Alert for animals or humans, Marissa followed the short
trail they'd taken the night before. After visiting the out-
house, she found the primitive bathing facilities and
washed quickly. Despite what she'd told Jed, she wasn't
perfectly comfortable out here by herself. Especially with
her clothes off.

The spider monkeys set up a loud chatter again. Looking
up, she saw them swinging from branch to branch, moving
rapidly toward a large kapok tree. Had Jed come out and
shooed them away?

Turning, she started back toward the house, her eyes
scanning the underbrush. Her gaze collided with the fender
of a jeep almost hidden from view.

Had it been there when she and Jed arrived last night?
Moving closer, she gingerly touched the hood. It was hot.
Not from the sun. From the engine.

Despite the heat radiating from her fingers, goose bumps surfaced up and down her arms. Someone else had found this place. Someone who didn't want them to know.

Her heart in her throat, she tiptoed back to the house, being careful to make as little noise as possible. She arrived in time to see a man standing in the doorway.

In the split second before he disappeared inside, it registered that he wasn't Jed. He was too short. And his hair was black instead of sun-streaked blond.

Chapter Fifteen

Marissa's mouth fell open when she realized who had stepped into the hut. It was Pedro Harara, the banker. He'd exchanged his usual broad-shouldered suit for peasant garb. What in the name of heaven was he doing here? And how had he figured out where they were?

Caution sent her to the side of the building. Screened by a small palm, she peered through one of the chinks in the bamboo wall. She could see Jed on his feet, shirtless and buttoning his pants. Harara was standing just inside the doorway pointing a pistol in his direction.

"Where's the *gringa* bitch?" he demanded in a voice he might have used to tell a delinquent loan holder he'd either have to pay up or go into bankruptcy.

"I don't know anyone who fits that description."

Harara jerked the gun at Jed. "Don't play games with me."

"If you happen to be referring to Marissa, she's not here," Jed said between clenched teeth.

Harara looked around the room, taking in the supplies on the table, the rumpled bed and the clothing on the floor. Being careful to keep the weapon trained on Jed, he reached down and scooped up Marissa's bra from the floor. Dangling it in the air, he fingered the silky fabric. "I presume this isn't yours. Unless you've been hiding some rather kinky proclivities." He laughed. "Is that why you were fired from your undercover job?"

Jed's eyes narrowed, but he didn't bother to answer.

"Did you have a good time in bed with her last night? Your wedding night, actually. You have the right kind of arrangement. Enjoy her while you're here. Then dump her."

He didn't succeed in provoking Jed, who remained silent.

Marissa wiped her sweaty palm on her pants. Shifting her grip on the revolver, she tried to decide what to do. She could probably maneuver in back of Harara, since his attention was focused elsewhere. But he'd still have a shot at Jed, and she couldn't risk that.

"I've heard she's frigid," Harara said conversationally.

Marissa locked her teeth together to keep from giving her presence away.

"Did you spend some time warming her up or just go ahead and take your pleasure with her?"

Jed stood like a stone.

Harara's expression changed. "If you don't want to brag about your wedding night, that's one thing. But there's still the question of where she is now. Maybe you're planning to tell her sister you couldn't get her out of Sanchez's compound alive. I assume the deal is that you get to keep the money they paid you. Fifty thousand dollars is a nice piece of change."

Marissa's skin went cold. Jed hadn't said anything about getting paid to rescue her. But now that someone had mentioned a cash payment, it made sense.

A terrible wave of hurt and betrayal swept over her, cutting off her breath. She'd been so grateful to Jed for rescuing her. And all along he'd done it for money. A lot of money.

In some corner of her mind a tiny voice argued that she wasn't exactly being reasonable. She and Jed hadn't been close before he arrived at the hacienda. Why should he risk his life for a woman who'd gone out of her way to keep him at arm's length?

Yet she simply couldn't make herself deal with her roiling emotions in cool, logical terms. She'd opened her vulnerable heart to Jed. She'd trusted him with her deepest, most damaging secrets. She'd given herself to him, body and soul. Now she felt a terrible choking sensation as she tried to come to grips with what sounded like betrayal.

Please, tell him you love me.

When Jed finally spoke, he made it sound as if she were nothing to him. "Congratulations," he answered in a gritty voice. "You figured it out. She's dead."

She held back a gasp. Jed was putting on an act. An act to fool Harara into dropping his guard. Yet she couldn't shrug off the sick, shaky feeling that had taken her over. It was like the way she'd been in the pitch-dark room before she'd climbed over to Jed's balcony. She was reacting the way she'd been conditioned to react for years.

"Oh?" the banker asked.

"She had an unfortunate accident early this morning."

"Show me the body." Harara stepped aside and motioned with the gun.

Jed walked to the door. "Sure."

"Keep your hands in the air."

Jed glanced at the machine gun in the corner, but he obeyed the curt order. "How do you know about the money?"

"When you've got a solid base of operation in the international financial community, you can find out about *anything* that has to do with money. I've had a team of computer experts digging up every scrap of information I could get on you. You deposited fifty thousand dollars in your bank account before you left Baltimore. And you arranged to rent several properties in San Marcos and have them stocked with supplies. You probably think you covered your tracks by working through third parties. But my computer analysts were able to match withdrawals from your account to local transactions. I checked here first, since this is the hideout closest to Sanchez's *finca*."

Marissa listened, the sick feeling inside her expanding as the men moved out of her line of sight but not out of her hearing. It was terrible to listen to Jed sounding so convincing.

"You went to a damn lot of trouble to get a fix on me," Jed remarked as Marissa edged along the side of the building.

"Don't flatter yourself. You're just small time. I've been monitoring my good friend Miguel's transactions for years. And now I've got something on him I can use. I know he's buying diamond mining equipment. My plans didn't include the *gringa* blabbing about it."

"So were you the one who turned her in that night at the reception?"

"No. I assume it was Clarita. Miguel told her she couldn't come to the party because she'd made a scene several times before. So she was out on the patio watching the festivities. Luckily for me."

"What happened to her last night? In the explosion."

"Why waste your time worrying about her?"

"I used to like her."

"She's in the hospital. I think she's going to be okay. Physically. Mentally…" He shrugged.

"Since you've studied my deposits and withdrawals,

you know I'm for sale to the highest bidder," Jed observed. "And you do owe me a favor for swinging your bank a big loan last year. Let's see what else we can work out now."

"After I'm satisfied your bride is out of the picture."

Marissa saw that Jed had chosen a trail that led away from the place where she was supposed to be. As he made his way through the jungle, he stepped on several fallen sticks, cracking them loudly in half.

The part of her mind still functioning on a rational level knew that he was trying to warn her—and that he assumed the banker was planning to kill him as soon as he saw the body. When Harara found out Jed was stalling for time, the result would be the same.

Struggling to stay calm, she looked around for something to distract Harara. Someone had discarded a pile of giant seed pods near the corner of the house where she was standing. Picking one up, she hefted it in her hand. It was fairly heavy. If she heaved it into the bushes, would Harara turn? If he did, she could take a shot at him.

She was about to step into the open when a noise from the other direction made her freeze. Seconds later, to her astonishment, another figure glided out from behind a screen of trees, Uzi in hand.

It was William Johnson. She stood like a statue, aware that if she'd come out of hiding a split second sooner, he'd have seen her.

"Drop the gun and turn around slowly," he called to Harara. "And, Prentiss, you stay where you are."

Harara didn't follow orders. Instead, he pivoted to face the newcomer and fired off a shot. As Johnson cursed and ducked, the banker dodged into the underbrush, palm fronds hiding him from view almost at once.

Jed threw himself behind the nearest tree as Johnson

recovered his presence of mind and squeezed off a burst of shots in the direction of the fleeing figure. Bullets slashed through broad leaves. But Harara didn't slacken his pace. Marissa could hear him crashing headlong through the dense vegetation. Just as she was sure he was going to make his escape, a bloodcurdling scream split the air.

"Dios. No."

Johnson hesitated, looking from the direction of the anguished cry to the place where Jed had disappeared. He went after Jed.

"Help me," Harara wheezed, his voice rising in panic and then choking off in an anguished gurgle.

Was it a trick? Would he come charging out of the bushes as soon as Johnson turned his back?

Marissa didn't know. But she had to act quickly. Praying that her left-handed aim would be accurate, she heaved the seed pod at Johnson. It struck him a glancing blow on the shoulder, enough to make him curse and turn to his left.

She was about to fire when Jed leaped out from behind the tree and brought the other man crashing to the ground. The machine gun flew out of Johnson's reach. Marissa sprinted forward, picked it up and backed away from the fighting men, who were now locked together and rolling across the group.

"Stop!" she shouted.

Neither combatant paid any attention.

Johnson got his arms up and wrapped his hands around Jed's neck.

Jed gasped, and Marissa watched in horror as his face darkened. She was going to have to take a chance and fire. Heart blocking her windpipe, she held the gun extended in both hands and tried to sight a clean shot.

Then Jed managed to jab at the other man with his knee. The mining engineer bellowed and loosened his hold. Jed wrenched away and landed a punch on Johnson's jaw. Stunned, the other man went still for several seconds. Marissa darted in and brought the butt of the gun down on the back of his head. He groaned and collapsed limply on top of Jed.

Coughing, Jed shoved the deadweight away and sat up. For several seconds he could only suck in great gulps of air.

"Are you all right?" Marissa asked. Kneeling beside him, she gently touched the finger marks on his neck. The skin was red. Later it would be bruised.

"I'm okay. What about you?" he wheezed.

"Okay," she whispered, not trusting herself to say more.

He took her in his arms.

She held herself stiffly, wanting to melt against him. But the hurt, frightened part of her spirit wouldn't let her. She'd wakened this morning happier than she'd ever been in her life. Now she felt as if sharp knives had slashed her insides.

"I'm sorry," he rasped.

"For what? You didn't know either one of them was coming."

"You were outside the hut. You heard us talking. I know what you're thinking now."

She couldn't hold back a small sound that started as a sob. She managed to turn it into a snort.

"Marci. I—"

"We've got to find out about Harara. Maybe that scream was just a ruse and he's waiting his chance to come back."

Jed muttered a curse under his breath. "You're right,

even if you've got the wrong reason. But as soon as we find out what happened to him, we'll talk.''

She nodded again, because she knew that if she spoke, it would be impossible to hold back her tears.

Jed glanced from Harara's untidy trail to the unconscious man on the ground. "I'd hate to have Sleeping Beauty wake up and come after us." As he spoke he reached into Johnson's pocket. "Thought I felt these!" he said as he pulled out a pair of handcuffs. Deftly he rolled the man over and secured his hands behind his back.

Marissa stood and stared toward the recently cut path through the foliage. She could see nothing. Hear nothing. But she sensed something bad was out there waiting for them. Either it was Harara or whatever had made him scream. Jed stepped in front of her. "I'll go first. Give me the Uzi."

Marissa handed over the machine gun. She wanted to hold on to Jed. She contented herself with clutching the butt of the pistol and following him as he moved cautiously through the trees, scanning the foliage for signs of danger.

Every time a leaf brushed against her face she felt a shiver go down her spine. Half expecting a wild animal to leap out from behind each new tree, she tried to penetrate the dim light. But she could see only a few feet into the tangle of vegetation.

When Jed halted suddenly, she almost bumped into him. "Over there."

She looked where he was pointing and saw a pair of legs stretched in front of them.

"Pedro?"

There was no answer.

Jed cautiously approached. Marissa followed.

Before he'd taken two steps he stopped in his tracks and

swore, grabbing Marissa's arm to keep her from moving forward.

"What?"

He pointed to what looked like a vivid red-and-pink ribbon almost hidden by one of the pants legs.

Marissa sucked in a sharp breath and took an automatic step back as she stared at the beautifully colored strand. That was no innocent ribbon! It was a coral snake, its bite an almost immediate death sentence, and Harara must have fled directly into its path.

She shuddered and clutched at Jed's shirt to hold him back. "Stay away from it!"

"Don't worry." Looking around, he found a dead branch hanging from a nearby tree and pulled it down.

Heart pounding, Marissa watched as he lifted up Harara's leg with the end of a stick. When the snake wiggled, he beat it with the improvised weapon. Marissa turned her face away.

The snake had stopped moving when Jed gingerly lifted it away and flung it into the underbrush. Then he turned the banker over. He was already dead, his mouth open in a silent scream, his face swollen.

Marissa shuddered, thinking that it could have been her a few days ago when she'd fled through the jungle.

"It couldn't have happened to a nicer guy. Except maybe Johnson," Jed said harshly. "And speaking of snakes, we'd better see if he's come around."

She nodded tightly.

"You think I did it for the money," he accused, startling her by changing subjects too abruptly.

"Did what?"

"Came back to San Marcos to rescue you."

"Didn't you?" She turned away and started up the trail, running away so he couldn't continue the conversation.

He kept pace with her. "That was part of it. I wasn't going to risk my neck for free, not after the way you'd treated me all these years. But I wouldn't have agreed if I didn't care about you. For that matter, I wouldn't have spent a couple of days in Santa Isabella finding out what had happened to you. And I wouldn't have gone to Baltimore to tell your sister." He was breathing hard as he finished the declaration.

"Maybe you needed the job." She kept her back to him, afraid that she was going to cry. To fend off the tears, she drew on every defense mechanism she'd ever learned.

"Damn you, stop running away and let me explain."

"I don't want to hear it!"

"I thought you'd changed," he said in a voice that seemed to issue a challenge.

"You were wrong," was all she could get out.

They had reached the clearing. Marissa gestured toward Johnson, who was struggling to sit up. "We've got other problems to deal with."

When Johnson spotted them he tried to move away but only succeeded in toppling to his side.

Jed righted him and hauled him against the trunk of a tree. "We're going to have a little chat."

"I don't think so."

"You may find you want to cooperate. Unless you'd like to spend the rest of your life rotting in a San Marcos prison."

"And who's going to put me there?"

"Sanchez."

"You think he's going to take the blame for trying to cheat his countrymen out of a fortune?" Marissa entered the conversation, her voice harsh. It felt good to focus her anger on Johnson. She knew exactly how to deal with *him*. "You're the one who's going to be his scapegoat. He'll have to explain why he was keeping a diamond mining operation secret. And he'll convince everyone you used him. You'll end up in front of a firing squad and there will be no one charging onto the field to sweep you out of the way of the bullets. Unless you turn the tables on him.''

Marissa could see by the panic in his eyes that he'd heard the story of her own eleventh-hour rescue.

''I'm listening.''

''All right, this is what we're going to do,'' she said, noting that she had both Johnson's and Jed's complete attention.

MARISSA'S HEART SLAMMED against her ribs as she followed William Johnson down the dark, silent hall to the room where she'd been arrested the week before. Behind her, a third pair of footsteps clicked on the tile floor. Jed. Even if she couldn't talk to him about their personal relationship, she was reassured that he was covering her back. He was a good man to have on your side. At least she was willing to admit that much.

She squeezed her eyes shut for just a moment while she forced the focus of her thoughts away from anything personal and back onto their present mission. God, she wished Jed or somebody else had told her this plan was demented. But he'd gone along with her proposition and made some astute suggestions that put the icing on the cake. Still, she knew that the two of them could be risking everything if the operation hit an unexpected snag. There had been so little time to think everything through. They'd been forced to act quickly before Sanchez figured out what they were up to.

But at least they'd gotten this far with no problem. The guard at the door hadn't questioned Johnson's authority to get them inside.

They reached *El Jefe*'s office, and Marissa heard the mining engineer suck in a deep breath. He was as nervous as she. Had he figured out some last-minute double cross that would get her and Jed killed? Or was he worried that Sanchez was going to come swooping down on them like a falcon from the clouds—tearing all of them to bits with razor talons?

The door closed behind them, and she felt the walls of Sanchez's private office close in around her. Like the night of the party when she'd been boxed up and delivered to a prison cell. Only this time she'd dragged Jed in with her. If anything went wrong, he'd get captured, too.

They'd almost reached the most dangerous moment of this whole operation, and Jed had insisted on being the one to take the biggest risk.

She glanced up to find him looking at her, and the mixture of pain and determination in his eyes made her heart squeeze. Even now, even when she knew it was all over between them, she wanted to reach for his hand. But she hadn't been able to let herself unbend with him since the scene with Harara at the hut. Emotionally, there was no way she could take that risk.

Jed held her gaze for another long second.

"You shouldn't have expected so much from me," he muttered. Then he turned his back and strode past her toward the little bathroom where she'd hidden the film and the camera. She heard him lifting off the top of the toilet tank.

Her mounting tension made it almost impossible to breathe. Even though she'd been subliminally waiting for it, the sound of the door crashing open made her gasp.

El Jefe stepped into the room, backed up by a contingent of armed guards.

Chapter Sixteen

"Got you," he snarled. "Come out with your hands up. Or my men will shoot your bride," he called to Jed. "And don't bother to hide the film of the incriminating documents. I know she put it in the toilet tank."

Marissa pressed a hand against her mouth.

Jed stepped out of the bathroom, his arms above his head, the plastic bag dangling from one hand like a flag of surrender. Sanchez snatched it out of his grasp and stuffed it in his pocket.

Marissa backed away from him. Being in the same room with *El Jefe* again made her hands tremble, and she pressed them against her sides.

He looked at her and grinned. "You should have left the country while you could. Your security was inadequate. My loyal friend managed to get in touch with me when you left him alone for a few minutes." He gestured toward Johnson.

The mining engineer moved to Sanchez's side, and the general clapped him on the back. "Well done."

Johnson looked uncomfortable.

"He's not your friend. He's your business partner," Marissa corrected, trying to keep her voice steady. "In a scheme to cheat your country out of millions of pesos."

El Jefe's gaze narrowed. "So you're the one who broke in to the building with my diamond mining equipment? I must say, you had a very unusual wedding night."

"Yes. Too bad we missed your explosive finale," Jed snapped. "If we'd stayed in your guest cottage, we'd have been blown to bits."

"That wasn't my idea."

Johnson reddened.

"But you went along with the plan," Jed clarified.

Sanchez managed to look regretful. "I wanted to trust you, *amigo*. But I couldn't. It's unfortunate you had to fall in love with Señorita Devereaux. I saw it bloom on your face like a hibiscus flower unfurling in the first morning light. You put her life above yours, and that was too dangerous for me."

Marissa went rigid as the general's words sank into her mind, sank into every cell in her body. Had she heard him right? Had he really said that he knew Jed loved her? She drew in a strangled breath and turned toward Jed. He was gazing at her with an intensity that made her heart skip a beat and then start up in double time. When her eyes met his, he looked quickly away—like a man unable to face the destruction of everything he holds dear. She understood in that blinding instant that the general had spoken the truth. And she'd been an utter fool.

Nothing else existed in the room besides Jed. She started toward him. But he was already speaking to Sanchez again. And she realized with sick desperation that she might not get another chance with the man she loved.

"Now that you've got us, at least tell me what documents she found in your files," Jed demanded. "Your agreement with Johnson to develop the diamond mines and steal the profits from San Marcos?''

El Jefe shrugged. ''I'll have to read the text to be sure. I have notes about the diamond mining operation, yes. Also my plans for having President Palmeriz declared incompetent so I can use the eighty-sixth amendment to our constitution to legally take over the government. I had the amendment pushed through several years ago. It allows the cabinet to elect an interim successor.''

''You?''

''Of course. But you've asked enough questions. It's time to get on with the good part.'' He grinned at Johnson. ''I like your idea of having a crew from the Televisión Nacional film the capture of these two American spies.'' He opened the door and Marissa saw a cameraman, sound engineer and lighting technician standing in the hall. ''We're ready for you now.''

All but one of the guards withdrew as the men began setting up their equipment. Sanchez ordered Marissa to Jed's side. She stood rigid, her heart thumping, her mouth so dry she could hardly swallow.

''Jed, I'm sorry,'' she whispered, pressing her shoulder against his, knowing in her heart that anything she said was inadequate. She was bursting with the need to turn and take him in her arms—to tell him she loved him. To make things right between them if that was still possible. But they were trapped here.

Sanchez came out of the bathroom where he'd been combing his hair in preparation for his performance.

''Let me do a test,'' the sound engineer said. He pressed a button and the conversation they'd been having about diamond mines and attempted murder began to play back.

''You fool,'' *El Jefe* bellowed. ''Erase that part.''

"Too late." A new, authoritative voice answered the general. "It's already been transmitted to the station, ready for broadcast when I give the signal. Thanks to the plans worked out by Señor and Señora Prentiss."

Sanchez whirled toward the door and found himself facing President Palmeriz, who stood with his shoulders back and his eyes glittering. He was flanked by Thomas Leandro, Louis Rinaldo and a contingent of municipal police. One of the officers disarmed the general's guard. The rest surrounded *El Jefe*.

As it dawned on Sanchez that he'd been trapped, his mouth dropped open and his eyes widened, making him look like a bug impaled on a specimen card. His gaze shifted rapidly from Palmeriz to Johnson to Jed and Marissa as if he couldn't believe what he was seeing.

The chief executive permitted himself a small smile as he enjoyed the expression on his rival's face. "In the past you've managed to hide your illegal activities. But this time you've just hanged yourself. We've got the proof on tape. Not just a sound recording, but video from your surveillance camera."

"No!" Sanchez bellowed, completely out of control. As he kicked at the men trying to restrain him, the toe of his boot collided with a chair leg, and he yelped in pain.

"Your gout acting up?" Marissa inquired.

Somehow her cool voice got through to him. He turned and glared at her. If looks could kill. Marissa shivered as the old cliché leaped into her mind. Jed put a protective arm around her shoulders and drew her against his side.

Marissa looked at him, seeing that his face reflected a mixture of anger and regret, and she felt a stab of pain for him. Once he and Miguel Sanchez had been friends. But she knew their wildly different values must have made the relationship an uneasy one for Jed. Then the general's murderous plans had proven he put his own interests before anything as trivial as friendship.

Jed pulled the film from the general's pocket and handed it to Palmeriz. "More evidence."

"*Gracias.*"

Sanchez growled low in his throat like a cornered dog.

"Your stranglehold on the country is over," Palmeriz said. "But there's one way you can keep from being arrested."

Sanchez straightened his shoulders.

Jed's eyes were cold. "Ask Marissa to give you the details."

She looked at him in astonishment. She and Jed had hashed out the arrangement with the president after he'd agreed to the plan. But she'd assumed Palmeriz would want to do the talking—especially in a country where the men jealously guarded their prerogatives. What kind of private deal had Jed struck with the president to get her such power? The implications were overwhelming.

Her vision blurred, and she struggled to keep from going to pieces.

"You earned it," he told her.

No. She'd made a mess of her assignment. And he'd bailed her out.

The president smiled at her. "After the way General Sanchez treated you, honor demands that you deliver my terms."

"I won't hear it from *her!*" Sanchez growled, his manner switching to his accustomed hauteur.

"Then rot in hell." Jed grabbed Marissa's hand and started toward the door.

They were almost out of the room when the general

called them back in a voice that had lost a great deal of its solidity. "Wait."

Marissa turned slowly, aware that all eyes were on her. She should feel jubilant now that she was the one in charge. But she was too numb with her own personal pain. All she wanted was to get this finished so she and Jed could leave. So she could try to make him understand why she'd stopped trusting him.

In a wooden voice she delivered the ultimatum. "You will announce that you have found diamond mines in one of the provinces. And you're such a patriot that you want to turn over the proceeds from the mining operation to the government to alleviate some of the country's pressing social problems."

"But I put in the development money," Sanchez yelped.

"That makes you even more of a benefactor. They'll probably put up a statue in your honor," Jed observed, his voice dripping with sarcasm.

"What about me?" Johnson interjected. "I'm losing a bundle on this, too."

"Your cooperation will be taken into consideration before charges are filed," the president responded. "You may get off with a simple deportation order."

Johnson had no time to argue further. Two policemen escorted him from the room.

With a bit more enthusiasm Marissa took up where she'd left off with Sanchez. This was the part she'd insisted on including because she wanted to help Clarita, even though the girl had treated her like an enemy. And she wanted Sanchez to face up to his family problems. "You're also donating some of your personal fortune to establishing a state-of-the-art mental health facility for needy citizens. You don't have to mention that you're anxious to get your own daughter the care she needs."

The general looked daggers at Marissa. Yet below the surface wrath she thought she detected a modicum of guilt—unless that was simply her own wishful thinking.

There was one more important stipulation. Marissa braced for a verbal onslaught. "You're also stepping down as commander in chief—for health reasons."

He drew himself up straighter and cursed her loudly, heedless that Palmeriz looked shocked and Jed's face reddened with anger. "That's going too far! I'm in perfect health."

Jed took a step closer and brought his foot down on the general's gout-ridden toe. He bellowed in pain.

Jed folded his arms across his chest and stared back evenly. Sanchez looked away first. "This is blackmail."

Jed shrugged.

"Things could be worse," the president interjected. "You don't have to go into retirement at your age. Señor Rinaldo has graciously agreed to allow you to personally head the mining operation for him."

"That would mean I'd be stuck in the middle of nowhere in Junipero Province."

"Which should help keep you out of trouble," Rinaldo muttered.

Palmeriz handed the general a statement to read to the nation in front of the live television cameras. Sanchez ground his teeth. But with the threat of exposure hanging over him, he sat down at the desk and held the paper in his rigid hands.

At least as far as the general was concerned, Marissa felt a profound sense of relief. This scam had been her idea; they'd managed to pull it off, and justice was finally being done. But she was too tense and worried to watch the broadcast. All she wanted now was to be alone with her husband. As the film crew resumed their preparations, she caught Jed's eye, and they slipped out of the room.

He started off down the hall at a rapid clip. She grabbed his hand. "Please. We have to talk."

"All right. I guess it might as well be sooner than later." Grim faced, he led her to a comfortably furnished sitting room with a view of the courtyard. He didn't give her a chance to speak first. Immediately after the door closed behind them, he turned to her and started in, his words coming in staccato bursts. "Let's get this over with. I agreed to stay and help Palmeriz stabilize the government. But you don't have to hang around. There's a ticket waiting for you at the airport on a flight to Miami this evening."

"Jed, please—"

He plowed on. "You can be back in Baltimore tomorrow. And that lawyer friend of yours, Laura Roswell, should be able to advise you on whether our marriage is legal and if you need a divorce to get me out of your life."

Marissa tried to swallow around the baseball-size lump in her throat. "Is that what you want?"

"What does it matter?" His tone was bleak.

"Oh, God, Jed." She twined her arms around his waist and held him close, trying to ignore his rigid posture. Despite her heroic efforts, the tears she'd been fighting so hard to hold back welled up and ran down her cheeks, and her shoulders began to shake.

"Don't. I didn't mean to make you cry," he said with anguish. "I don't seem to get it right, do I?" His hand brushed the back of her head, clasped her for a moment and then dropped away.

She struggled to control her sobs, fighting to get out the words she needed to say. She couldn't let him think this mess was his fault or that she had come in here intending to leave him. Or perhaps that was what he really wanted, she thought as sudden cold fear stabbed into her. Every self-defense mechanism urged her to cut and run. But she stood her ground. She had turned away from him this morning. The only way she might get him back was to risk everything. "Jed...I...love...you." Once she'd said it, she realized how much she wanted him to know what was in her heart. Whatever happened next.

He went very still, surprise and hope mingling on his countenance. "Marci?"

She lifted her tearstained face to his. "I love you. I don't want a divorce." With the back of her hand she swiped at the tracks of moisture running down her face. "Jed, I'm so sorry. When Harara started talking about the money something inside me went cold and stiff." She fumbled for words. "One moment I was so happy. The next I was afraid of getting hurt all over again. I was still reacting like the old Marissa Devereaux. The woman who was afraid to trust you. But I know what kind of risk you were taking to come down here and save me. You could have bailed out any time, but you stuck with me."

"I'd never have left without you."

"You did what nobody else could. You got me out of there *alive*. But you did a lot more than that. You rescued me from the bleak life I carved out for myself. And you made me ache to make our marriage real. I want to stay married to you. If you'll still have me."

"If I what?" Then his mouth came down on hers—hard, possessive, insistent.

She cleaved to him, opened to him, poured her soul into

him. And he returned the fervor, measure for measure. When he finally lifted his lips from hers, her head was spinning. But she heard his heartfelt words. "I love you, Marci. I thought I'd messed up. I thought I'd lost you forever."

"No, Jed. No. I'm the one who messed up. I was too afraid to trust my happiness. I was afraid to tell you that I want to be with you—always. Our wedding ceremony was the most important thing that ever happened to me." She gave a wry little laugh. "Well, maybe it's a toss-up between that and our wedding night."

His hands stroked the curve of her back, gently touched her face, her hair as he told her wordlessly that he felt the same way.

Yet his eyes were still shadowed. "Before you make a final decision, don't forget about my big liability. You're sure you're willing to be saddled with a guy who nods off at inconvenient times?"

Her face shone with her love for him. "If his name is Jed Prentiss."

The look of wonder on his features made her heart contract.

"Marci. Marci."

They kissed again with aching passion.

"And don't *you* forget I know how to wake you up," she whispered.

"Oh, yeah." Jed looked around, located the door and locked it. Then he pulled her close once more, and there was no mistaking his intentions.

Her eyes widened. "The president's out there," she whispered. "And the camera crew. And all the guards."

"So? They know better than to bother a couple on their honeymoon!" He laughed and led her to the couch, and she stopped thinking about anything besides the joy of being with her husband once more.

HARLEQUIN®

Live the emotion™

American **ROMANCE**®

Heart, Home & Happiness

HARLEQUIN®

Blaze™

Red-hot reads.

Harlequin® **Historical**
Historical Romantic Adventure!

HARLEQUIN®

HARLEQUIN ROMANCE®

From the Heart, For the Heart

HARLEQUIN®

INTRIGUE®

Breathtaking Romantic Suspense

Medical Romance™...
love is just a heartbeat away

Ne**xt**™

**There's the life you planned.
And there's what comes next.**

HARLEQUIN®

Presents

Seduction and Passion Guaranteed!

HARLEQUIN®

Super Romance®

Exciting, Emotional, Unexpected

www.eHarlequin.com   HDIR106

Harlequin® Historical
Historical Romantic Adventure!

Imagine a time of chivalrous knights and unconventional ladies, roguish rakes and impetuous heiresses, rugged cowboys and spirited frontierswomen— these rich and vivid tales will capture your imagination!

Harlequin Historical... they're too good to miss!

www.eHarlequin.com

HHDIR06

HARLEQUIN®
Presents

The world's bestselling romance series...
The series that brings you your favorite authors,
month after month:

Helen Bianchin...Emma Darcy
Lynne Graham...Penny Jordan
Miranda Lee...Sandra Marton
Anne Mather...Carole Mortimer
Susan Napier...Michelle Reid

and many more uniquely talented authors!

Wealthy, powerful, gorgeous men...
Women who have feelings just like your own...
The stories you love, set in exotic, glamorous locations...

HARLEQUIN®
Presents

Seduction and Passion Guaranteed!

www.eHarlequin.com

HPDIR104

HARLEQUIN®
INTRIGUE®

BREATHTAKING ROMANTIC SUSPENSE

Shared dangers and passions lead to electrifying
romance and heart-stopping suspense!

Every month, you'll meet six new heroes
who are guaranteed to make your spine tingle
and your pulse pound. With them you'll enter
into the exciting world of Harlequin Intrigue—
where your life is on the line
and so is your heart!

THAT'S INTRIGUE—
ROMANTIC SUSPENSE
AT ITS BEST!

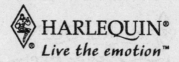

HARLEQUIN®
Live the emotion™

www.eHarlequin.com   INTDIR06

HARLEQUIN®

SuperRomance®

...there's more to the story!

Superromance.
A *big* satisfying read about unforgettable
characters. Each month we offer *six* very different
stories that range from family drama to adventure
and mystery, from highly emotional stories to
romantic comedies—and much more! Stories
about people you'll believe in and care about.
Stories too compelling to put down....

Our authors are among today's *best* romance
writers. You'll find familiar names and talented
newcomers. Many of them are award winners—
and you'll see why!

If you want the biggest and best
in romance fiction, you'll get it
from Superromance!

Exciting, Emotional, Unexpected...

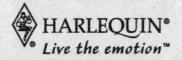

HARLEQUIN®
Live the emotion™

www.eHarlequin.com   HSDIR06

Invites *you* to experience lively, heartwarming all-American romances

Every month, we bring you four strong, sexy men, and four women who know what they want—and go all out to get it.

From small towns to big cities, experience a sense of adventure, romance and family spirit—the all-American way!

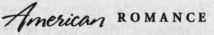

Heart, Home & Happiness

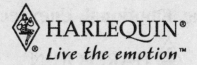

www.eHarlequin.com   HARDIR06

HARLEQUIN ROMANCE

The rush of falling in love,

Cosmopolitan,
international settings,

Believable, feel-good stories
about today's women

The compelling thrill
of romantic excitement

It could happen to you!

EXPERIENCE
HARLEQUIN ROMANCE!

Available wherever Harlequin Books are sold.

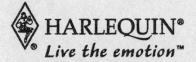

HARLEQUIN®
Live the emotion™

www.eHarlequin.com

HROMDIR04